PRAISE FOR THOMAS TESSIER!

RAPTURE
"Ingenious. A nerve-paralyzing story."
—*Publishers Weekly*

"Nerve-tingling suspense."
—*Booklist*

"Truly scary."
—*Kirkus Reviews*

"Top-flight terror!"
—*Washington Post Book World*

"Shocking. As horrifying as a novel can be."
—*Rocky Mountain News*

"Superb!"
—*Chicago Sun Times*

"Completely frightening!"
—*Richmond Times Dispatch*

FINISHING TOUCHES
"A novel of erotic cruelty...
seductive and compulsively readable."
—*Publishers Weekly*

"A decidedly adult horror
novel that deserves a wide audience."
—*Library Journal*

"A beguiling read through a compact
yet splendidly evocative—even mesmerizing—
novel of style and high entertainment."
—*Booklist*

"One of the most terr
—*Ran*

MORE PRAISE FOR THOMAS TESSIER!

LISTENING TO REASON

Sean returned his gaze. Jeff had reached a dead end: he had come here and aired his warped fantasy, but now he had nowhere to go. Sean felt sorry for him, but it was time for a change of scene. Standing here and arguing was too bizarre, and probably only made matters worse.

"Okay, Jeff. You don't want to discuss it at home with Georgianne, and I can understand that. But I don't see what I can do for you. We're wasting each other's time here. I'm going to try to forget all about this, and I hope you will too. But whether you do or not, I don't want to see you again. Stay away from my house, stay away from Georgianne, don't even try to get through on the phone—and I'll let it go. But do yourself a favor, Jeff, and get some help. You need it."

"Oh, you put your house first, then Georgianne," Jeff said. "Is that the way it is? I might have known. You think you can tell me—"

"You heard me," Sean interrupted, jabbing a finger at Jeff's heart with enough force to push him back on his heels. "*You heard me.*"

He turned and began to walk away, back toward the street. It was too much for Jeff, who rushed after him, grabbed a handful of his hair, and yanked his head back violently. At the same time, he reached behind his back, up under his sweatshirt, and pulled out the .22....

Other *Leisure* books by Thomas Tessier:

FINISHING TOUCHES

RAPTURE

THOMAS TESSIER

LEISURE BOOKS 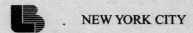 . NEW YORK CITY

For Alice, again.

A LEISURE BOOK®

August 2006

Published by

Dorchester Publishing Co., Inc.
200 Madison Avenue
New York, NY 10016

This is a work of fiction. Names, characters, places and incidents are either the product of the author's imagination or are used fictitiously. Any resemblance to actual events or locales or persons, living or dead, is entirely coincidental.

ISBN 0-8439-5558-9

Printed in the United States of America.

Visit us on the web at www.dorchesterpub.com.

TABLE OF CONTENTS

PART I

The Girl in the Very Long Dream

CHAPTER ONE

This business with Diane was a bizarre flourish in Jeff's life. Their sessions were trivial but vaguely worrying. Should he be carrying on like this? At his age? But maybe this *was* the right age for such behavior to start manifesting itself. He didn't like that thought at all. Fortunately, Diane rescued him, as she so often did.

"Honey . . ."

The voice of a teenager. She was standing with her back to him, slowly tugging a pair of tight shorts up over her girlish ass. She knew he loved to watch her, especially from behind. When they were together, she spent most of her time composing herself in pictures for him. The rest of the time, they fucked.

"Hm?"

"You gonna come see me again soon?"

"Of course."

"My folks are always out, you know. . . ."

He nodded, smiling as he tied his shoes.

3

"Daddy's always working," she went on in that little-girl tone, her face a mild pout. "And my mother can't stand to be around the house. She's out somewhere with her friends every day."

"I know," he said agreeably.

"They leave me all alone here. . . ."

She had turned to face him, and now stood twirling her long blond hair idly in front of her breasts. They weren't quite as full as Jeff would have liked, but they weren't far off either, and he knew this could never be the ideal situation of his dreams.

"You know I'll be back," he told her.

"Really? Promise?"

He was nearly a foot taller, and she had to look up at him as he stood before her. She pressed her lips with her thumb like a shy, fearful child. It always amazed him how she could invest her appearance with so much vulnerability. It was strangely moving, and he knew that was what he liked most about Diane.

"Yes," he said. "I promise."

She smiled sweetly. Now he could go. She pulled on a T-shirt and accompanied him to the door. He gave her a long, lingering kiss.

"You won't tell your parents?" he asked.

"Not if you come back."

"You got me."

He winked, and left. Traffic was light at this hour, and he was soon out of Los Angeles, heading into Ventura County. How lucky he'd been to find Diane! None of his previous attempts had worked out the way he had hoped. Diane was an angel. A real find, no question.

Still, he told himself a moment later, the whole thing was really rather silly. He turned on the radio so he wouldn't have to think about it any more.

His telephone was ringing when he unlocked the door of his condominium. Odd—not just because of the hour, but because he rarely received calls at home.

"Hello?"

"Jeff? Is that you?"

The voice was old and somewhat frail. He hadn't heard it in several years, but he knew it at once. He grasped the situation at once. A scenario he had run through his mind many times over the years was now, finally, about to be played out. He was ready for it.

"Yes, Kitty, it's me."

"Goodness, it sounds like you're just across the street," his aunt exclaimed.

"How are you?" he asked, smiling.

"Jeff, I'm sorry to call so late, but I've been trying to get you all evening and—"

"I was out," Jeff interrupted. "In fact, I just came in the door this minute."

"Jeff, I'm afraid I have some bad news to tell you. . . ."

She was obviously quite uncomfortable at having to use the telephone for this task.

"That's all right, Aunt Kitty," Jeff said, trying to make it a little easier for her. "I expected it sooner or later."

"Yes . . . Your father . . ."

"I know. I understand."

"His heart . . ."

They talked a while longer, and then Uncle Roy managed to get on the line and exchange a few words.

5

He wanted to assure Jeff that he would make all the necessary arrangements for the wake and the funeral.

"Will you . . . uh . . . ?"

"I'll be on the first plane I can get in the morning," Jeff said, wondering if they really thought he might pass up his own father's burial.

Jeff reserved a seat on an early flight. Then he dialed a number in Van Nuys. Ted Benedictus, groggy with sleep, was soon alert and concerned as Jeff explained the situation.

The only alcohol in the house was half a bottle of Scotch that Jeff hadn't touched in ages. Now he poured a large measure into a glass with some ice. He smoked a cigarette, drank, and thought.

He hadn't been home in—what was it?—seven or eight years. His whole life was here now, in California. But his past, or at least the most important part of it, was there, on the other side of the country. He felt eager and excited about going back.

And the best part of it was that Jeff had spent the last several hours thinking about Georgianne.

CHAPTER TWO

Jeff drove with all the windows down. The air was like warm syrup, but he didn't turn on the air conditioner, because he hated sealing himself in a car, even on a scorcher of a day like this. It was the middle of the afternoon, early May, and Connecticut was experiencing a premature heat wave. Sweat trickled down Jeff's back, sides, and chest beneath his half-unbuttoned shirt.

It should have taken two hours to get where he was going, the town of Millville, up in the Brass Valley, but traffic and tolls had slowed him. The car, which he'd rented at La Guardia Airport, was only a year old, but it moved like a pig. One of the speaker wires must have been loose, because there were bursts of static that soon forced Jeff to turn off the radio.

So his father was dead. Chopping wood on a hot afternoon at the age of seventy-six. The damn fool. What did he expect? Who bothered to chop wood at the beginning of May? Perhaps his father simply didn't care any more. Jeff lit another cigarette.

The wake was tomorrow, the funeral the day after. Jeff thought he should feel sorrier about his father's death, but the truth was he didn't. It was more of an inconvenience than anything else, just about the only thing that could force him to travel clear across the country. But now that he was here, he felt a curious sense of anticipation. It might yet prove interesting, after all this time.

Jeff and his father hadn't been close in a long time, and they had hardly communicated at all since his mother died several years ago. There wasn't any open hostility between them, but neither was there any real warmth. Father and son were alike in this regard: each was a very separate, private person.

The traffic on I-95 thinned out a little after Westport, and Jeff was able to make better time. Connecticut looked unfamiliar to him, what he could see of it from the highway. He had been living in Southern California for twenty years and had no desire to be anywhere else. He had it made out there.

The Waterbury sign appeared just after Bridgeport, and Jeff drifted into the right lane. He fell in behind a semi with its signal light blinking. He knew the exit was just ahead, although he couldn't see it, but he suddenly felt hesitant and indecisive. The truck stayed on the highway, and he followed it, passing the Waterbury exit. He cursed as he put his foot down and swung the car out to pass, but he didn't know whether he was angry with the truck driver or with himself. Now he would have to take route 63 north, the old New Haven Road. He knew it well enough, having traveled it many times. When you were in high school in the Brass Valley, New Haven was an attractive place to visit.

He caught the beginning of rush hour at New Haven, which slowed him some more. Once he got out of the city again, he was pleased to find route 63 in better shape than he remembered it. He seemed to fly up through Woodbridge and Bethany in no time. The road was wider, and there were new buildings everywhere. Twenty years ago it had still been vaguely rural, but now it was just another stretch of suburban America.

As Jeff approached Millville he slowed down to an almost stately cruise. Now he knew every side street, and the changes were even more glaring. A meadow that had been used as a picnic ground had given way to tract housing. High on one hill was a cluster of condominiums. The drive-in was still there, but it apparently no longer played creature features for audiences of impassioned high-school kids. Now—sign of the times—it showed three X-rated "adult hits" nightly. A little farther along, he discovered that the driving range had been replaced by a small industrial park. Across from it, two national hamburger chains had pitched their gaudy camps.

He spotted a familiar mailbox ahead on the right. It was the same, still there, with the name Slaton painted in black on the side. Jeff had known the Slaton family well when he was in high school, and the sight of their mailbox made him smile. But then, abruptly, he pulled the car off the road and stopped.

He had just noticed, a couple of yards from the Slaton driveway, a For Sale sign with the name and telephone number of a local realtor. It was a shock, and Jeff felt as if another fragment of his youth had just died within him. He got out of the car.

The driveway, exactly as he remembered, ran about a hundred yards up a gradual slope and then swung around behind some trees to the house, which was only partially visible from the road. It was impossible to tell if anyone was there. But the bushes along the drive spilled over onto it, and weeds sprouted up through wide cracks in the asphalt. The mailbox, and even the For Sale sign, looked dirty and neglected. They had to be gone, Jeff thought sadly. Perhaps Mr. Slaton had been transferred somewhere else, and they had moved without waiting for the house to be sold. Then Jeff shook his head and smiled, realizing that he had lost track of time. By now Mr. Slaton was probably retired, the family scattered. Time to sell the house and move to a smaller place, a better climate. Yes, that was the most likely explanation. Not that it made him feel any better.

He drove on into Millville. Many of the businesses on Main Street had changed, but the old buildings were still the same. No hint of a new skyline here. Millville was aptly named. It was an old mill town, struggling to survive in a new era. That industrial park on the edge of town was probably only a recent flicker of hope. A few of the kids Jeff had known would still be here, but most, like him, would have gone elsewhere to make their lives.

Jeff drove through the quiet residential streets on the east side of town, and finally parked in front of a small, blistering, white Cape Cod house. Uncle Roy and Aunt Kitty came out to the front lawn to greet him. They looked fragile, but their movements were energetic, and he felt surprising strength in them as they hugged him. Still pretty sturdy, he thought. No doubt his father had been the same, right to the end.

"How long has it been?" Uncle Roy asked as they went into the house.

It was a perfectly natural question, but the old man immediately realized his mistake, and his wife flashed him a nasty look in case he didn't.

"I'm ashamed to say I haven't been back here since Mom died," Jeff admitted promptly.

Aunt Kitty nodded sorrowfully and tried to smooth it over by fussing about some food. Jeff declined, saying he had eaten on the road. It wasn't true, but he wasn't hungry. He merely felt tired now, very tired. Uncle Roy brought him a cold beer that was so good Jeff drained the can in minutes, then leisurely sipped a second.

"Let me get your suitcases out of the car," Uncle Roy offered while Jeff relaxed.

"No. Leave it."

"Well, later, then."

"No," Jeff repeated. "I'm going to stay over at my father's house tonight."

"We've got the spare room all ready for you," Aunt Kitty protested. "You don't want to stay at the other house all alone."

"That's right," Uncle Roy echoed.

11

The two of them were so kind and well-meaning that Jeff hated to disappoint them, but his mind was made up.

"Thanks, really," he said, "but it's still my house and I want to spend the night there. At least tonight. I have a lot of old junk stored there and I want to begin sorting through it."

"Maybe tomorrow, then," Uncle Roy said quietly.

"Uh . . . you said that Dad didn't suffer. Is that right?"

"Yes," Aunt Kitty confirmed. "Next-door neighbor, Mr. Hall—remember him? He called us right after he called the ambulance. Said he'd seen George chopping wood in the backyard. It was a hot day, just like this one."

"We've been having a helluvan early hot spell," Uncle Roy put in quickly.

"Anyway," Aunt Kitty continued. "Next time he looked that way, he saw George lying on the ground. He didn't wait; he called the ambulance right away, then us, and then he ran outside. He told us later that your father seemed to be gone already when he got to him."

"He couldn't tell," Uncle Roy added. "But he said he seemed to be gone. He couldn't find no pulse or breath in him at all."

"I'm just glad he didn't go through a lot of pain."

"No, he didn't. Thank God for that," Aunt Kitty said. She showed Jeff his father's obituary in the local newspaper, and while he tried to read the brief notice she told him how good the ambulance crew was at CPR, how they'd got to the house in seven minutes, according to Mr. Hall, and . . . Jeff found himself blinking to keep his eyes open. The flight, followed by the long hot drive, was catching up with him. The beer was good, but it made him sleepier. He rose from his seat to leave.

"I'm sorry," he said. "I guess I'm jet-lagged."

"Sure you are," Uncle Roy said, understandingly. "Here's your dad's keys. This one's the house and this one the garage."

"Thanks." Jeff put the keys in his pocket. "I haven't even thought to ask how Nancy is."

Nancy Lisker was his cousin, two years older and, like him, an only child.

"Oh, she's fine," Aunt Kitty said. "She'll be there tomorrow, in the afternoon and in the evening."

"Good," Jeff said. "It'll be nice to see her again."

"You know where the Butler Funeral Home is?" Uncle Roy asked. "Sure you do. The wake's there, from two to four in the afternoon and from seven to nine in the evening."

"You come around for breakfast in the morning," Aunt Kitty told him. "Anytime'll be fine."

"I'll call you first," Jeff said. "Uh . . . is there something I should do or somebody I should see about any of the arrangements? There must be a lot of things to get squared away."

"The wake and the funeral and burial are all taken care of," Uncle Roy said soothingly, a hand on Jeff's back. "Just get yourself a good night's sleep, and we can talk tomorrow. Dick Hudson's your dad's lawyer. He'll be at the wake, and he'll fill you in on any unfinished business."

Jeff hugged Uncle Roy and Aunt Kitty again, and finally got away. They were fine people, but he wasn't in the right frame of mind to enjoy their company. As soon as he got in the car, he felt more awake.

It took less than ten minutes to drive to his father's house, *his* house, on the other side of town. It was another Cape, but with a better yard and on a nicer street. Had it been repainted in the last seven or eight years? Probably, but Jeff couldn't be sure. He pulled the car into the small driveway, took his two suitcases out of the back seat, and went inside.

The place was warm and stuffy from being shut up for a couple of days, but impeccably neat and tidy. Jeff opened several windows. In addition to a few items of food, he found a couple of cans of beer in the refrigerator. He took one and drank it while wandering from room to room. The house seemed remarkably impersonal, as if his father had taken care of every possible aspect of his private life and died leaving not so much as a scrap of paper out of place.

Jeff left the lights off as he sat in the front room for a while, drinking the beer and watching the dusk darken into night outside. Cool air gradually filled the house. He felt relaxed, even peaceful, and no longer quite so weary.

Next time I come back here, he thought, it'll be for Roy's funeral, or Kitty's. Unpleasant thought; he liked both of them. Roy would probably go first. Either way, there were at least two more return visits in Jeff's future.

At least? Now what does that mean, Jeff wondered

as he went into the kitchen to get the other beer. He smiled at himself and at the way his mind sometimes surprised him. Something was taking shape, but what? Maybe nothing.

He was thinking about the Slaton house again. Almost as much as his father's death, that For Sale sign seemed to signify a door shutting on the past. The Slaton house, the mere name Slaton, held many bittersweet memories. They were still real, twenty years later.

The father—what was his name? He was some kind of engineer, wasn't he? A soft-spoken, more or less invisible man. Successful in his chosen field and within his own limits, but not the sort of person you noticed much, even when you were in the same room with him.

The mother—Dora, or Doris? She was a bit of a snob, in the silliest ways. She always left her latest book-club purchases on the coffee table. Once, out of the blue, she'd asked Jeff: "Have you read Mr. Mailer's latest?" She had a habit of talking to teenagers with that ridiculous mock-seriousness some adults think is real communication.

There were two Slaton boys, both of them several years younger than Jeff. He couldn't remember their names either. At the time, they had been kid brothers, occasional pests, nothing more. It was odd to think of them now as grown up, living their individual lives, somewhere.

And one daughter, Jeff's classmate and good friend: Georgianne Slaton. They had never been boyfriend-girlfriend to each other, but they had spent a great

deal of time together. There had been a bond, a close-
ness between them that had lasted for four or five
years. It was something good in his life to remember.

Jeff couldn't count the number of double dates he
and Georgianne had been out on together. He with
one of his three successive high-school romances,
Georgianne always with Mike Rollins, her steady.
Wherever Georgianne was now, it surely wouldn't be
with Mike. He may have been a good high-school
date, but she must have done better since then. Mike
was jolly and energetic, but it was mostly surface
flash. He'd probably found a place in marketing somewhere, but he couldn't have held on to Georgianne.

She had gone to college in Boston, as Jeff recalled.
He didn't know where Mike had gone. A couple of
months after graduation, Jeff had gone out to UCLA.
He'd soon lost touch with Mike and Georgianne.
High-school friendships, however intense at the time,
often prove to be the most perishable.

Jeff put the empty beer cans in the kitchen. His old
bedroom, he found, was almost completely stripped
of personal items. It was like a guest room now, or a
motel room, but at least the bed was made up. Jeff's
body was tired, but he was awake for a long time,
thinking, before he found his way to sleep.

CHAPTER THREE

Jeff woke up about ten minutes before the alarm was due to go off feeling rested and eager to get on with the day. He showered, toweled himself dry, and opened his suitcase to get some clean clothes.

It came as something of a surprise to find the pistol tucked in among his shirts. Now why the hell did I bring that, Jeff wondered. It was a cheap .22, and he had owned it for five years or more—ever since his company had landed its first significant defense contract. At the time, buying it had seemed the thing to do, for reasons he could no longer recall. Yet he had continued to carry it with him most of the time, and he had obviously packed it for this trip without even thinking about it.

He picked up the gun and looked at it as if it belonged to someone else and had come into his possession by mistake. Oddly enough, he thought, there was more of a rationale for the weapon now than at any previous time. His company had just begun an extremely sensitive military project. But did a California gun license have any legal status in Connecticut? Could he get in trouble simply for having the pistol? He put it back in the suitcase. It would stay there, and he'd be back in L.A. in a few days.

He drank the bitter remains of some orange juice, made instant coffee, and smoked his first cigarette of the day. Next, he called Uncle Roy and said he'd be over later in the morning, explaining that he'd already had breakfast. Then he found Dick Hudson's number in the telephone book. The lawyer came on the line at once and said he'd be glad to see Jeff anytime.

"Thanks. I'll stop by in about an hour."

"Fine, fine. You know where we are?"

"Church Street?"

"Right you are."

Jeff went into his bedroom to finish unpacking. His suit was rumpled from being left in the suitcase overnight, but he knew Aunt Kitty would be glad to give it a quick press for him. After putting it by the front door, he busied himself by disposing of the rest of the perishables in the kitchen. They filled less than half a trash bag.

Dick Hudson's office was definitely the establishment of an unpretentious small-town lawyer. The chairs were leather, but worn and scuffed. The carpet felt like it wasn't there, and the rest of the furniture might have come from a forties movie. But it all looked somehow reassuring, and it wasn't uncomfortable.

Hudson was a large, middle-aged man with fleshy

hands and a full head of graying hair brushed tightly back over his skull. Property deals, wills, and probate were the mainstay of his practice, with two or three divorce cases a year thrown in for good measure. He spent a minute or so commiserating with Jeff about his father and a few more on idle pleasantries. Then he got to the point.

"I suppose you want to know about the will. That's understandable, perfectly understandable," he soothed. "You probably want to get back to California as soon as possible."

"Right," Jeff said. "But I'm mostly interested in knowing how involved I'll have to be in the process."

"Ah." Hudson looked at Jeff for a moment, as if he was unsure of what he had heard. "Well, it takes a few months, and there's nothing we can do about that. It's just the way the system works. But your presence isn't really required, if that's what you mean. You'll have to sign a lot of documents, but I can ship them out to you by Express Mail and you can return them to me the same way."

"That's what I wanted to hear."

"Good. Now as for the will itself"—the lawyer looked mildly embarrassed—"your father left some money in the bank, but not much. Couple of thousand. He was getting by on Social Security, as you probably know."

"Right, yes."

"And there's the house and its contents, furniture and tools, and . . . uh . . . that's about it."

Jeff nodded; he sensed there was more to come.

"Anyhow," Hudson went on, "you and your uncle Roy are the only two living blood relatives."

"I know."

"Okay. Well." Another deep breath. "The will specifies that the house and everything in it be sold, and that the net receipts be divided equally between you and your uncle."

Hudson looked at Jeff as if he expected the younger man to explode and begin tearing up the office.

"Fantastic," Jeff said as soon as he grasped the news. "That's fantastic."

"Uh . . ." Still wary.

"No, really, I'm delighted my father did that," Jeff explained. "Uncle Roy and Aunt Kitty have been retired for quite a while now, and I'm sure they can use some extra money. That's fine with me. Really." He felt a new measure of respect for his father.

"I see." Hudson's face relaxed somewhat. Wills tended to bring out the worst in people, but apparently not in this case. "I'm glad you feel that way. Everything should go smoothly. It'll just take a little time."

They exchanged addresses and telephone numbers, and then chatted for a few more minutes. Jeff was distracted, though. Glancing out the window, he caught sight of the dome skylight over the reading room of the Millville Public Library. He'd spent countless afternoons and evenings there, and now a vivid image took hold of his mind. Georgianne was at one table, doing homework. She was wearing a miniskirt and those patterned black tights that were popular back then. From where he sat, Jeff had an excellent view of her legs under the table, the glorious reach of her thighs. It was as if Georgianne were a picture, composed only for Jeff. She looked up, distracted momentarily, and noticed him. She smiled and winked before going back to her homework.

The image was so powerful Jeff couldn't remember saying good-bye to Dick Hudson, although he knew he must have. He had lunch with his aunt and uncle and his cousin Nancy, a divorced dental technician. It was pleasant. They sat around the kitchen table eating roast beef sandwiches and drinking lemonade. He was able to talk easily with his relatives, the recollection of Georgianne now a kind of delicious aftertaste. Aunt Kitty lightly ironed his suit.

They got to the funeral home half an hour before the official start of the wake. Jeff spent ten minutes sitting alone with his father's body. They had done a good job. Not too heavy with the make-up, no signs of disfiguration or pain. He could still see the strength of character in George Lisker's face, even in death. His father had the features of someone who'd been his own man. Worn, weathered, and battered with age, and now submissive to death, they were still, somehow, strong. Well, I got that much from you, Jeff thought, even if we didn't understand each other most of the time. It had been worse when his mother died. Now, Jeff felt remarkably peaceful, and he wondered about it. There was something cold in you, old man, and maybe there's something cold in me, too. Did it have to be? There was warmth in Mom—but didn't she have strength as well?

Jeff shook himself slightly and left the room for a

cigarette. It had been hard enough talking to his father in life; there wasn't much point in trying now.

The afternoon passed quietly. Not many people came, but those who did stayed until four o'clock. Nearly all of them were older people who had known Jeff's parents over the decades. They were very kind and friendly to Jeff, asking about his life and work in California and telling him, sincerely, nice things about his father. It was a different and more enjoyable experience than he had anticipated.

The evening session was even better. More people came, and many of them told Jeff that his father had always thought highly of him.

"Maybe he didn't show his feelings much," one elderly woman said. "But he had them, and we all knew how proud he was of you, Jeff. I don't know if he really understood, or liked, you know, computers and all that high-tech stuff you do. You know what we old folks are like—can't stand anything new. But he knew that was the way the world was going, and he was proud of you."

Jeff was touched. How strange to learn now what his father had felt about him! Was it all true? Maybe if Jeff had been around more often over the years, or if he'd paid closer attention, he would have gotten the message.

But did George Lisker ever know how his son felt about him? Probably not, Jeff thought. I did love you, but you made me feel I could never measure up, and that still hurts.

A few minutes after nine, as Jeff and his relatives were about to leave the funeral home, a fat, sweaty man rushed up to them.

"Jeff! Boy, am I glad I caught you. I tried to get here earlier, but I was stuck in a meeting. I feel real bad about it. Hey, I'm sorry about your dad."

He was shaking Jeff's hand vigorously while he talked. It was Mike Rollins, Jeff finally realized.

"Mike. That's all right. Thanks for coming. I really appreciate it. It's good to see you again."

He had to remind himself that twenty years had passed since they were last out on double dates together. Mike must have gained fifty or sixty pounds. He was virtually unrecognizable. Jeff introduced Mike to his relatives before they left. Then he and Mike stood talking under the awning in front of Butler's.

"You look great, buddy," Mike was saying.

"So do you."

"Yeah, like a house." Mike laughed, evidently not bothered by his weight. "What're you doing now?"

"Just going back to the house."

"How about a drink?"

"Okay, sure."

"You got a car? You still remember how to get to Ike's? I'll see you there in five minutes."

Ike's, one of Millville's many bars, had opened in 1956 and was named after President Eisenhower, who was re-elected in a landslide that year. Older townspeople still told each other that Ike's should have been called "Mamie's."

Jeff caught up with Mike at the back of the bar. After they found an empty booth, Jeff lit a cigarette. He noticed that Mike was still sweating.

"So what've you been doing all this time?" Mike asked as they clinked glasses.

"Oh, I've got my own little business, outside L.A., and I live nearby. Otherwise, not much."

"The land of movie stars and beach bunnies, eh? That's great. What is it—computers, did I hear?"

"Sort of," Jeff said. "We design special systems. We have one foot in theory and the other in application."

"Nice." Mike shook his hand loosely. "You always did have a brain for that kind of stuff. I bet there's a lot of money in it, right?"

"How about you?"

"I'm superintendent of the Street Department. How do you like that?" Mike grinned proudly.

"No shit? Superintendent?"

"Head honcho," Mike confirmed.

"You've got it made," Jeff said. "That's a job for life."

Mike didn't dispute this, contenting himself with a smile. "Hey, Millville isn't the liveliest place in the world," he said. "But it's home, you know. And somebody's got to stay here and look after it; otherwise it'll fall apart."

Jeff wasn't sure that was such a bad idea, but he didn't say so. They talked for more than an hour, shuttling back and forth between the good old days and the present. Jeff caught up on a great deal of gossip he really didn't care about and good-naturedly indulged several of Mike's fantasies about life in Southern California.

"Tell me," he said eventually, "what happened with you and Georgianne? You were a steady pair, but I lost touch after that last summer. The summer after graduation."

"Yeah. Georgianne. Right." Mike had a dreamy, faraway look in his eyes. He was on his third gin-and-tonic, the glass all but lost in his meaty grip. "That was a great summer, wasn't it? Best damn time in a person's life, as far as I'm concerned. After that it's just . . . shit and more shit. . . ."

"So what happened?" Jeff sipped a tall glass of tap beer.

"Yeah, well. Let's see. Georgianne went to college in Boston, I went to UConn, and we stayed in touch. We talked on the phone, we saw each other when we were home for holidays and breaks. I think I went up to Boston to see her a couple of times. But . . . well, you know me, Jeff. I wanted to screw everything in sight, and the big difference in college is there you can almost do it. So . . . uh . . . Georgianne and I kind of drifted apart. No big breakup, no heavy scenes, but . . . you know how it is."

"I thought sure you two would get married."

"Ha. I was a cowboy, man," Mike said. "I got married, all right, but not until I was twenty-eight. And even then I couldn't tell you how it happened. Everybody slips up sooner or later. You're married, aren't you?"

"Married, then divorced two years later," Jeff said. "Too much time working and not enough time home with my wife. She took up with her flying instructor, and for all I know they're still getting their rocks off at ten thousand feet."

"That's what I mean about California," Mike said obscurely. "Lemme buy a free man a drink."

"So what happened to Georgianne after that?" Jeff asked when Mike had returned with a fresh round. "I drove up the New Haven Road on my way into town and I saw that the house is for sale."

"She got married ages ago. Some guy I never heard of. I don't think she lives around here, or I would have heard about it sooner or later, and I haven't heard anything about Georgianne in years."

"Her family still in the house? Or did they all pack up and move out?"

"I couldn't tell you," Mike said. "That's a state road, and I haven't been down it in a long time. Christ, I drove up and down it enough times in high school to last the rest of my life."

"That's true."

"Georgianne was a sweet kid, though. A real beauty."

"She was," Jeff agreed quietly.

"Funny thing is . . ." Mike rambled on. "I'll tell you, though I hate to admit it, but the fact is, for all the time I spent with her, all those hours wrestling in the back-seat of my old man's car, then my car, at the drive-in or out on that dirt road in Gunntown, for all that, I never did get in her pants. Not even a finger." He shook his head, as if he still found it hard to believe.

I'm glad to hear that, Jeff thought, surprised both at the minor revelation and at the sudden intensity of feeling it occasioned.

Yes, I'm very glad to hear that.

"Georgianne was one of those gorgeous, unattainable blondes, you know," Mike continued.

"In high school," Jeff said, "none of us got laid nearly as often as we said we did at the time."

"Now that's the truth," Mike exclaimed, seizing the point gratefully. "But we sure did kiss like there was no tomorrow, and kissing Georgianne was some kind of experience in itself."

"I'm sure it was."

The conversation had become unpleasant and distasteful to Jeff, but at the same time it seemed strangely important to him. Something was taking shape.

Back at the house a little later, Jeff followed a hunch. Cognac was the only form of spirits George Lisker ever touched. It took a few minutes, but Jeff found the solitary bottle, on the shelf in the broom closet. He didn't need another drink, but he wanted one, and poured a double measure.

He sipped the liquor slowly, enjoying it. As he drank and smoked, the grin on his face would not go away.

So, he thought, Mike had never made it with the wonderful Georgianne. Never even got a finger in, as he had so charmingly put it. Jeff still couldn't say why this pleased him, but it did, undeniably. Enormously.

CHAPTER FOUR

The funeral service was short and dignified. Once again, more people attended than Jeff had expected. After the burial, everyone went back to Uncle Roy's place. By the time Jeff got home it was early afternoon. He stripped off his clothes and stood under a cold shower for twenty minutes. Then he sat on the edge of his bed, a large towel wrapped around his waist, and stared at the floor.

There were things to be done around the house, but he couldn't concentrate on them. His mind didn't seem to be functioning smoothly. Putting on a pair of light slacks, a sport shirt, and his loafers, he went out for a drive, acutely aware that he was surrounded by scenes of his past. The high school, the football field, the baseball diamond were all still there, more or less unchanged. But Ramona's Pizzeria had been absorbed into a plastic pizza chain and some of the bars had new names. The Alcazar movie theater was now a roller disco, and a rather forlorn-looking one at that. Next to it was an alcohol-free teenage night club. Jeff felt old.

He parked and went into a package store. A few minutes later he was driving again, a can of cold beer wedged up against his crotch and eleven others stashed under the seat. It was stupidly enjoyable, this cruising of the old ground, even if he was thirty-eight. He hadn't done this in about twenty years, but it still felt good. Sometimes it was the best thing you could do in a small town.

After a while, he got on the New Haven Road, heading south out of Millville. He was curious, but he still wasn't sure he had enough nerve. It could be terribly awkward or embarrassing. Would he really be able to think of anything sensible to say?

When he got there, he hesitated, but turned the car onto the Slaton driveway and went right up and around to the house. A small brown pickup was parked in front of the garage. Jeff turned his motor off and sat for a moment, looking at the house and the yard. The windows were uncurtained and the lawn needed mowing, but the place still had a peaceful, secluded feeling about it. The nearest neighbors were a couple of hundred yards along the road, in both directions, and at the back of the lot was a wooded hillside that rose steeply. The birdbath and swing set remained, but Jeff knew the Slatons were gone. Yet he was glad he had come.

Getting out of the car, he walked slowly toward the house, went up the half-flight of stairs to the back porch, and knocked on the door. The kitchen, he saw through the window, was completely bare. Not a single appliance or piece of furniture had been left. But someone was inside; he could hear a power tool in use. He knocked again when the loud buzzing stopped for a couple of seconds, but it started again. He tried the door, which was unlocked.

He went through the kitchen, which seemed too small, then the dining room, which also appeared to be cramped, and finally came into the living room, which was larger and closer to what he remembered. The place was empty, even the built-in bookshelves on one wall. The good feeling he had experienced only a few minutes ago now seemed to be leaking out of him, and he thought about turning around and leaving. But the power tool upstairs went silent again.

"Hello!" Jeff called out quickly.

"Yeah," a voice answered. A young man, perhaps in his late twenties, clumped down the stairs in a rush. His face, arms, and hair were covered with a fine dust. "Yeah, what can I do for you?"

"Uh . . . is this your house?" Jeff asked. There was a very slight chance this person was one of Georgianne's younger brothers.

"Yeah, the sale's gone through now, but the agent hasn't taken his sign away yet. Sorry, if you were interested."

"No, it's not that. I used to know the Slatons years ago," Jeff explained. "I wondered if they were still around."

"Oh. No, the Slatons are gone."

The young man made it sound as if the entire family had been wiped out.

"Gone?"

30

"Yeah. To Florida, I think."

"Did you know them?"

"No, not me. They moved out before the house was sold. It was a while ago now."

"Okay." Jeff gave the room a last quick glance and started to go. "Thanks anyhow."

"If you want to get in touch with them, you could ask Mrs. Brewer," the young man said. "I think she knows where the Slatons can be reached."

"Mrs. Brewer?"

"First house up the road on this side."

"Going toward town?"

"That's it."

"Okay, thanks. Maybe I will."

Jeff turned the car around in the back-in with the netless basketball hoop and drove down to the road. He shifted into neutral and sat there for a moment, trying to make up his mind. Did he really want to take this thing any further? What was the point? She wasn't even your girlfriend, he reminded himself unhappily. He had gone through Kathy, Joanne, and Betsy, and a couple of minor flirtations, during the years in which he had doubled with Mike and Georgianne. But of all those he'd known, friends and classmates, Georgianne was the only one who still interested him. He had thought about her many times. In fact, he realized, he'd never quite stopped thinking about her. Georgianne had always been there, somewhere, in his mind. And this could well be the last chance he would ever have to do anything about it.

He put the car in gear and began driving slowly toward the center of Millville. As soon as he saw the house, Jeff smiled. A woman was weeding a flower bed along the front walk. He took it as a good omen: he was meant to know what had happened to Georgianne. He pulled the car over to the side of the road and left the engine idling.

The woman stood up to face him. She wore a checkered bandana on her head, slacks, sneakers, and a print blouse of hideous design. She was pudgy and sixtyish, but, with a three-pronged garden tool in her hand, she looked ready for anything. Jeff put on his best smile.

"Mrs. Brewer?"

"Yes."

"My name is Jeff Lisker, and I grew up here in Millville. I used to know the Slatons real well. Georgianne was a good friend and classmate of mine, but we lost touch as the years went by. I live out in California now and I'm just back on a visit to see my family. I thought I'd catch up with the Slatons, but they've moved, and I was wondering if you could tell me where they are now."

The elderly woman had listened to this little spiel carefully, and now she considered it for a few seconds before deciding that it sounded reasonable enough.

"Oh, the Slatons. They're a wonderful family," Mrs. Brewer said. "You know that Jack died five, no, six years ago."

"No, I didn't. I'm sorry to hear that."

"Yes. He had the cancer, but it come on him real sudden and it didn't take long. So he didn't suffer the way some do."

"Well, that's something."

"Now, Donnie, he went to college down in Florida, and then he got a job teaching there, in Tampa. And little Jack went to UConn, and got himself a good job at Anaconda, right up here in Waterbury. But the whole company moved to Chicago about four years ago, and he went with it. Both the boys are married now and have kids of their own."

Jeff nodded with every sentence, trying to keep the woman moving along. Apparently she was going to tell him the whole tedious story.

"Well, the winters got to be too much for Doris," Mrs. Brewer continued enthusiastically. "That driveway is murder when there's any snow at all. And ice? Oh! It's impossible. And being all alone up there in that house just wasn't good for her. So she finally put the house on the market in January, which wasn't a good time for that, but she'd had enough and she moved down near Donnie in Tampa. Now she has a nice bungalow-style condominium. I've got some snapshots of it inside."

"Good for her," Jeff said impatiently. "But—"

"Now, you said you were Georgianne's friend?"

At last. "That's right," Jeff said.

"Well. Georgianne worked in Boston for a year or two after she finished college, and then she married a young man by the name of Sean Corcoran. Did you know him?"

"No, I don't think so."

"I've met him a couple of times," Mrs. Brewer said, "and he's a very nice person, very nice."

"That's good."

"They have one child, a daughter. Her name is Bonnie. Now if you're a friend of Georgianne, you know she was always very bright."

"Yes."

"Right. Well, I hear from Doris how the kids are doing, you know, and Bonnie is just fantastic at schoolwork. They say she has a brain like a computer."

In the computer field this is no compliment, but Jeff didn't tell Mrs. Brewer that. Now that he was finally hearing some real news about Georgianne, he was having a hard time absorbing it.

"They live in Foxrock, over near Danbury," the elderly woman went on. "Sean teaches high school there. They have a very nice house. But it's kind of sad, isn't it, the way families are so scattered these days. Connecticut and Chicago and Florida . . ."

Jeff nodded sympathetically and took a step back toward the car. He had what he wanted, more or less.

"Thanks very much for your help."

"I'll tell them you were asking for them. Doris still calls up from time to time. What'd you say your name was?"

"Lisker," Jeff replied softly, turning away. "Thanks again." He got into the car.

"What was that?"

Mrs. Brewer hadn't caught it, but she knew she'd heard the name the first time. It would come back to her sooner or later. She had read about this somewhere. The trick was not to try to force it. Once you saw or heard something, it was in your mind for good. Maybe you couldn't always find it just when you wanted it, but eventually it would pop up again. All it took was patience.

She watched the young man drive away, noticing the New York license plate on the back end of the car, and then she got on with her weeding.

CHAPTER FIVE

Jeff's talk with Mrs. Brewer had left him determined to finish his business in Millville as quickly as possible. He no longer had the slightest reason to linger. He took Uncle Roy and Aunt Kitty out to dinner, and then spent all of Wednesday morning sorting through personal effects at the house. It was a strange experience. Most of the things to be thrown away belonged to him, not his father. Junk, he considered it, left over from childhood and adolescence, things he'd never bothered shipping out to California. When he was done, he had filled several trash bags.

Tuesday night, after taking Aunt Kitty and Uncle Roy back to their house, he had come home and sat in the living room watching television and drinking the rest of the beer he had bought. It was another silly luxury, like cruising around that afternoon. In California, he saw little television. Now, in the house where he'd been raised, it was impossible to resist, and the shows were right out of his past: Wally and the Beaver, Bilko, *Dobie Gillis*, *Twilight Zone*, *The Honeymooners*, and *Love that Bob*. It was like being on vacation, something he hadn't done in more than ten years; and it had taken a funeral to achieve it.

Perhaps if he had been able to do something like that with Audrey, something as simple as sitting up late once in a while and watching old TV shows . . . She had divorced him because he was a workaholic, and because he showed no willingness to change. But he knew it was foolish to think that anything could have saved their marriage.

Audrey had never understood or accepted that he simply couldn't afford to take much time off from work. He and Ted had just started their own company, entering one of the riskiest and most competitive areas of the computer-science field. For the first five years, neither of them had ever put in less than ninety hours a week. To do so, they were convinced, would be suicidal. Then they'd be damaged goods; they'd never get the money or the business to start over.

You had only to glance upstate to Silicon Valley to see how many others there were, breathing down your neck, and to learn the lesson of all those hundreds of failures, bankruptcies, and personal catastrophes. Somehow, amazingly, Jeff and Ted hadn't burned out. Jeff had lost a marriage and Ted was a walking pharmacy, but they reckoned they were lucky. The pace was still furious, but they were down to sixty-hour weeks, and the company was secure now, thriving.

Jeff had sat up watching the reruns with a Connecticut road map open on his lap. He kept glancing down at it, as if he expected it to change. He had forgotten all about I-84, the highway that had come through Waterbury about the time he had graduated from high school. He hadn't paid much attention to it then, but it fascinated him now. It was an alternate route to New York and, judging by the map, a quicker one. But the interesting thing about it was that it passed through Danbury.

After piling the trash bags in the cellar Wednesday morning, Jeff took care of the rest of his business. He arranged for the gas to be turned off and the telephone service disconnected. He filled out a change-of-address card at the post office. Hudson had asked him to leave the water and electricity on; they would be useful when the realtors showed the house. As agreed, Jeff delivered a slim folder of outstanding bills and other papers to the lawyer's office.

Back at the house, he packed his suitcases and checked every room one more time. I'll never see this place again, he thought, and for a moment he couldn't get his feet to move. Yes, on the whole he had been happy here. Happy enough, and that was probably as much as anyone could hope for.

He locked up, put his things in the car, and drove across town to say good-bye to Uncle Roy and Aunt Kitty. He gave them the house keys and a card with his office address and number on it.

"I think I'll take I-84 back to New York," he said as they stood out on the front lawn.

"I should've thought to tell you," Uncle Roy said. "It's faster that way, and a better ride."

"It goes through Danbury, doesn't it?"

"Yeah. Well, *over* it."

"Danbury's getting to be quite a big city," Aunt Kitty said, offering last-minute Connecticut news. "Lot of new business and development."

"Yeah, Union Carbide set up headquarters there a few years ago," Uncle Roy added. "Quite a setup."

"That's right," Jeff said quietly. He was suddenly interested. "I remember now hearing that Union Carbide was in Danbury. When that Bhopal disaster was in the news."

He was genuinely sorry to leave his aunt and uncle. They had always been good to him. As he drove north toward Waterbury, he had to face again the unhappy thought that this might be the last time he'd see them both alive. Yet, to him, the whole damn Brass Valley reeked of death, and he was glad to be leaving it. Even the brass giant, Anaconda, had packed up and moved away, according to Mrs. Brewer. Old industry had made this gritty area, but that was the past. New technology had taken over, and it would rule supreme at least through Jeff's lifetime.

Traffic was light Wednesday afternoon as he headed west on I-84, leaving Millville, Waterbury, and the Brass Valley behind. It was a short drive to Danbury, and he hardly noticed the miles passing. Too many thoughts were crowding his mind. A lot of things had happened in a few days, some by accident and some by design. On Sunday he had missed route 8, the Waterbury exit, the immediate result of which was that he had come up the New Haven Road instead, past the Slaton house. Then, when he'd gone to the house on Tuesday afternoon, it could have been locked up and empty, but it wasn't. The new owner had been there to steer him to Mrs. Brewer, who in turn had been out in her front yard, making it impossible for him to drive by without stopping. Then, looking at the road map, he had discovered I-84, a way back to La Guardia Airport through Danbury. Not to forget the conversation with Mike Rollins, which seemed to have a bizarre significance for Jeff. Something had been taking shape in his mind, and now he knew what it was. Since he was here, and since it was possible, he wanted to see Georgianne again. Once would be enough, he thought. It was just too good an opportunity to pass up.

He nearly lost his nerve, letting two or three Danbury exits pass before he finally got off the highway. With no sense of direction, he drove around the outskirts of the city until he spotted the Mortlake Motel. It was neither great nor terrible, but, like most motels, bleakly adequate. The package store across the road was a plus. After checking in, he bought a six-pack, returned to his room, and picked up the phone.

"Lisker-Benedictus Future Systems. May I help you?"

Jeff loved to hear that. More than his own name, those four words told him who he was, what he was. Lisker-Benedictus Future Systems. Beautiful. Once in a while he used his outside line to call the front desk and hear those words; then he'd hang up, satisfied. They had considered shortening it to Future Systems, but eventually discarded the idea because Jeff was so opposed to it. He loved the sound of it the way it was. A few seconds later he was put through to Callie Shaw, personal assistant.

"Callie, this is Jeff."

"Hello," she said brightly. "How are you? Where are you?"

"I'm fine and I'm still in Connecticut. I wanted to check in with you because I've been in and out a lot the last few days and I didn't know if you'd been trying to reach me."

"No. There's no real news here, Jeff. Nothing exciting or important to report, so I didn't want to bother you."

"Just the usual day-to-day madness."

"Right, yes," Callie said with a laugh. "We're coping. Pretty well, I think."

"Okay, glad to hear it. Now listen, Callie. I'll be staying on here for another day or two, which will bring us into the weekend, so you might as well not expect to see me until Monday."

"Fine. I'll make a note of that."

"I won't be at the number I gave you," Jeff said. "In fact, I can't really give you a number, because I'm doing a lot of running around, seeing people and tying up loose ends—family business. What I'll do is give you another call, either this time tomorrow afternoon or else the first thing Friday morning. Your time. All right?"

"Fine. Got it."

"You can give Ted the message," he added. "I assume he hasn't been trying to get me."

"He would have told me, I think," Callie said. "He's completely wrapped up in the project."

"Of course." *The* project. Sigma Tau, so sensitive they were forbidden to use those two words on any telephone—not even on the company's internal system. It was such a sweet contract that Lisker-Benedictus could probably survive on it alone for the next five years.

After Jeff hung up, he sat back on the bed and lit a cigarette. It was Wednesday evening, and the last twenty-four hours had been tiring.

What was he really doing here? It seemed like the kind of fool's errand that could easily turn into a colossal embarrassment. He hadn't seen her since they were teenagers. She was married now and had a teenage daughter of her own. That in itself was so hard for Jeff to fathom that it almost paralyzed him.

He opened a can of beer as he flipped through the Danbury telephone directory. There it was, Foxrock. A short section for a small town. He turned the pages slowly, enjoying his search. It didn't take long. There were only two Corcorans listed: Bonnie, on Indian Hill Road, and Sean R., also on Indian Hill Road. For a moment, Jeff wondered what the R. stood for—something Irish, like Rory? He tried to picture the man. Florid, freckled, red-haired? He smiled. Georgianne marrying an Irish stereotype? Fat chance of that ever happening.

What about the daughter? He tried to construct a chronology. Georgianne should be thirty-eight, or nearly so. If she hadn't given birth until after college, Bonnie would be fifteen, sixteen at most. Did she look like Georgianne at that age? It was a dazzling, terrifying thought. But Bonnie didn't really interest him. He was curious about Georgianne, not some teenager who probably dressed like Madonna.

Should he dial the number and talk to her? Now? That was what he had come for, but Jeff was hit by another attack of uncertainty. He could still avoid this moment of possible contact. He could check out of the Mortlake Motel and get to New York at a reasonable hour. Catch a late flight to L.A. or else spend a night in Manhattan, where there were good restaurants, music, films, any number of pleasant things to do. It would make a lot more sense than sitting out in the middle of nowhere drinking beer and acting silly about a girl, no, a woman he hadn't seen in twenty years.

Even if he did call the number, her husband might answer. Then what? Or if he did get Georgianne on the line, he might just dry up and not know what to say. His professional manner would desert him. The whole thing was a whim, a bad idea really, nothing more. The kind of thing that seems irresistible until you actually do it. Then you understand what a mistake it was all along.

Jeff scrawled the two telephone numbers on the road map and put the directory back on the bedside table. He went into the bathroom and urinated, then sat down on the bed again and stared at the floor. All right. He had a plan, of sorts. He called Bonnie's number, and she answered on the second ring.

"Hello."

"Is Harold there?"

"Who?"

"Harold. Harold."

Jeff nearly laughed, because he was doing such a good job of altering and coarsening his voice.

"There's no Harold here," Bonnie Corcoran said. "What number did you want?"

"Who's this?"

"Bonnie. What number—"

"Sorry."

Jeff hung up and fell back across the bed, his whole body shaking with excitement. Jesus Christ, that voice! As though it had come right out of his own head, not from the other end of a telephone line. It was like honey poured in his ear, lighting up the center of his brain with a warm glow. Bonnie sounded like Georgianne, as he remembered her. The voice of a teenager—deliciously appropriate, so right, so true to the voice he had carried in his mind all these years.

That did it. He had to see her. Not the daughter—he didn't care about her—but the mother. Georgianne. No matter how it might turn out—awkward, embarrassing, a disaster—he had to see her.

And why worry? Now that he had made the first move, he was sure the rest would fall in place. It required a little careful thought, that was all. Plan it, make it nice, smooth, relaxed. Something that would become a fine memory for all of them.

Lighting a cigarette and opening another beer, he began to piece it all together. It was a special project, but nothing he couldn't handle. Jeff was good at special projects.

44

CHAPTER SIX

Foxrock wasn't much more than a village, off route 7 north of Danbury. Jeff got there just before eight o'clock the next morning. It was a rural community, and the houses were widely scattered along country roads rather than closely packed on neat residential streets. It took him nearly another half hour of driving around before he found Indian Hill Road.

When he spotted the Corcoran mailbox, he took care not to slow down, and glanced only briefly at the house. As soon as it was convenient, he turned the car around and drove back. The second time he passed the house he noted the two cars in the driveway, one a blue compact, the other a deep-red or maroon wagon. The usual suburban scene.

Back at the T-junction, he turned left, away from the center of Foxrock and stopped just before the first bend in the road, about a hundred yards along, where he pulled onto a grassy verge. He turned the car off, adjusted the rear-view mirror, and propped a road map conspicuously on the steering wheel. Next, he took the lid off a cup of coffee he'd picked up at a fast-food place on the way. Still hot. He waited.

The wagon appeared fifteen minutes later and turned in the other direction. Two people in it. Precisely what Jeff had expected. Sean and Bonnie going to school. Hadn't Mrs. Brewer said Sean was a teacher?

Now, Georgianne. He had no intention of barging in on her this early in the morning, having visions of her in some drab housecoat, her hair mussed, surrounded by breakfast dishes. It wouldn't be fair to either of them. She needed time, and he was prepared to wait.

So he was startled when he saw the blue compact stop at the junction only a few minutes later. It headed toward town. Pushing the map aside, he started the car, and turned it sharply around. He put his sunglasses on and hung back as far as he could; all he wanted was to keep her in sight. No passengers— it looked good. The thought came to him that there might well be more than one blue compact on Indian Hill Road, but when he had to come up close behind her at the red light in the center of Foxrock, he was sure it really was Georgianne. The blond hair . . . He cupped his hands in front of his face, lighting a cigarette with difficulty. He was trembling.

He followed her all the way into Danbury, where she left her car in a municipal lot. Jeff parked there as well, though some distance away. Then he trailed her for two short blocks. She went into a place called the

Reinecke Fitness Center. Jeff continued walking slowly along the other side of the street, trying to figure out what to do. If Georgianne was a customer, she would most likely be out in an hour or ninety minutes. But if she worked there, she might not reappear until lunchtime, or even the end of the afternoon.

He bought a newspaper, found a convenient diner, and sat at the counter, by the front, where he could keep an eye on the entrance to the Fitness Center. He ordered coffee, orange juice, and a Danish. Later he had to ask for another coffee, but he hardly ever looked at the newspaper.

What was she wearing? He had been trying to remember, but he didn't have a clear picture in his mind yet. He had been so concerned about keeping her in sight without getting too close that he hadn't been able to focus on details. A light summer skirt and blouse, appropriate for the May heat wave? It was maddening. For twenty years, whenever Jeff had thought of Georgianne, she had always come to mind in sharp, vivid images, so real he would sometimes think he could actually speak to her or touch her. But now, when he had finally seen her in the flesh, she was so elusive he didn't even know what she was wearing.

Eventually he couldn't sit still any longer. He had to do something, move. So he walked back to the parking lot, got in his car, turned to the sports pages, and tried to concentrate on an article about the Lakers.

A little after eleven, he looked up and saw Georgianne at her car. She tossed something—a gym bag?—onto the front seat and locked the vehicle again. He was out and following her as she walked away in the opposite direction from the Fitness Center. She went into an art-supply shop.

This is it, he told himself as he gazed absently at another store's window display. Putting his sunglasses in his jacket pocket he patted his hair. He was ready now to talk to her, and he was so excited his whole body felt charged. And yet he was very calm. After all the uncertainty, he knew he was not making a mistake.

Then Georgianne was back on the sidewalk, coming in his direction. Jeff turned to face her.

"Georgianne," he said clearly when she was less than ten feet from him.

She stopped and stared. The blank look on her face changed to one of amazement. The shock of recognition, Jeff thought happily. But she hadn't put it together enough to say anything yet.

"You look beautiful," he told her, smiling broadly and stepping closer.

"Jeff? Jeff Lisker? My God, it's you!"

They threw their arms around each other, hugging and kissing. Then they stepped back a pace and looked each other over once more, as if to make sure they weren't having a hallucination. And they hugged again.

"Oh, Jeff, how are you?"

"I'm just fine. And you?"

"Fine. Stunned."

Jeff smiled. "You look great," he said, gazing at her with deep affection.

"So do you." Now Georgianne laughed. "I still don't believe this. That I'm standing here talking to you."

"Well, you are," he said. "It's great to see you again. It's been so long. *Too* long."

Georgianne was truly beautiful, somehow much more so than he had either remembered or expected.

"I thought you were living out in California."

"That's right. I've been there ever since college."

"And you're back now for a visit."

"Several things," Jeff said vaguely. "But before we get into that, where are you going right now?"

"I was just on my way home. I live about ten miles from here, in Foxrock."

"Well, no," Jeff told her. "You're on your way to lunch with me, instead."

"Great. I'd love that."

"Okay. Let's see. The restaurants probably don't open until noon. How about a Bloody Mary first?"

"Sure," Georgianne said. "Do you know Danbury?"

"Not a bit."

"There's a fairly decent cocktail lounge just around the corner. I don't know how the kitchen is, but they serve lunches and dinners, too."

"Let's give it a try."

Jeff couldn't take his eyes off her as they walked. Georgianne had more than doubled her age but she seemed to be immune to time. Her face was still unlined. Her hair, shorter now, was thick and lustrous, the blond having mellowed into a rich honey color that glowed in the sunlight. She was radiant, her skin not rosy but almost golden. Jeff had found what he'd come looking for—the girl in the very long dream.

"How long has it been?" Georgianne asked. "Not since we—"

"More than half our lifetimes ago," Jeff said, and he was immediately annoyed with himself for sounding so pompous. "Twenty years, to be exact."

"Twenty years. Is there a reunion?"

"Other than this one? Not that I've heard of."

They entered a tidy, middle-class bar. The furniture was dark-stained wood and there were prints of country scenes on the walls. It was unpretentious and, at this time of day, empty. They sat at a banquette and a waitress appeared to take their orders.

"Well, to us," Jeff said, raising his glass, when she had returned with the drinks.

"Why not," Georgianne said, smiling warmly. "To us." She touched his glass with hers.

Jeff already knew he wanted to spend the entire day with this woman. She was glad to see him, to be with him. Nothing awkward or embarrassing about it. He was sure now he hadn't made a mistake in seeking her out.

Georgianne's eyes, which Jeff thought he remembered as being green, now seemed to be silvery gray. But there was no denying the sparkle in them, the fire of life. He tried not to stare at her too much, but he was still on the high of simply seeing her and being in her presence. She met his gaze with no hint of self-consciousness.

"Tell me," she said, "what are you doing here in Danbury? How did this happy accident come about?"

"It's not entirely an accident," Jeff replied. "I had to come home for my father's funeral."

"Oh, Jeff. I'm sorry."

"I would have been coming back anyhow," he continued. "I have some business with Union Carbide in Danbury, and the two things just happened to coincide, more or less."

"I see."

"Anyhow, I was on the New Haven Road the other day and I saw the For Sale sign outside your house. Somebody told me you were living in this area, so I thought I'd see if I could find you while I was here. And then, this morning, almost as soon as I get here, who do I see walking toward me on the sidewalk?"

"It's amazing, it really is." Georgianne shook her head slightly, smiling. "And what are you doing—your work?"

"Computers," Jeff explained. "I have my own company, just outside Los Angeles. We design special systems for—well, for whoever needs them."

"That's fantastic. And you're doing a job now for Union Carbide?"

"Not yet. We're still in the talking stage and it may or may not come off. It's a very complicated deal."

"How exciting!" Georgianne said, evidently impressed. "But we always knew you'd do well at something like that."

"Yeah, but it's just work," Jeff said, "and it seems that's all I do. I can't tell you what a treat it is to see you. This is the first time I've been away from the office in years, and if it weren't for you, the whole trip would have been nothing but the funeral and business."

"I'm glad to see you, too." Georgianne squeezed Jeff's arm lightly.

"Tell me about yourself."

"Oh, it's pretty boring," Georgianne said. "When I was in my second year of college I fell in love with a great guy. We got married right away, I quit school, and we've been together ever since."

"Terrific," Jeff said quietly.

"We have a daughter," Georgianne went on. "She's about to graduate from high school, if you can believe that. Sean—my husband—teaches in the middle school here in Danbury. We built our own house, piece by piece, and it took two long years. And . . . what else can I tell you? Sean's a jogger; I go swimming every morning. Oh, and I do some pen-and-ink sketches—not very good, but it's better than just watching the soaps. It's all pretty quiet and normal, I guess."

"Not at all," Jeff said. "It sounds great. The main thing is you like it and you're happy."

"Right. I do and I am."

"That's all that matters then. Tell me about your husband and daughter. Just the one child?"

"Yes." The note of regret was clear in her voice. "Bonnie came early and lightning never struck again."

"You would have liked more."

"Sure, but we were lucky to have Bonnie at least. She's a great kid. Did I tell you she's graduating a year early? She's only seventeen. We're very proud of her. And Sean—he was a junior stockbroker when I met him, but he hated it and gave it up after a year."

"Good for him," Jeff said. "A lot of people don't have the nerve to make that kind of move."

"You must be married, Jeff."

"Ah. I'm the one who's normal there," he said with a smile. "I *was* married, but it didn't last long. You could say it was a California romance. I was working sixteen-hour days, trying to get the company off the ground. She ran off and I let her go. Eventually we got around to the formality of a divorce."

"That's a shame," Georgianne said.

"It was all wrong from the beginning," Jeff added. "If I had been honest about it, I wouldn't have married her in the first place. I knew I'd be working all hours as far ahead as I could see, and that's no basis for a marriage. You've been very lucky."

"I know. Sometimes I look at my daughter and think, It's a miracle, nothing less than a miracle, that she's the person she is. That she hasn't been messed up or damaged in some way. Maybe I'm wrong, but it seems it was easier when we were growing up."

"I know what you mean," Jeff said politely. He had his own thoughts about the past, and they had nothing to do with that kind of middle-class paranoia.

They had a second round of drinks and then ordered lunch. Jeff didn't want to move. They talked about old friends and acquaintances, where they were now and what they were doing, and Georgianne told him about her everyday life in greater detail—things that ordinarily wouldn't have interested him at all, but that now, in her presence, he found strangely fascinating. He could listen to her talk all day, and all night, too, probably. Just so long as he was with her.

After the meal, Jeff ordered a cognac and persuaded Georgianne to have something else. She settled on Irish coffee.

"I never drink this much," she said, "and it's beginning to catch up with me."

"That's all right. It's a special day."

"It certainly is," she agreed merrily. "Where are you staying, Jeff? The Hilton?"

This threw him momentarily. The Mortlake Motel made little sense for someone supposedly in town to do business with Union Carbide. He was annoyed that he hadn't anticipated the question.

"Uh . . . no. I just drove down here this morning and I was planning to go back to the house in Millville tonight."

"It's not that far," Georgianne said. "How long will your work keep you here?"

He shrugged. "It's a day-to-day thing, but I expect to be back in California by Monday."

"Oh, well, you must come to dinner. I'd love to have you meet my husband and daughter."

"I'd like that very much," he said. "But first I'd like to take you out. How about dinner tonight, all of us?"

Jeff had worked this out beforehand. In his mind it was important that he take the Corcorans out first. Dinner at their house—he had expected the invitation, of course—had to come later.

"That would be wonderful," Georgianne said. "But you don't have to do that, Jeff."

"I want to. Really."

"Well, Bonnie can't make it. She has a party tonight. But Sean and I could come."

"The three of us, then. You pick the place, and make it the best. My treat."

"All right, but then you're coming to our house for a good home-cooked meal," Georgianne insisted. "Tomorrow night?"

"You're on."

She smiled and took Jeff's hand in hers and held it for a few moments. He felt a charge from her touch surging through him. They agreed that the easiest thing would be to meet again at the same cocktail lounge, have a drink and go on to another restaurant. Jeff hated to leave Georgianne at all, even for a couple of hours, but he knew it was necessary.

From the Mortlake he phoned the Hilton and was able to get a room for that night. He checked in within the hour. Georgianne had asked if he'd like to stay with them, but he had declined. It was tempting, so very tempting, but too risky. Being with her all the time, but with her husband and daughter around too . . . Jeff was not sure he could handle it. And it would require much more of an effort to keep up the Union Carbide charade. No, the offer delighted him, but he was right to turn it down.

After unpacking, he surrendered to a nap. The meal and drinks had made him drowsy, but he drifted in and out of sleep, as if his mind couldn't quite let go. He kept seeing Georgianne, her face at this angle or that, her hair catching the sun, her eyes shining in the dark interior of the cocktail lounge. Her neck and throat were so elegant, showing no signs of age. Her body looked as firm and gorgeous as ever, from the glimpses he'd had of her legs to the way her breasts filled out that snug knit top.

What was it about Georgianne, he wondered dreamily.

She had grown up into a perfectly ordinary woman, it seemed. A wife and mother, bright but not too brainy. You didn't have to compete with her to make simple conversation—no small pleasure in itself. And she appeared to be content with her life. Jeff envied her that. Few people managed it, from what he knew.

But she still had that—that air of magic, or whatever it was. He couldn't put his finger on it, but it didn't really matter. There was something special about her. You wanted to be with her. You liked to listen to that clear, true voice, regardless of what it was saying, simply because it was so clear and true. Most of all, you wanted to feel that charge she gave off, the electricity of life—everyday life, as you should be able to live it.

There was more, but Jeff hadn't figured it out yet. Something to do with the future, the past. But for now he was happy to have found her, and he felt younger and more alive than he had in years. Georgianne had matured into a beautiful, still-young woman who outdazzled the high-school image in his memory. That in itself seemed proof enough that he was on the right track.

CHAPTER SEVEN

Sean Corcoran was friendly but quiet. Jeff wanted to like the man, but had a hard time getting a fix on him. He had a sly sense of humor, which Jeff might have appreciated if he hadn't thought it was at his expense. When Sean had something to say, he glanced up at you, but most of the time he kept his eyes on his wife or his drink. Maybe he just felt uncomfortable being the odd person at this private reunion, but that didn't make it any easier to like him.

"Georgianne tells me the two of you double-dated all the time but never actually dated each other," Sean said. His fingers absently traced lines in the condensation on the side of his beer glass, and now he looked across the table at Jeff, eyes mischievous. "How did that happen?"

"He never asked me," Georgianne said promptly. She was sitting in the middle of the banquette, between the two men.

57

"She had a steady boyfriend," Jeff replied. "Hasn't she ever told you?" Then, to Georgianne, "Mike Rollins, in case you don't remember."

"Would rather not remember," she corrected.

"And you've been in California all this time?"

"Just about," Jeff said.

"Do you jog?"

Jeff laughed. "No. I smoke cigarettes."

"So I see," Sean said. "I thought it was against the law not to jog in California."

Jeff smiled but didn't bother to respond. This man was no threat, he told himself. The wonder was that he'd ever managed to marry Georgianne in the first place. He might have been handsome, and he still wasn't bad-looking—dark curly hair and a lean, wiry build; just under six feet tall. And he might be a capable, even clever man, in his own way, but he seemed all wrong for Georgianne.

"And you're designing some kind of monster computer," Sean went on. "Is that right?"

Again Jeff smiled politely. "Not quite," he said. He was going to say something else, but let it go, deciding instead to concentrate his gaze on Georgianne.

"I'm all in favor of computers," Sean said, in a way that made it clear he was not.

"I understand you designed and built your own house," Jeff said, just to change the subject.

"Now, that's true," Sean replied. "The height of my creativity, and I must tell you that ninety percent of it came from other people's plans."

"That doesn't matter," Jeff said. "A house is a house, and it's a hell of a job to build one on your own."

"The American dream," Sean agreed. "And do you know what holds it together? Yugoslavian nails."

Georgianne groaned. "He loves to tell people that."

Jeff laughed, as he was expected to, but he wondered about Sean Corcoran. Was he always like this? Could anyone be obscurely antic on a full-time basis? It occurred to him now that Georgianne might have married Sean because he'd got her pregnant, and somehow they'd made a go of it. It was one possible explanation, and Jeff was looking for an explanation because Sean was definitely not the man who would, or should, be Georgianne Slaton's husband. The odd part was that they got along. Jeff could see that, but he wrote it off as mere habit, the familiarity of routine.

"I'm at the Hilton now," Jeff told Georgianne. "Got a room there after I left you this afternoon."

"Oh, Jeff. You should have stayed with us," Georgianne said. "I told you we had plenty of room."

"That's right," Sean confirmed. "Why stay at a hotel when you could stay with friends?"

Jeff smiled, pleased by the disappointment Georgianne showed. By contrast, Sean's remarks seemed perfunctory.

"Thanks. I appreciate it," he said. "But I'd only disrupt your household, coming and going at odd times. Besides, the hotel is a tax-deductible business expense, and if I don't bring a few of them back my accountants begin to get jumpy."

"It's up to you," Sean said.

They left the cocktail lounge after two drinks and drove to a restaurant somewhere outside Danbury.

Georgianne rode with Jeff, in case he lost sight of Sean on the way.

"Your husband's a nice man," Jeff said as he followed the blue compact out of the city.

"Oh, I hope you do like him," Georgianne said. "He *is* a good man, a very good husband and father."

The gambit was refused, or ignored. Jeff thought he'd opened a door for her, but Georgianne's response was bewildering.

"What more could you want?" he forced himself to continue. "No, I really meant it. I like him."

"I'm glad. Not everybody does."

"Oh?" A note of hope.

"Well . . . Sean does rub some people the wrong way. They think he's being sarcastic, when he isn't really. It's just the way he talks."

"As long as you're happy. That's the only thing that matters. Other people don't count."

"I know."

It took a few seconds for Jeff to realize that she hadn't said, *Yes, I am happy*. It was, he thought, a significant omission. He reached for her hand and squeezed it. She smiled back at him. The hem of her dress was perched demurely on her knees, and his eyes lingered briefly on her legs. Then suddenly he had a strange feeling. It had to do with being in a car with Georgianne again. This time, at last, they were alone. An old picture came into his head, and he instinctively glanced at the rear-view mirror. Once, many years ago, he'd been in the front seat with Joanne, and he'd looked up to catch a glimpse of Georgianne buttoning her blouse. What had she and

Mike been doing? It didn't matter. What stuck in his mind was that brief, tantalizing curve of breast, before it was covered.

"Funny, isn't it?" he said, savoring the memory.

"What?"

"Oh, you know—what your husband was saying about the two of us. How we went out together all those times but never really on a date."

"Like I said, you never asked me."

"Ah, well . . . Mike."

"Mike was no big deal," Georgianne said. "Lots of kids went steady because it was easier that way. Mike was good company, but he was never a real heartthrob. I guess that's why there was no pain on either side when we went our own ways." Then she added, "Anyway, if you'd asked, I would have gone out with you, Jeff."

It was a flat statement, a plain comment on something that had never happened. Georgianne put no special emphasis on the words, but they shook Jeff deeply. Back then, he'd wanted to ask her out. Many times. But he'd never worked up the nerve to do it, and he'd always explained his hesitation in terms of Mike Rollins. Now that excuse was gone. Hearing what Georgianne had just said, he felt a confusion of sadness and anger. In a way, it was the best thing she could have told him, but it still hurt.

"Really?"

"Sure," she said. "Why not?"

"My mistake, I guess."

"I thought you weren't interested."

"No. That wasn't it."

You were afraid, Jeff told himself. It was fear, and nothing else. The fear that she would reject you—that would have been unbearable. But as long as you didn't ask, you weren't rejected, and the dream survived. It was pathetic. Yet he knew this was what he had come here to learn. The reunion was more than a whim, more than simple curiosity. He'd sought her out for this bit of truth.

"Oh. Well, you were so busy with Joanne and Kathy, and Betsy," Georgianne said lightly, as if she sensed that this was no longer idle chat and wanted to defuse the subject. "You went through a few girls in high school, you know."

"Yeah, I guess I did." Because none of them was right, none of them was the girl he'd really wanted. The sadness was offset to a certain extent by the one priceless new fact that, yes, Georgianne would have gone out with him.

The restaurant, the Gray Door, was better than Jeff had expected. Sean warmed up a little bit during the meal as Jeff became less mysterious and formidable to him. He didn't seem to mind Jeff and Georgianne reminiscing about the old days. When they were about to proceed with coffee and cognac, a trio of musicians appeared, and a few couples took to the small dance floor at the back of the restaurant.

"Georgianne and I haven't danced together since the senior prom," Jeff said briskly. "May I steal your wife?"

"Be my guest," Sean said affably.

The music was medium tempo, slow enough so you

could hold your partner and talk, if that's what you wanted, but fast enough to keep middle-aged people moving without inducing cardiac arrest. Jeff thought fondly of the old body-groping slow numbers he'd danced to in high school—never, alas, with Georgianne. He held her as close as possible now. She didn't press against him, but neither did she hold herself away. She felt fantastic in his arms, their thighs brushing, her breasts just touching his chest, the feel of her hair on his cheek, the scent of her . . .

"You know," he whispered.

"What?"

"I do remember dancing with you once at the senior prom. We all danced with each other's dates once. It was the polite thing to do."

"Mm-hmm."

"Well, it's much better this time."

Georgianne pulled her head back to look at him. She was smiling, and Jeff thought it was the most luxurious, sensual smile he had ever seen.

"That's very sweet," she said softly. "Thank you. It's so nice to see you again, Jeff. I'm really glad it happened."

"So am I."

They stayed on the floor for two dances. Jeff noticed Sean making his way to the men's room as the second song wound down. He and Georgianne went back to the table.

She was so at ease with herself. So many of the women Jeff encountered were either sharp and aggressive, out to make it in a man's world, or else resolutely, it seemed to him, confused . . . muddled housewife types who no longer knew who they were. But here was Georgianne, solid as bedrock, at peace with the person she was and apparently content with the life she had.

Content? Or resigned? Jeff wondered if Georgianne could look this radiant if she wasn't really happy. What kind of life was it, actually? Unexciting, unremarkable, and surely modest if they were getting by on Sean's teacher's salary alone. This still puzzled Jeff, because he had expected something else, something different. Georgianne was the kind of girl you thought would end up married to a rich doctor or lawyer. That Jeff should find her in such cozy but diminished circumstances seemed wrong. A mistake.

CHAPTER EIGHT

It was a little after eleven-thirty when Jeff got back to the hotel. Still early, as far as he was concerned. He felt wide awake, and he didn't want to sit around in his room. He had stayed in the night before, planning, drinking beer, and watching the X-rated cable channel the Mortlake Motel provided for its guests (he'd seen *Debbie Does Dallas* for the third time). But the Hilton offered no such distractions. He went to the bar and ordered a beer.

He seemed to be full of nervous energy, and this might help him to settle down, collect himself. The big event, dinner with the Corcorans, had passed. Ordeal, challenge, opportunity. He thought it had gone well enough, generally. There had been no awkwardness, no unpleasantness. Sean was a drag, but it could have been worse. And if one door had finally shut, perhaps another had opened. . . .

There were quite a few people in the bar, most of

them businessmen. Unmistakable, Jeff thought. Then he wondered if he looked like one of them. Was he just as obvious? It was a forlorn thought.

He glanced down the length of the bar. A few seats away, a young woman sat alone. He had noticed her when he came in, and he'd thought she was with someone. Now she looked at him and smiled, stirring her drink with deliberate slowness. She had dark hair and wore a metallic blue dress with a wrapped front. It wouldn't have reached her knees when she was standing, and it didn't come close as she sat. He turned to stare at his beer. A moment later the girl took the seat next to him.

"Hi," she said, all throaty.

"Hi."

"Nice night, isn't it?"

"Not bad."

"Could be better, right?" she said. "I know what you mean. . . ."

Jeff turned to face her. She wasn't bad. Her hair was a little too dark, and her manner, of course, was completely wrong, but he had time to kill.

"Are you a working girl?"

"Ha, ha, that depends."

Jeff noticed that the bartender was hovering a few yards away, projecting an air of watchful neutrality. He lowered his voice, but still spoke bluntly.

"How much?"

The woman's eyebrows arched slightly and she smiled, studying Jeff for a few moments before responding.

"Are you a cop?"

"No." He laughed. "Why would you think that?"

"They're no good at small talk either."

"At least it's not my clothes."

"No, you don't dress like a cop," she conceded, becoming friendly again. "But I like to ask."

"I understand."

"Want some company?"

"Not really."

"Just a drink, then. Hm? Why not? It's pretty quiet now," she added, as if to explain.

Jeff looked around and discovered that the crowd had all but vanished. A group on its way to a party, perhaps, he thought. Or, more likely, good little businessmen off to bed so that they would be fresh for their business breakfasts. They reminded Jeff of himself and the way he'd lived and worked for so many years—with the single-mindedness of a mole, pushing ahead stupidly and seeing nothing. Maybe now, this special night, was the time to admit to himself that he didn't like it, that he was tired of it all, and that there would have to be some serious changes made. A new beginning.

"I'll have another beer," he said to the woman. "What would you like?"

"White wine spritzer, thanks," she replied at once, smiling. She shifted slightly on her seat so that Jeff would be treated to an extra measure of thigh, should he care to look that way.

The bartender brought the drinks, added the charge to Jeff's bill, and then wandered away, no longer interested.

"I'm Lorna," the woman said, raising her glass.

"I'm Sean," Jeff said, raising his.

"Sean—that's nice. I like that."

"Were you ever busted?"

The woman gave a short laugh, but she wasn't surprised. She had Jeff sized up as just another bored, jaded businessman. If they weren't nervous as hell, they drove you up the wall with lousy jokes you had to laugh at convincingly. She hadn't met one yet who was any good at small talk.

"Once," she replied. "Not here. It was just a case of beginner's bad luck."

"What was it like?"

"A drag. A nuisance, that's all. Why?"

"Oh, I was just thinking," Jeff said. "Suppose a woman knocked on a hotel-room door and went in, and the guy turned out to be a cop. He'd be in a pretty good position, wouldn't he? I mean, with the girl."

Lorna smiled. Another one who thinks he's clever. If they only knew how alike all these silly routines really are. But their imaginations are firmly stuck back in adolescence.

"He could be," she admitted. She didn't tell him that any girl who worked that way deserved whatever happened to her, because that wasn't what this man wanted to hear. No, Sean was interested in the game. So Lorna said, "Yeah, it could be an interesting situation . . . exciting."

Jeff looked frankly at her, his eyes surveying her body. He sipped the beer. Soon he reached into his pants pocket and took out his room key. He held it in the palm of his hand, below the bar, displaying the piece of sturdy plastic that identified the hotel and his room number. Then he finished the rest of his beer and stood up to pay the bar tab.

"Guess I'll go watch some TV," he said. "Be seeing you, Lorna."

"Sure. Thanks for the drink, Sean."

"Anytime."

Upstairs in his room, Jeff switched on the television set but turned the volume all the way down. He left the room lights off. The place was cast in a gray-green light, pale and ghostly, that flickered and changed. He stripped to his underwear and took five bills from his wallet and set them on the corner of the bed nearest the door. After locking the wallet in his suitcase, he sat leaning against the pillows, staring at the silent television.

She tapped lightly on the door a few minutes later. Jeff let her in. She stayed by him while he locked the door, and when he turned, she pressed herself expertly against his body, her fingers dancing on his arms.

"I'm alone, honey," she whispered like a little girl. "Can I be with you for a while?"

They swayed together briefly, and Jeff ran his hands down her back. He led her into the room and sat on the bed as she stood and looked around. She noticed the money at once. Jeff nodded, and she put the cash in her pocketbook, which she then set on a side table.

"Spooky," she said in a hushed voice. "It's so spooky in here." But she smiled to show she liked it.

"Take off your shoes," Jeff said. "Are your legs bare?"

Lorna removed her open-toed high heels. The wrap dress, cinched around her waist, parted easily as she took off her tights and tossed them onto her pocketbook. Then she fumbled with the front of the dress, as if to rearrange it, carefully flashing more of her legs. She contrived to open it more above, too, revealing cleavage and a sheer bra.

Jeff held one hand out, low, almost at knee level. She stepped forward so that her leg filled his grip. He touched her for a few seconds, then let go and stood up.

"Sorry," he said. "I'm a cop."

"Oh, no."

"I'm going to have to arrest you."

"I knew it. Oh, please."

"Hands up, against the wall, spread your legs."

She did as he said.

"Oh, please," she whimpered effectively. "I'll do whatever you want . . . anything."

"Sorry."

He went up close behind the young woman and searched her, running his hands down her arms even though her dress was sleeveless. Down along her sides to her hips. Then up her legs, the backs of her thighs, slowly under the dress. Lorna made her body tremble and began to breathe quickly through her mouth, so that he could hear it. She let her head hang down between her upraised arms. Her buttocks tensed as his hands slid under the flimsy panties she wore and snaked around to the front. He leaned over her, his knees up against the backs of hers, and she gasped as he probed between her legs. She was open, moist, ready. He kept one hand there and brought the other up to the top of her dress, testing the texture of that silky excuse for a bra, pulling it down, and exposing her breasts. She made little cries in her throat. Her whole body moved to his touch.

"Please . . . anything . . ."

Cries of pain and pleasure. Her hips rocked on one of his hands, her breasts thrust against the other. He was almost ready, and he slipped off his underpants. Then he pulled her dress up over her ass and removed her panties.

"Please, please," she begged.

"I have to arrest you."

"No, no, sir . . . just teach me a lesson."

Jeff grabbed her hair, firmly but not roughly, and turned her around. She kept her eyes tightly shut, knowing that's how he would want them. He opened her dress completely and sucked one breast, then the other, and he held the nipple between his teeth, biting it carefully to make her moan. Finally, he brought her to her knees, so that she could take him the rest of the way.

"I'll have to remember that," Lorna said later, as she was about to leave. "It's different, and fun."

Jeff's face tightened. He said nothing, but he was annoyed. She had to open her mouth and blab something like that. He should have carried it through all the way, showing her out the door with a gruff warning, like a stern cop, before she got around to talking. But he hadn't, and now she'd gone and ruined the whole thing, destroying the illusion.

"I'll be around tomorrow night, if you are," she said.

"So long." Jeff rolled over on the bed, away from her, like a child sulking and wanting to be left alone.

"Yeah, okay, so long." Lorna made a face, turned, and walked out of the room, thinking, They're not all assholes; it only seems that way.

When the door clicked shut, Jeff lit a cigarette. He turned up the volume on the television and sat for a while at the foot of the bed, watching David Letterman and Jamie Lee Curtis talk about her body.

CHAPTER NINE

Jeff woke up a little after one. He didn't feel as bad as he had expected, just sleepy. After a long shower, he pulled back the drapes, and the room filled with sunshine. Another hot, cloudless day, apparently. He called his office again and was pleased to hear that Callie had no news of any importance to pass along.

He dressed and ate a light late lunch in the hotel restaurant. Then he took a drive to Union Carbide and cruised around the massive complex. He felt slightly ridiculous, but thought he should at least see what the place looked like, in case there was any mention of it over dinner. Sean had brought up the subject once or twice the night before, but Jeff had put him off with a few boring comments of a technical nature.

It was nearly three o'clock when he parked downtown in Danbury. He had just realized he was low on money. He found a bank that honored his California cash card, then wandered around for a while, and finally entered that same cocktail lounge for a cold beer. The place was quiet, dead, at this time of day. He sat at the end of the bar, enjoying the cool darkness.

The beer was good, settling him. How strange to have so much free time on his hands, and to be doing so much drinking! Two luxuries he hardly ever enjoyed in California. He told himself that he looked forward to getting home and back to work. The time would be eaten up then, as it always was, consumed in great, easily digested chunks. That's the way life should go. If you sat around too long, you'd go crazy . . . wouldn't you?

But, at the same time, he knew it would be different now. Everything was changed by the fact that he'd seen Georgianne. The question was: Changed how? It was absurd to think of anything beyond the simple pleasure of this reunion. When he returned to Los Angeles, it would be over. Georgianne would slip back into the past. Finis.

Jeff couldn't accept that. This reunion was a way of saying A, and a favorite old chess maxim had it that if you say A, you must say B. . . . His real problem was to figure out what B was. Of course, the obvious solution would be for Sean to pack up and bow out gracefully.

Did he really think that? He lit a cigarette and smiled at himself in the mirror behind the bar. He had a weird grin on his face, and he kind of liked it because it was so new and unusual. Well? Yes, it was a crazy idea, and one that probably had no real chance at all. But why throw it out? Why not enjoy it for a while, as a purely theoretical possibility? She *could* fall in love with him, she *could* decide to break with Sean. That kind of thing *did* happen. Every day.

Jeff was sure he and Georgianne could be very good for each other. He was in a rut at work, and she could get him out of it, help him enjoy life again. By the same token, she was in a kind of rut too, a suburban stupor. He didn't sense any edge in her life. She deserved better. So did he. If nothing else, this trip east had given him a new determination to improve the way he lived, to transform his life. He had the financial means and, now, the desire. They were both still in their thirties; it wasn't too late yet.

The second beer was even more soothing, and Jeff relaxed into his daydream. Oh, he knew it would almost certainly come to nothing, but it was so damn pleasant to think about . . . he couldn't let it go. It wasn't new. It had come to him many times over the years. But now, finally, he had seen her and touched her, and that made the dream half real.

He left the lounge just before five and drove back to the hotel. After he brushed his teeth again and changed, he made his way to Foxrock. Georgianne came out the front door and walked across the lawn to greet him.

"I'm a little early."

"Not at all," she replied, kissing him lightly on the cheek. "You could have come anytime this afternoon, you know. Sean probably has a drink ready for you."

This was to be a relaxed at-home evening. Georgianne looked casual for it, but gorgeous. She wore a pair of white shorts, snug but not too tight, and a madras shirt with the tails tied across her bare, flat midriff.

"You look terrific," Jeff said as they walked to the house. "I love the shirt."

"I knew you would. That's why I put it on."

"Really?"

"Sure. Don't you remember how popular madras shirts and jackets were back in high school?"

"Yeah, of course."

He was immensely pleased that she had dressed for him, and that she had chosen something from the memories they shared. No matter what she says or does, he thought, it turns out even better than I could hope.

They found Sean in the kitchen, a tray of ice cubes in one hand. He wore sandals, jeans, and a Mets T-shirt.

"Hello, hello," he welcomed Jeff merrily. "What'll you have for openers?"

"Uh . . . well . . . what're you drinking?"

"Harp lager, good and cold."

"I'll join you."

"Right you are." Sean went to the refrigerator. "Honey, what about you?"

"Can I have a white wine spritzer?" Georgianne asked.

"Certainly, certainly."

Jeff showed no reaction, but the image of the hooker's asking for the same drink at his hotel the previous night flashed briefly through his mind.

"Ah, that's good," Jeff said after sipping the can of beer. He knew it had been bought specially for him, for this occasion; surely Sean couldn't afford to drink Harp all the time. He took it as another sign of the man's insecurity.

Georgianne had things to do in the kitchen and suggested that Sean give Jeff a quick tour of the property. They went out the back door, onto a flagstone patio. The Corcorans had just over an acre of land, with some fine old trees. Sean had put up a split-rail fence around the front and two sides. The back gave way to tall grass, briers, and a gradual downhill slope. They had a vegetable garden, flower beds, and a modest grapevine.

The house itself was a gambrel, with cedar siding that had weathered to an attractive silvery gray. Inside, the post-and-beam construction created an old, country feeling, solid and homey, rural but not of the wilderness. They had an ornate soapstone wood stove.

The cellar comprised a small cold-storage room for food and a large main area that contained the laundry appliances and Sean's workshop. Jeff had never seen so many tools. Not even his father, who had been a professional carpenter, had owned this many.

"Don't ask me if I need them all," Sean said, as if reading Jeff's thoughts. "When you build a house yourself you tend to accumulate all sorts of things."

"I'm impressed."

"Ah, well. I've come to the conclusion that a house is really just a big inventory of things that need to be repaired, changed, adjusted, or refinished. You keep

77

doing them, one after another, but the list never gets any smaller."

Jeff smiled. "The rigors of ownership." His five-room condominium was elegantly furnished, but decidedly uncluttered.

"Exactly," Sean said, leading the way back upstairs.

"I love it." Jeff pronounced his verdict as they went through the kitchen.

"Thanks," Georgianne said, smiling. "So do I."

Fresh cans of beer in hand, Sean and Jeff went outside to sit on the patio. The Adirondack chairs were comfortable and looked recently painted. Jeff was going to say something about them, but decided not to—he didn't want to hear that Sean had made them himself.

They chatted about the winters, summer vacations, the Mets and the Dodgers, cars and computers. Sean didn't like computers, and on his home ground he was less reserved about saying so than he had been the previous evening. Jeff didn't bother arguing. He found it amusing and rather pathetic. He had the luxury of being on the cutting edge of technology. In the cellar, Jeff had seen a huge display of tools, but they were the old tools, the tools of the past. Still useful, of course, but undeniably quaint, as far as he was concerned. Sean struck him as one of those people whose idea of common sense is to go back to some simpler, earlier way of life. The only technology needed to accomplish this was H. G. Wells's time machine. Jeff could smile at this without being aware of the irony.

"You must come jogging with me," Sean said, returning from the kitchen with more beer. "I go out early in the morning. It's beautiful."

"No way," Jeff replied, setting the full can of lager next to the one he hadn't yet finished.

They heard a car stop in front of the house. A door slammed shut, and the car drove away. A minute later Georgianne came out to the patio with a teenager in tow.

"Jeff," she said, "I'd like you to meet our daughter, Bonnie." Her voice was proud, her smile radiant. "Bonnie, this is Mr. Lisker, a friend of mine from grammar school and high school."

"Jeff'll do fine," he said, standing. His heart hammered in his chest, and he was afraid his face had changed color. "Hi. How are you?"

"Hi. Pleased to meet you."

The girl smiled shyly. She was stunning. She was an inch or so taller than her mother and she had her father's darker hair, but otherwise Bonnie Corcoran fulfilled in almost every way the twenty-year-old image of Georgianne in Jeff's mind. Breasts perky and girlish beneath a thin T-shirt, obviously no bra. Legs long and slender in tight designer jeans, a compact but definitely female ass that Jeff could hardly bear to look at. Most of all, the face and eyes, so like her mother's. Jeff had to make an effort not to stare at Bonnie, but he ached inside.

"Can I have some wine?" Bonnie asked her father.

"All right," Sean said. Then, to Georgianne, "Water it down a bit for her, would you, hon?"

The women went inside.

"Did Georgianne tell me that Bonnie's about to graduate from high school?"

"That's right," Sean said. "And she's only seventeen."

"She's a beautiful girl."

"The price is more or less constant terror," Sean said. "You think it'll get better as a child gets older, but it doesn't. Just the opposite."

"I can imagine."

"Bonnie looks like any other teenager, and she is, in most respects, but God gave her a great brain. She's highly motivated and she seems to know exactly what she wants to do. Her SATs were fantastic."

"That's great," Jeff said. "Where is she going to school in September?"

"Harvard."

"Wow!"

"And they're paying just about everything, which is just as well, since I couldn't."

"What does she want to study?"

"Molecular biology." Sean had a helpless expression on his face. "She can tell you about it; I can't. My knowledge of biology is limited to giving electric-shock treatment to dead frogs."

Jeff laughed. "Me too."

The four of them ate at a large redwood picnic table on the patio. The food was simply prepared but excellent. Cold shrimp, which they dipped in a spicy sauce, was followed by a platter of soft-shell crabs and a spinach salad with mushrooms and hot pieces of crispy bacon. For dessert they had chunks of watermelon that had spent the afternoon soaking in iced vodka.

Throughout the meal, Jeff and Georgianne took turns

telling old high school stories. It was a kind of mutual self-indulgence, but Sean and Bonnie seemed to find it entertaining. Afterward, they sat back and relaxed. Then Georgianne went inside to prepare the coffee, and Sean followed her to mix some vodka-and-tonics.

"So . . . you're going to be an Ivy Leaguer in the fall," Jeff said to Bonnie. The girl nodded, smiling shyly again. "You'll like Boston, Cambridge—well, Cambridge might as well be a part of Boston," Jeff continued. "I've been there a couple of times."

Bonnie nodded her head enthusiastically. "We went up for my interview, and we walked all around Harvard afterward. I really liked the look of it, but we didn't see much of the city. Cambridge was nice."

"You'll like it," he repeated.

There was a brief silence between them. Jeff felt he should say something more; he wanted to talk to the girl, but the words wouldn't come. Bonnie had a way of looking directly at him, open, almost expectant, and it had an effect on him. Jeff realized, amazingly, disturbingly, that he was unsure of himself. Was this what he had been like with Georgianne, years ago? Suddenly, it was hard to tell. The past and the present had merged into a moment of confusion.

"Mom says you live in L.A."

"Outside the city," Jeff said. "But close by. Just a short drive on the freeway."

"What's it like?"

"Like any other city," Jeff replied promptly, grateful that Bonnie had taken the lead. "But the state of mind is different. I don't think anyone has figured out what that is, yet."

Bonnie laughed, another trivial gesture that sent waves of delicious sensation through Jeff.

"That's just my residual New England prejudice," he added. "I really like L.A., and I wouldn't live anywhere else."

"I'd like to do my graduate work in California," Bonnie said. "Unless I end up liking Harvard so much I can't bear to leave it."

"Well, you certainly—"

"Are we in graduate school already?" Sean asked, returning with two tall glasses. "Here you are, Jeff."

"Thanks."

It was a strong drink, and Jeff wondered if Sean was trying to get him drunk. Not that he cared. He was annoyed with Sean anyhow. The conversation with Bonnie had just been getting off the ground, and now Sean had killed it. Jeff wanted to talk with the girl, but it was impossible with her father sitting in on every word. It didn't matter at all that Jeff really had very little to say to Bonnie. He had enjoyed being alone in her company, and now the spell was broken. There would probably never be another opportunity.

Perhaps it was that feeling of annoyance, in combination with the alcohol, that got him in the trouble that followed. Whatever the reason, by the time the coffee arrived, Jeff had agreed to accompany Sean to the Gorge at seven o'clock the next morning. They would jog together. It was madness, and Jeff didn't know why he'd been so foolish. The Gorge was a park, a stretch of countryside that jutted into Foxrock. Sean jogged there every morning. Jeff smoked and had no desire even to try running, but

Sean talked, wheedled, dared him into it, convincing him that the Gorge was beautiful to see and promising that they'd mostly just walk anyway.

Later, Jeff would tell himself that the real reason he had agreed to jog with Sean was because it would give him one more chance to see Georgianne and Bonnie. The plan was that they'd go out at seven, run or walk for a while, and then return to the house for breakfast. He thought he'd drive down to New York in the afternoon. He had reached the point where he wanted to leave Danbury.

It was getting dark and cool outside by the time they'd finished their coffee. Bonnie cleared the table and cleaned up in the kitchen while her parents sat in the living room with Jeff. Georgianne dug out some albums of old photographs, which they looked through with a mixture of disbelief and amused embarrassment. She had a lot of pictures Mike Rollins had taken—he had been a Polaroid enthusiast. The result, Jeff discovered for the first time, was a number of snapshots of himself with two girls, his date at the time and Georgianne. He was fascinated to look at them now. How odd he appeared to himself! Weedy, angular, stiff. But there was something nice about it. He wished he had some of these photos, because he saw it would be possible to crop out the other girl, leaving pictures of himself with Georgianne, alone.

"My hair didn't start to grow until I got to college," he said absently.

Georgianne looked great in every snapshot, as he knew she would, and Bonnie's resemblance to her became even more apparent. Mike, in various poses, showed great fat-bearing potential, which Jeff now knew had not been left unfulfilled. Kathy, Joanne, and Betsy looked almost like strangers to Jeff. None of them was quite as pretty as he remembered, although in one picture, as a result of an optical illusion or a pair of falsies, there was definitely more to Joanne's bosom than Jeff had ever encountered. They were still going through the albums when Bonnie came in to say good night. Not long after that, Sean began yawning and hauled himself to his feet.

"I'm always early to bed," he explained. "And I've got some catching up to do for last night."

"I should be going," Jeff said.

"No, no, stay and finish your drink," Sean insisted. "Georgianne will fix you another one, if you like. You two haven't talked in twenty years, and I'm sure you still have a lot of ground to cover."

"He goes to bed at ten o'clock every night," Georgianne confirmed.

"Just make sure you're here at seven sharp," Sean warned, "or I'll come down to that hotel and drag you out in your pajamas. You're going to do some jogging."

"I know," Jeff said, nodding his head reluctantly. "I may be unconscious, but I'll be here on time."

"You *do* need another drink," Georgianne said when Sean had gone upstairs. "Come on."

"I've had more to drink this week than I have in the last year," Jeff remarked, following her into the kitchen.

Georgianne poured two more tall vodka-and-tonics. They touched glasses to toast each other once again. Jeff leaned back against the counter, Georgianne beside him at a slight angle.

"I told you yesterday that you'd done well," he said. "Meeting your husband last night, your daughter today, seeing you in your home and how you live, I have to say it again, kid, only more so."

"Thanks, Jeff." Georgianne looked down at her drink, which she held in both hands at her waist. "You know, I told Sean last night, on the way home after dinner, that the reason you and I were such good friends in school was because I always felt safe with you around. We all did. Even Mike. You know the kinds of things he could get up to—I think he felt freer and could be a little wilder as long as you were there, because you knew how to take control when things started to get out of hand."

Jeff shrugged, but he was deeply touched. "I'm glad we never had to test it." He took her hand, squeezed it, held on. "Twenty years later," he joked softly, "and I'm finally getting to hold hands with you. How about that?"

Georgianne smiled back at him, then tugged gently. "Come on. I've got to sit down. The drink is catching up with me."

They returned to the living room and sat together on the couch. Hands still held between them, they stretched out their legs on the coffee table. Jeff was beginning to feel dizzy, but not from the drink. The back of his hand, holding hers, rested lightly against bare thigh where Georgianne's shorts ended. The feeling was devastatingly wonderful, but at the same time he was a little frightened by it. What was happening? Was she seriously flirting with him? It was another bizarre echo of a past that had never occurred—on the couch with Georgianne while her old man slept upstairs. This time her husband, not her father. Jeff felt anything but self-possessed now. This moment was precisely what he had wanted and dreamed of so many times. But he didn't know what to do with it.

"How has it felt being back here?" Georgianne asked. "Make you think at all about moving back to Connecticut?"

"No, not really," Jeff replied, glad to have something to say. "Where you are, here, is the nicest place I've seen. But the old Brass Valley is even more depressed, and depressing, than it was when we grew up there. Besides, I've made a home for myself in California that I can't see myself leaving, not in any foreseeable future."

"It doesn't really matter where any of us lives," Georgianne said. "As long as we live well in ourselves."

"Right."

Side by side they sat, close, comfortable together. It felt so very good, but Jeff was afraid to turn and look at her. Afraid of what might happen. But suppose that was what she was waiting for . . . ? Could he be reliving his own unnecessary hesitancy?

Jeff finally turned to say something, but the words were lost as he was transfixed by Georgianne's madras shirt. The top three buttons were undone. They had been that way all evening, he realized, but now the image meant something more to him. She still wore a shirt like a high-school girl—open like that but with no cleavage visible. It seemed peculiarly girlish, and Jeff couldn't explain why but he thought it was the most beautiful, telling quality that Georgianne possessed. He knew he should look away, but he couldn't move his eyes. Georgianne gave no indication that she was aware of how intensely poignant this moment was for him. She simply held his hand and gazed absently at her drink. Finally, he leaned forward, his face closer to hers. She looked up at him and smiled.

"I should be going," he said.

And cursed himself silently. Even now, he thought, you're hesitating, hoping she'll take the initiative and kiss you. He felt desperately miserable. At the same time, he couldn't believe that Georgianne really wanted him to try anything. She had made the point about feeling safe with him. The wrong move now would destroy that. He had waited twenty years, and now he had come this close to her; he could wait a while longer to get the rest of the way.

"Think you'll make it here at seven?" she asked.

"Yeah, somehow."

They stood up and walked across the room to the front door. Georgianne stepped outside with him.

"Thanks for a great meal and a great evening," he said.

"Thank *you*," Georgianne responded. "For last night, and for coming tonight."

She seemed subdued, in a dreamy, wistful kind of

way, as she leaned back against the door frame and looked at him. He was no longer a successful businessman, he wasn't even an old acquaintance enjoying a nostalgic reunion. He was a trembling schoolboy saying good night to the girl he had never really stopped wanting in his life. And she looked better than ever, a picture he would keep, if only he could. . . . He brought his hand up into her hair and kissed her. It wasn't a passionate kiss, but gentle, lingering, open-mouthed. It was a moment he wanted never to end, the past made perfect in a simple act of innocent but deeply felt affection. No, not just affection—love.

"Jeff . . ."

Instinctively, he kissed her on the cheek to lighten the moment. But secretly he was thrilled. He had finally done it. He had kissed her, not like a brother or a harmless friend, but the way a man kisses a woman. And it had done no apparent damage.

"See you at breakfast," Georgianne whispered. Then she pulled back slightly, a small but clear step.

On the drive to his hotel, and until sleep overtook him, Jeff wondered about that last look on her face in the doorway. It was impossible to decipher, but endlessly fascinating. Had he seen sorrow in her expression? Perhaps, but happiness, too—he was sure of that. And there was more—a fire, an undefined longing for something . . . or someone. Had he awakened that in her? He wanted to believe that more than anything, but he knew it was too early to tell. Still, it was all beginning to drift in the right direction as far as he was concerned; that much was undeniable.

Jeff sprawled across the bed and started laughing quietly. The laughter grew, a rhythm that took hold of his entire body. You're delirious, he told himself, enraptured, enthralled, on your way off the deep end. You know that, don't you?

"Yes, yes, yes, yes, yes . . ."

CHAPTER TEN

"I didn't think you'd make it," Sean said.

"Neither did I."

"How do you feel?"

"Fine, more or less."

"Think you can do some jogging?"

"Sure, but not very far."

"Well, I'll be easy on you," Sean promised unconvincingly, "seeing as how you're a smoker and all."

"Thanks."

Sleepy but not too hung over, Jeff had made it to the Corcoran house on time. Sean was already in the driveway, going through a routine of stretching exercises. He wore a proper running suit and shoes, whereas Jeff had on slacks and a T-shirt and an ordinary pair of sneakers. He resented having to go through with this nonsense, but he kept thinking ahead to breakfast with Georgianne.

Sean parked the wagon on a side street near the entrance to the Gorge. There was a plaque mounted on a boulder just inside, where several paths diverged.

"It's a beautiful place," Sean said, leading the way. "Every September we have a real invasion of out-of-towners, who come to see the leaves turning color."

Within a few minutes, the trail they had taken brought them to the edge of the Gorge itself. An old rail fence had been put up in places to keep people from wandering off the edge. It was a steep drop to the Bullet River, a narrow band of violent water rushing through a rocky cut. Jeff was impressed by the wild, raw look of it.

"Two or three people fall in every year," Sean said.

"Really? It does look dangerous."

"Outsiders who don't know their way around, or kids who've had too much to drink. Some of them survive, and some don't." Sean pointed ahead. "You can see places where there's no fencing, just undergrowth. Foxrock's a small town, so there's not a lot of money, and this isn't a managed park. It's just ground that's too wild and rocky and hilly to be developed. The river runs through town, bringing this finger of land with it. Nobody's figured out what to do with it, and I hope they never do. I like it just the way it is."

They had walked perhaps a quarter of a mile, with the rocky Gorge always nearby on their left. The ground was heavily wooded and thick with tall grass and brush, but the path was well worn. It never ran straight for more than a few yards before dipping to the right or left, then rising again, swinging up, looping around stone outcrops, threading past clumps of birches. In spite of himself, Jeff liked the place, liked the idea that it was so close to town yet so wild and secluded.

"Ready for a little run?"

"Uh . . . yeah, I guess so."

"Keep me in sight, because we'll be crossing other paths, and give a holler if you want to stop and catch your breath."

Sean took off at a slow trot, and Jeff stayed close behind. At first it wasn't as bad as he had expected. He had no trouble keeping up with Sean, as he quickly found an easy rhythm for his breathing. The only awkward part was the ground itself, which was so rough and irregular that he had to keep his eyes on it all the time to avoid a misstep. They were moving gradually away from the Gorge, he reckoned, since he could no longer hear the roaring river. But they hadn't gone too far when Sean surprised him by stopping.

"Okay?"

"Yeah, I'm still here," Jeff said, bending over and gulping air.

"Teenagers," Sean muttered, kicking a rusty beer can off the path. "I wish they'd take their litter with them. Listen, the path widens from here, and we can pick up our pace a bit, if you want. Or would that be too much for you?"

Jeff caught the tone of that last sentence all too clearly, and he couldn't refuse the challenge. If nothing else, it served to crystallize the amorphous dislike he felt for Sean.

"Why not?"

"Are you sure?"

"I'll stop if I have to," Jeff said irritably. He straightened up. "Otherwise, let's go."

"Okay."

Sean sped away, and Jeff trailed gamely behind, telling himself, The man's a fucking asshole. He was determined to make a fire of his anger, and to warm his hands at it. Make the effort, make the effort, he told himself. Just this once.

But it was too much. He was competing with Sean on Sean's terms, and he didn't have a chance. Sean steadily increased his speed, and Jeff drove himself to keep him in sight. The rhythm he'd found earlier eluded him now. His legs began to hurt, in the calves, knees, and thighs. He felt a tiny red dot form on his breastbone. It burned as it grew, and pressure seemed to be building up beneath it, as if a hot poker were being pressed into his chest. He pushed himself on, though his breath came in loud, jagged gasps. Then a metal band started to tighten around his forehead. He could still see Sean, but only as a blur, a floating figure that bounced in and out of view. I ought to die here, now, he thought dimly. Serve the bastard right—let him live with guilt for the rest of his life.

He stumbled to a halt, unable to move another step. He swayed on his feet, his whole body heaving. His mouth was dry and gummy, and black spots danced across his vision. He got down on one knee and bent over—that's what he'd been taught in school, he remembered: put your head down when you feel dizzy. But as soon as he did it, he was shocked to find himself puking furiously. It looked like everything he had consumed the night before was coming up. That's beautiful, he thought with self-loathing, just beautiful. Now you've really made Sean's day. When the spasms finally subsided, he moved away from the smelly mess. He stood up carefully and wiped his face. He felt shaky but calm. The dislike had become a pure white flame of hatred within him.

"Are you all right?" Sean asked, walking up casually. Then he noticed the pool of vomit on the ground. "Oh boy, I was afraid of that."

Afraid? More likely you were looking forward to it, Jeff thought bitterly. He stared at the other man without speaking, and he could tell that his look was so icy cool it unnerved Sean, who was compelled to fill the air with noise and chatter.

"Sorry about that. Barfed myself the first time out. Almost everybody who starts running does, you know. Really. You can't push yourself too hard. You have to break into it gradually. I did it on Main Street, for all to see."

"Yeah, well, forget it. I feel okay," Jeff said, walking away. He could no longer bear listening to the fool prattle on.

"I thought you were doing pretty well," Sean said as he caught up. "We must have covered a mile or so, anyway. You're in better shape than I thought."

That was a lie, Jeff knew. He hadn't run anywhere near a mile. Everything that came out of Sean's mouth was inane. But Jeff was enjoying the situation, too. He had submitted himself to an indignity in order to gain a psychological edge of some sort, and he felt he had achieved that.

"I'm okay, really," he said, forcing himself to sound reasonable and unruffled. "I should have slowed up a little sooner, that's all."

"Right, right," Sean agreed quickly. "But it was a bad idea after a night of drinking and so on. My fault entirely. I'm the experienced runner. I should have known. . . ."

And he babbled on. How typical, Jeff thought, that Sean was now so eager to shoulder all the blame. It was another roundabout way of rubbing it in, for all his apparent sincerity. Yes, he was the experienced runner—which only persuaded Jeff that what had happened was precisely what Sean had intended. The man was like cheap window glass, weak and transparent.

"Do you want to stop and rest some more?"

Jesus Christ! "I'm all right," Jeff answered, the edge back in his voice. "I didn't have a heart attack."

Sean kept up his line of talk, though it diminished some in the face of cold silence. They came out of the woods onto the street and drove back to Indian Hill Road.

"You're a good sport, Jeff," Sean said as he parked the wagon in the driveway. "Sorry it turned out to be a bad idea."

Jeff nodded curtly. A good sport—what a thing to say! It was as good as admitting that the whole thing was a prank. Once you get into Sean's shallowness, there's almost no end to it, he thought, and then he nearly laughed out loud at the contradiction. Georgianne came out of the kitchen when she heard them at the front door.

"Hi there," she said brightly. "How was it?"

"I'm no runner," Jeff replied with a genuine smile. She looked terrific, as usual, although she was dressed only in faded denims and a gray sweatshirt. "I'm just going to wash up," he told her as he headed for the bathroom.

"Beautiful morning," he heard Sean say.

As he stepped through the bathroom doorway, Jeff caught a glimpse of Sean making a gesture with his finger in his mouth, not quite as exaggerated as Joan Rivers, but just as obvious and tasteless. Son of a bitch, he thought, furious again. That was totally unnecessary. He shut the bathroom door, found a bottle of mouthwash, and gargled for a full minute. Telling Georgianne was uncalled for, telling her in such a crude fashion was totally unforgivable. Sean had had his fun with Jeff; the least he could have done was keep it between the two of them. But no, that was the whole point. He had to let Georgianne know, so that Mr. Computer Wizard from the West Coast would be cut down to size. Jeff spat out the mouthwash and rinsed his face with cold water. He felt calm, cool, full of hate. In other words, just fine.

"You okay?" Georgianne asked when he walked into the kitchen a minute later.

"Yeah, sure." Jeff sat down at the table, which was set for breakfast. He ignored Sean, smiled at Georgianne. "I am, really," he added tightly, since she looked unconvinced.

"Think you can eat any breakfast?" Sean asked in an even tone.

"As a matter of fact, I'm starved," Jeff replied. He knew he wasn't sick, so he had no fear that he'd throw up again. "And I know I have room for it." He forced his expression into a broad smile, and held it.

"How do you like your eggs?" Georgianne asked.

"Any way you serve them," he said. "You know, the next time, I think I'll go swimming with you and leave Sean to his running around in the woods." He gave Georgianne a deliberate wink.

"You got a date," she responded cheerfully.

"How's that Union Carbide business coming?" Sean asked. "Are you going to be back here at any time in the near future?"

There was nothing remarkable about the way Sean put these questions, but his feelings were clear to Jeff, who wished he could come up with an answer that would leave the other man in a state of private torment. But what could he say? He knew it would be a mistake to carry the Union Carbide charade too far.

"You know how it is with an outfit that big," he said. "They have a lot of people to rope into line before they actually commit themselves to anything. We'll see how it turns out. Dealing with them makes me glad I've got my own company, though. It's just the right size, a good team, and if we want to do something, explore this or that line of research, we go ahead and get on with it."

Bonnie stumbled into the room, eyes half-closed, hair tousled. She wore a boy's white shirt, definitely too small to be one of Sean's castoffs. The cut of the shirttail gave a brief glimpse of bikini briefs and fanny. Georgianne rolled her eyes and sighed disapprovingly at this display.

"We've got company for breakfast, you know," she reminded her daughter.

Bonnie sat down at the table. "Oh, hi," she said to Jeff with a sleepy smile.

"Good morning."

It was difficult for him not to keep glancing at Bonnie, she was such a beautiful girl. A window on the past. He could look at her now and see what Georgianne looked like first thing in the morning, right out of bed, half awake and sensual. It was a distracting sight.

"When is your flight?"

This came from Georgianne, and Jeff noted sadly that they were already adjusting to his departure. Life would soon return to normal, and he and she would forget about each other until the next time—if there ever was a next time. People live by the routines, and the Corcorans were anticipating the resumption of theirs. The excitement of the reunion was fading fast. Life goes on—like a small death, Jeff thought. But he hadn't forgotten about Georgianne in all this time, and he wouldn't start now.

"I don't know," he said. "I may stay overnight in New York and fly out sometime tomorrow. I haven't seen the city in ages. Or I may decide to fly out this evening. Either way, I'm driving down this afternoon."

Georgianne served mounds of scrambled eggs, bacon, and a plate of toast. The coffee perked like a drum roll, and they all started eating.

"Even if this Union Carbide business goes through," Jeff suddenly volunteered, on a whim, "it's not that big a deal, to tell you the truth."

"No?"

"Well, it'll be very nice, of course," he continued. "But our main work, our most important work, is with a couple of other large companies, on the West Coast." Georgianne and Bonnie looked interested, but Sean's expression said he couldn't care less. Jeff thought, I'll change that. "I'd appreciate it very much if you'd keep this to yourselves," he went on. "The fact is, we're working on an important aspect of the SDI."

Georgianne didn't get it, but Bonnie's eyebrows went up, and Sean understood. He looked as if he didn't know whether or not to believe Jeff.

"Star Wars," Bonnie exclaimed. "Wow!"

Georgianne nodded in recognition now.

"Are they spending money on that already?" Sean asked.

"The money, well . . . money is always there," Jeff said with a condescending smile. "Several companies have been working on various parts of what will be the SDI package for years now. That's how it goes. This project is irresistible. And once private work and research get to a certain point, everything else falls in place, and the government money starts pouring in— it's on the way now. Of course, it's a great project, and absolutely necessary. There's no future in building only more warheads. We've done that trip."

"What's your part of it?" Bonnie asked. "I mean, if it's not a state secret." She was genuinely interested, which pleased Jeff.

"It's incredibly complex," he told her. "And I can't go into any kind of detail. But, basically, we're trying to develop a preliminary set of sensor signature codes for the computer banks. So they can tell the difference between a missile being launched and, say, a natural-gas flare-off, or a truck exploding in an accident . . . anything like that."

"I don't know," Sean said gloomily. "Why don't they save a lot of time and money and just dismantle all those nuclear weapons everywhere?"

Again Jeff smiled at the other man's naïveté. "Right up the street from me in Santa Susana," he said, "North American Rockwell has the world's largest land-based laser, and it's fully operational. You can't stop research. These things have a life of their own. Once you say A, you must say B."

"Oh, really?" Sean had a look of cool cynicism on his face, as if he finally understood Jeff.

But Jeff was paying no attention to Sean. He had been addressing his remarks to Georgianne and Bonnie, and now he realized that the teenager was a potential ally. He should have seen it sooner. It was hard not to think of her as just a sexy little high school kid, but she was a brilliant student on her way to Harvard. Bonnie was the only one here who could understand the significance of his work. She looked impressed.

"I may have a job for you in a few years," he told the girl. "The other really exciting frontier we're working on is the marriage between molecular biology and supercomputers."

Bonnie's eyes widened, and then she grinned and said, "I'm interested, I'm *very* interested."

"Okay. Do well at Harvard and you can write your own ticket. The possibilities are infinite."

Sean wore his gloomy expression again. Jeff stopped talking, satisfied that he had achieved his purpose. It wasn't at all like him to tell others about himself or his work, but it had been necessary this morning, and he felt he had regained the stature he might have lost by emptying his belly at the Gorge. Now, whenever they heard Star Wars mentioned, they'd think of him. He had evened things up with Sean somewhat, although he still disliked the man intensely.

After breakfast Jeff persuaded Georgianne to show him some of her sketches. She didn't want to, was surprisingly shy about them, but she gave in finally. Jeff liked them very much, though he admitted that he knew nothing about art.

"That's all right," Georgianne said. "It's not art; it's simply therapy. Which one do you like most?"

Jeff picked out a sketch of an old, falling-down barn, with a stone wall and a cluster of birches in the background. Georgianne gave it to him, rolling it up carefully and putting it in a cardboard tube. He would have preferred a self-portrait of Georgianne, but she did only country scenes. He promised to have it framed and to hang it on his wall as soon as he got back home.

"And now I have to go," he said, looking at his watch.

Bonnie was upstairs dressing, and Georgianne went to get her. Sean led Jeff out to the front step.

"If you're back this way anytime, do call and stop by," he said. "Come and stay with us next time; never mind about a hotel."

"Thanks very much. I really appreciate your hospitality. I've had a great time, meeting you and your daughter, and of course seeing Georgianne after all this time."

"I mean it," Sean repeated. "Come see us."

The mistake, Jeff thought. Typical. He had to say he meant it. You can trust some people to show how false they are by overemphasizing their sincerity.

"You've got a wonderful home and a wonderful family," Jeff said, since that seemed to be what Sean wanted to hear.

"Ah, I know it. I tell you, Jeff, sometimes I think teaching kids is a bit of a drag, you know. It stops being exciting or even fun after a few years. The administration, the parents—it's all a load of crap, for the most part. But then I think, Hey, I have a woman I love dearly, who loves me dearly, and we have a beautiful, very bright daughter who shares the love and makes us proud every day. And we have this house, so . . . what it all adds up to, I guess, is that however much I might want to gripe or complain, I know I've got the world by the balls. I mean, as long as we're healthy, we should all be grateful for what we have, and consider ourselves lucky. Right?"

"That's exactly right," Jeff said, putting his hands in his pockets so he wouldn't punch Sean in the mouth. What a smug little bastard this guy was. I've got it, I've got mine, the wife, the daughter, the house. So long, pal, and come back in another twenty years if the smoking hasn't killed you in the meantime. That's how it all translated to Jeff, a kind of gloating dismissal.

Then Georgianne and Bonnie came out of the house, and he didn't have to suffer Sean alone any more.

"Well, good luck with the work and all that," Sean said as he shook Jeff's hand.

"Thanks. Take care of yourself," Jeff said. "And these two fine women."

"I will."

Bonnie was wearing cutoffs and a blouse now, and her hair was brushed. She stepped forward to shake Jeff's hand.

"It was nice to meet you, Mr. Lisker," she said rather too formally.

"Jeff," he corrected, smiling. "And it was nice to meet you. I'll expect to hear that you're knocking them out at Harvard. I know you're going to do really well."

"Thanks." She smiled at him.

He turned to Georgianne. "You know," he told her, "it's impossible for me to look at Bonnie and not see you. She looks so much like you did in high school." Georgianne smiled warmly, a little embarrassed perhaps, but proud. "It's been very good to see you again," he continued. "Really very, very good . . ."

"And you, Jeff," Georgianne said.

She hugged him, and he squeezed her tightly to his body, holding her as long as he reasonably could, and then a little longer. He knew that if he did nothing in the future, if he failed to come up with an idea, this embrace might have to last him the rest of his life. They kissed each other, like friends, on the cheek. Then they promised to keep in touch, perhaps by letter but more likely with the occasional telephone call.

Jeff thanked them all again, got in his car, and, after a final wave of the hand and honk of the horn, he drove slowly back to Danbury.

Sean will think, Good riddance, Jeff told himself as he rolled on out of Foxrock. Bonnie would probably forget him within the hour. And Georgianne? The memory of Jeff's visit would stay alive in her for a few days, perhaps, a week at most. But then she'd be back in her little groove, and he'd be three thousand miles away.

He had to shower, pack his suitcase, and check out of the hotel. Then on to New York, Los Angeles. He still hadn't made up his mind whether to take the first available flight or to waste a night in Manhattan. But he was glad to be on the move again.

He had reached the point where it hurt to stay in Danbury and see Georgianne with Sean. His curiosity was now completely satisfied, and the visit had been worthwhile. To see Georgianne looking so glorious, and to meet Bonnie . . . he envied them Bonnie. It could have been different, he thought, so very different. Georgianne could have been his wife, Bonnie his daughter. But that was another lifetime, and he had misread it all, back then. Seeing Georgianne now had cleared it up for him, and that was another part of the hurt.

A wonderful, terrible truth had been revealed to him on this trip east. He understood now, consciously and clearly, as he never had before, that he loved Georgianne—and that he *wanted* her, more than ever. He'd been secretly in love with her all the time they'd been in school together, so secretly and so deeply that he'd never managed to articulate it to himself, much less to her. But the spell was never quite broken in all the years that had followed. And there had been times over the years when he had actively thought about Georgianne, and he had done things he would rather not dwell on now. . . .

He had to do something now, that was now painfully obvious. If Sean was turning Georgianne into a house plant, Jeff could see that he had been turning himself into a zombie with his work obsession. The two of them, Jeff and Georgianne, had been drifting blindly through-life. They needed each other, and a way out. Jeff began to see himself and his life in a shocking new light. He hated what he saw, but at the same time he felt a new sense of exhilaration.

Georgianne was there, ready to be won—of that Jeff had no doubt. She had been married to a twerp long enough for any passion to have died, and now her daughter, her only child, was about to leave home for college. It was a real turning point in Georgianne's life; a point of access and an advantage for Jeff. He wouldn't pass it up. He couldn't. Ideas blossomed like strange new flowers in his mind as he parked the car in the hotel lot and switched off the ignition. He sat there for a few moments, staring ahead but seeing nothing except his inner visions. Georgianne would fall into his arms, and Bonnie would come with her. Sean was on the way out; he just didn't know it yet. And why not? *Why the fuck not?* Jeff pounded the steering wheel with his fist and started to laugh.

"Take her," he said aloud. "I'll just take her!" And

as he said this over and over again, he fell in love with the words, what they meant and the sheer beautiful sound of them. He seemed to be completing a sentence he'd begun to form during some previous incarnation.

PART II

A Friend
of the Family

CHAPTER ELEVEN

It was nearly eleven in the morning when Jeff awoke. Saturday, the middle of June. He wasn't going to the office, not even for a few minutes. A change. But then, he'd been out drinking with Callie and Ted and a couple of other people after work the previous night, and that too was something of a change. While he showered, he wondered if he was beginning to drink too much. In the past, he had never been much of a socializer, and hardly ever drank. Never when he was alone.

The trip east had done it, he knew. He had downed a lot of beers and no small amount of spirits in Connecticut. Not out of any determination to do so; it had just happened that way. He had brought this renewed taste for alcohol back to California with him. The change was undeniable, and while he sometimes had his doubts, he was, in general, pleased with it. One of the first things he had done after his return was to stop at a package store and buy a supply of whiskey to have around the house. Some Scotch, which he enjoyed with ice and a little cold bottled water, some bourbon for when he wanted more of a kick, and some rye, which was a mistake, he discovered the first time he tried it. He continued to drink beer, but as little as possible, since it made him feel bloated, smelly, and leaky if he had much of it. Now—after his journey to Connecticut—he was no longer averse to having a drink with his colleagues after work. Nor did he feel bad about a large solo nightcap back in his condo.

Jeff dried himself, put on a black robe, and went into the kitchen, where he poured a glass of orange juice. Next he put the kettle on and spooned instant coffee into a cup. He had become a bit more sociable, that was all there was to it. And it was a good thing, he believed. Ted and Callie approved, and he could tell that others at Lisker-Benedictus had noticed the change.

The kettle whistled. Jeff filled the stoneware mug with boiling water and stirred it thoroughly, until it looked almost like real coffee, which he was too lazy to make today. Then he went out onto the small balcony off the living room and sat in a plastic deck chair. Every condominium in Ravenswood Estate was designed to afford a good view of the canyon and to provide maximum privacy. It hadn't been cheap, but to Jeff it was worth the cost.

He lit his first cigarette of the day. It had been five, maybe even six, weeks now since he'd seen Georgianne. No cards, letters, or telephone calls. But that was as he thought it should be. He would have been delighted if Georgianne had phoned him, but that was perhaps too much to hope for, and he had made no attempt to communicate with her. Only a week before, he had debated whether to send Bonnie a graduation card, but once again he had decided that it would be a mistake to force himself into their lives at this distance. A plan was taking shape in his head, and although he knew only the rough outline of it so far, he didn't want to ruin it by any precipitous action.

Georgianne was in his mind all the time now. After twenty years of being little more than a ghost, the object of vague and submerged yearnings, she had become the focal point of his conscious thought. At work he had to make an effort to concentrate, not to daydream about her. He had a whole new library of mental pictures to summon up and browse through lovingly whenever he liked. They went well with the lode of images of Georgianne in high school that came rushing back to him now. And then there was Bonnie, another person but somehow almost an alternate version of Georgianne. It wasn't hard for Jeff to see himself with both mother and daughter. That was the perfect picture.

He stubbed out the cigarette and finished the cup of coffee. Inside, he picked up the telephone and began to dial a familiar number.

"Hello."

"Diane? Hi, it's Jeff."

"Oh, hi, Jeffie," she said, her voice changing instantly. "Where've you been? I've really missed you. It's been ages, absolute ages since you came by. . . ."

"That's what I was thinking," he said. "And I've got that book to return to you. How about this afternoon?"

"Uh . . . just a sec." Then, "Jeffie, that'll be fine if you can come early. My mom and dad are going to be out, but they'll be back later."

"So . . . two o'clock?"

"Yeah, or one-thirty would be even better."

"Okay, one-thirty."

After they'd talked a little longer, Jeff hung up, made a second cup of coffee, and went back out to the balcony. He had known Diane for about a year, and he regarded her as a friend. Of course, it was a bizarre relationship—he had to admit that. But it wasn't something new in his life. There had been others before Diane. Not one of them had been as good as Diane, and none had lasted this long. But even with Diane it was the same kind of thing, a facet of his needs and his behavior that he didn't really like but had come to accept. He could only hope that his plans for Georgianne came to fruition, in which case Diane would be redundant.

It was a shame about Georgianne. A woman falling for the wrong guy was an old, old story, Jeff knew, but he still found it hard to fathom. First Mike Rollins, then Sean Corcoran. It was up to Jeff to turn her around, to save her, in a sense, from herself. When she told him in Danbury that she would have dated him if he had ever asked, the dream had started to become real. In the weeks since, he had analyzed her words, her expressions, the sound of her voice. He replayed in his mind every second of his time with her,

and he subjected everything she had said, every gesture she had made, to an intense and objective
scrutiny. It all added up to the same thing: Yes, she
could love him; yes, she wanted to love him; yes, only
he could help her out of her present situation. Georgianne didn't understand this yet, but she would in
time. Meanwhile, the more Jeff studied it, the more
obvious and irrefutable the truth became.

He made a tomato-and-cucumber sandwich and ate
it in the living room. He smiled at the sight of Georgianne's pen-and-ink sketch of the old barn. The
brushed-metal frame he'd bought was perhaps too
modern for the picture, and it looked rather lonely
because he'd never bothered to put anything else on
his walls, but he loved it. Anyhow, he told himself,
someday dozens of Georgianne's drawings would be
hung here.

Diane rented a two-story so-called maisonette in Uni-
versal City. Jeff parked his Camaro around the corner.
When he rang the bell, as usual he couldn't bring
himself to look directly at the eyehole in the door. He
was tense, but excited. The door opened, he walked
right in, and it locked behind him.

"Hi, Jeffie."

She had longish, streaked blond hair and wore a
boy's white shirt, open to the fifth button. She had a
way of holding her head slightly down and looking up
from behind a fall of hair, like Veronica Lake. Her
smile was shy but knowing.

"Hi, Georgianne." Jeff felt the goose bumps on his

113

arms. It was the first time he'd ever actually called her that! "Are your parents still here?"

"No, they're out for a while."

"Oh, here's the book I wanted to return."

He took an envelope out of his pants pocket and handed it to the girl.

"Thanks . . . So, what've you been doing?"

"Nothing much."

"I'm just playing records. Come on."

"Okay."

He followed her up the stairs, appreciating the way her thighs moved and her shirttail rode her fanny. They went into a large bedroom with a deep shag carpet and a wall of mirrors. Jeff stepped out of his loafers.

"Want a drink? I've got some of my father's whiskey. He never even notices it's gone."

"Okay, sure."

Jeff watched her get the drinks at the vanity table, where she had a tray with a Scotch bottle, some ice and mixers, and a couple of glasses. He enjoyed the way she bent over, the way she walked back to him and bent over as she served his drink. They sat cross-legged on the floor. Music played softly on the stereo system.

"Your parents would kill us if they found us like this," he said, smiling.

"They're in Disneyland. I told you they won't be home until later."

"How come you didn't go with them?"

"I'm too old for that, Jeffie. Or haven't you noticed?"

"Yeah, I guess you are."

"Seventeen."

"I know. I've been watching you, Georgianne."

"You have not." She pouted. "You never notice me. You hardly even look at me in school or in the library."

"But I do, really," he insisted. "I saw you at the library the other day. You were in the reading room, and I sat and watched you for nearly an hour."

"You did? How come?"

"You were wearing a miniskirt and black tights with some kind of pattern in them."

"You were looking at my legs?"

"Mm-hmm."

"Oh. Well, you were at that party last weekend, and you didn't ask me to dance. Why not?"

"I . . . don't know. . . . I wanted to, but . . ."

"That's all right," she said sweetly. "Would you like to dance with me now?"

"Sure, yeah."

They clung to each other, moving only minimally to a slow song. She held one of his hands against her chest, in the open shirt, close to but not touching either breast. He put his face in her hair and dreamed, and it seemed as if locks and knots were dissolving throughout his body. He felt lighter, happy and free. He stroked the small of her back, occasionally daring to reach a little lower. She wore no panties, and the curve of her flesh beneath the soft cotton shirttail felt wonderful.

"I like being treated like a grownup," she whispered. "Daddy still thinks I'm his little girl."

"You're a young woman now, Georgianne."

"Mmm, you dance so nice, Jeffie."

When the song ended, they sat down to their drinks again, but this time she leaned back against the foot of the bed, her legs stretched out. She flapped the front of her shirt.

"It's so hot. . . ." Her face brightened. "Hey, would you do me a favor, Jeffie? Would you put some rubbing alcohol on me? It's so-o-o fantastic the way it cools your skin. It's refreshing and relaxing at the same time."

"Sure, if you want."

"Oh, I do." She went to the vanity table and returned with a plastic bottle, which she gave to Jeff. "Don't get up. I'll stand here and you can rub it on my legs."

She turned her back, but stood almost on top of him, her legs spread, her hands clasped behind her neck, and arched her back slightly. Jeff splashed some alcohol into his hands. He did the calves quickly, then the backs of her knees, one of his favorite parts of the female body. He took his time with her thighs, slowly enjoying every inch of them, until his hands were up under the shirttail, brushing, caressing her bottom. His fingers glided around her hips, flirting with that exquisite hollow in front before retreating to the back again.

"Oh, Jeffie, that feels so good . . . don't stop, please don't stop . . . this is how I wanted you to touch me . . . my belly, between my legs . . . oh, Jeffie, Jeffie . . ."

With one hand she pulled her shirt up a little more, and he began to kiss her skin with his cheek and lips.

"Ooooh . . . Jeffie . . ." A few minutes later she

knelt down, keeping her back to him. She slid her shirt off her shoulders and spoke in that little-girl voice. "Would you do my neck now?"

Jeff rubbed more alcohol on her. Then he came closer, so that she could lean her head back against him and he could do her front. She had a lovely, slender throat and neck. She seemed to let her body melt on him, and she made soft moaning sounds that intensified when he reached lower. The shirt fell around her waist, and he massaged her breasts. It thrilled him to see how the combination of cooling alcohol and his warm fingers could bring her nipples to life.

When he felt he had done enough, he sat back on his heels, and then she did something he adored. She turned around on her knees to face him, and as she did so she held the collar of the shirt up to her mouth, only partially covering her breasts. She held her head down, hair falling across one side of her face, and peeked up at him. She was a perfect picture, and Jeff was transfixed.

"Georgianne . . . Georgianne . . ."

"Can I do you now?"

How could she manage it, he wondered dimly. How could she sound so shy, but breathless and eager too?

"Georgianne . . ."

"Please, Jeffie. I want to. Please let me."

"Georgianne . . ." He was helpless.

"Don't you want me to?"

"Yes." His voice very quiet; his eyes avoided hers.

"Here, give me the bottle of alcohol. Now stand up. You have to let me take off your shirt and pants. I want to do everything, Jeffie. Everything. You can close your eyes if you feel shy about it. It's okay, it's okay. Isn't that so nice and cool and silky? It's okay, Jeffie, it's really really okay. . . ."

"Georgianne . . ."

"I'm so glad you came today," she went on soothingly. "I thought about this so many times, I wanted to do this with you and have you do it with me. I never touched anyone else or let them touch me like this. I wanted it to be you, Jeffie, only you. . . ."

"I was afraid . . ."

"Both of us, like this."

"You'd say no."

"It's okay now, Jeffie, it's all right now. . . ."

"Georgianne . . ."

CHAPTER TWELVE

"By the way," Jeff said, "I won't be around at all next weekend. Unless—"

"No problem," Ted Benedictus replied without bothering to raise his eyes from the charts he was studying.

"Going away?" Callie asked.

"Yes. I'm going on a twenty-mile hike."

Now Ted looked up. He took his glasses off and gaped at Jeff.

"A twenty-mile hike?" He pronounced the words carefully, as if testing each one before going on to the next.

"That's right," Jeff said, grinning.

"I don't believe it," Ted declared flatly.

"It's true."

Ted sat back in his chair, smiling. "Jeff, Martha and I, and Callie too, have been telling you for years to take time off from work, to get out and do more for yourself. I think it's great that you're finally starting to take our advice, and what you do is your business. But when you come in here and tell me you're going to hike twenty miles, I simply don't believe it. Your idea of strenuous exercise is lugging the Sunday papers home from the store."

Callie did a good job of restraining her smile. She was enjoying this. A bright, professional woman, she had been with Jeff and Ted from the beginning. Neither of them had ever made a pass at her, a fact she deeply appreciated. She liked both men, and she was proud of the company she had helped them to establish.

"That's true enough," Jeff said. "But, well, I got talked into it by a very nice young woman."

"Ah." Ted nodded approvingly. "She must be pretty special, to get you out on something like that."

"I think she is," Jeff said. "We'll see how far I get— uh, no pun intended."

"Where are you going?" Callie asked.

"Somewhere up in Los Padres." Jeff knew he didn't have to be specific. Besides, the national park covered parts of three counties and thousands of square miles.

"You'll come back on crutches," Ted predicted. "But it'll be good for you."

"I just wanted you to know," Jeff said, "so you wouldn't try to reach me next weekend. Nobody will be able to get in touch with me, where I'm going."

Ted shook his head, amused. "Jeff, do me a favor, do Callie, here, a favor, and most of all do yourself a favor. Get lost in the woods with that woman for a month or so. It would be the best thing that could happen to you. And we'll survive here—don't worry about that."

One base covered, Jeff thought later as he drove toward Los Angeles. He wasn't going directly home after work that evening. He had an appointment. Diane had given him a name of sorts, Knobs, and a telephone number. Diane was the only one Jeff knew who might be able to help. She had refused to act as go-between, but she did refer him to this other person. Some ridiculous hugger-mugger had ensued, ambiguous phone calls and instructions for him to send a certain kind of photograph of himself to a post-office box in Santa Monica. He had done as he was told, waited a week, and then called again. Everything was set, and now he was on his way to conclude the deal. It was necessary—Jeff had no doubt about that. But the whole procedure seemed juvenile, and in spite of all the money he was carrying and the risk he was taking, he felt silly rather than nervous. Is this what it seems like to everyone who gets involved with illegal goods, he wondered, something of a prank, until the cops take you in? Never mind, he told himself, it'll be over in less than an hour.

Jeff drove into Hollywood. He found the right street and the taco stand just around the corner from Sunset. A small crowd of typical street people were hanging out in front of the place. He pulled over, shifted the car into park, and sat with his signal light blinking. He had decided not to wait more than one minute, but almost at once the passenger door opened, and a large, heavy young man got into the car. One look at the way he filled out his T-shirt explained the man's nickname. He had long, wispy side-burns, and his hands were empty, which puzzled Jeff at first.

"Hi, you're a friend of . . ." The man deliberately left the sentence unfinished.

"Diane," Jeff said. "And you're . . ."

"Knobs, right," the man replied in a way that discouraged jokes. "Let's go."

Jeff put the car in gear and drove down the street at a moderate speed. Knobs picked up the folded news-paper on the seat and let the envelope in it slip onto his lap. God, Jeff suddenly thought, what's to stop him from jumping out at the next corner and disappearing with my money? But nothing like that happened. Knobs held the envelope on his lap and counted the bills.

"Very good," he said. "Very good."

He crammed the cash into his right front pants pocket and tossed the envelope on the floor—a gesture that annoyed Jeff.

"Turn here and swing back up to Sunset," Knobs said, pointing. He reached behind and fished something out of his back pocket. He slipped it into the newspaper, which he refolded and set down on the car seat. "You're all set, pal. It ain't much, so if you want more, give me a call. You know the drill now."

"Uh, yeah . . ."

Jeff thought he should inspect his purchases before Knobs left, but they were at a traffic light at Sunset now. Knobs got out of the car and disappeared into the crowd before Jeff could bring himself to say anything. Well, if I've been burned, it serves me right, he thought. At least it's over. He'd spent less than five minutes with Knobs, but he'd been uncomfortable the entire time. He drove carefully back to Santa Susana, stopping for every yellow light. That is what is so damn stupid about all this, he reminded himself. If a cop finds these things on you now, you're fucked, plain and simple.

When he got home, he flung the newspaper down on the coffee table and poured himself a large Scotch to steady his nerves. He took a couple of gulps and lit a cigarette before examining the items he'd bought. There were two Manila envelopes, each about the size of a grocery clerk's pay packet. In one was a small plastic bag containing white powder, in the other a piece of hard plastic.

He had no desire to try the cocaine, but he touched it with a moistened fingertip and tasted it. Bitter, definitely alkaloid, as it should be. Satisfied, he got some flour from the kitchen, along with a spoon and a small bowl. He dumped the coke into the bowl, added an equal amount of flour, and stirred them thoroughly. Then he poured the cut mixture back into the plastic bag and hid it in his bedroom.

The other item was no less important. It was a phony state of California driver's license. The tiny photograph was the one Jeff had sent to the box in Santa Monica, and the physical description of height, weight, hair, and eye color matched his own. But the license was in the name of Philip Headley, who might or might not actually exist and who supposedly lived out in Loma Linda. Jeff was pleased that the license looked every bit the real thing, and he made a mental note to practice the signature until he could dash off a good approximation of it. He placed the laminated license between two volumes in the bookcase, and left the Manila envelope on the shelf in front of them so he wouldn't forget the location.

As he sat down to enjoy the rest of his whiskey and smoke another cigarette, he was starting to feel something like pride in what he'd done. He wanted to believe that he'd taken the first step toward the solution of his problem. Perhaps he was just indulging in a fantasy, but he thought it was better to do something, even if it subsequently failed to bear fruit, than to continue doing nothing at all. Maybe he'd fall short. Maybe he didn't have any real chance of winning the woman he wanted and loved. But if he lost Georgianne again, this time it wouldn't be for lack of trying.

He thought about calling her. Just to hear the sound of her voice on the telephone. But he knew he couldn't do that; it would be a mistake. No matter. She was more alive in his mind now than ever, and he had the extra comfort of knowing that his plan was finally getting underway. He was doing something—something about and for Georgianne.

If it didn't work out, there was still Bonnie. Now *that* was an exotic thought. Was he too old for her? In four years, when she graduated from Harvard, she'd be twenty-one and Jeff would be forty-two. Exactly twice her age, a significant difference. But not impossible. There were many instances of men marrying women who were thirty or even forty years their junior. Besides, Jeff wouldn't necessarily have to marry her; a steady, intense, long-term affair would do just as well. He'd made up his mind before he left Connecticut that when Bonnie was in her final year at Harvard he would offer her a good job, an excellent salary, and relocation expenses.

He began to laugh out loud. The audacity of it! Now he wanted both women, mother and daughter. It was crazy. But at the same time—why not? Go for broke, he told himself, you have nothing to lose and everything to gain. You might even pull it off. He still wasn't sure if he was serious, or if he was merely letting his mind go too far . . . but it was a line of thought he was eager to follow. Bonnie was not out of the question, not by any means. In fact, the more Jeff considered the situation, the more certain he became that it was entirely in his favor. And that could only help him with Georgianne.

But did he really want either of them? And if so, why? How he felt was answer enough; what he had carried around inside him for over two decades was more than justification. Yes, he wanted Georgianne, because he had finally come to face the truth that life was unacceptable without her. And, with or without Georgianne, Bonnie would inevitably come.

CHAPTER THIRTEEN

At lunchtime the next day, Jeff went out and bought a jogging suit. It was gray, with maroon trim. He also picked up an expensive pair of running shoes. He had no intention of taking up jogging, but when he got home that evening and tried on the outfit, he was surprised by how comfortable it felt. He could picture himself lounging around the house in it.

Jeff went nowhere that weekend. He stayed indoors, smoking, drinking, and staring vacantly at the television. Occasionally he nibbled a piece of fruit or a raw vegetable. He slept in his underwear and didn't bother to shave. He never turned on a light, and he kept the drapes drawn. Because he'd switched the air conditioner off, his rooms were not merely hot, but stifling. He stayed away from the bath and shower, didn't brush his teeth or even splash cold water on his face. He sat in the dark or wandered from one room to another. He seemed to be sweating all the time, but it wasn't just from the heat and it certainly wasn't due to anxiety. He thought of it as a kind of purification, as if his body were literally and physically exorcising a deadness within itself. This ritual was a rebirth, and if he'd been able to shed his skin, he would have done so proudly.

All he'd have had to do to make a plane reservation was pick up the telephone and dial one of the airlines, but as early as Friday night Jeff knew he wasn't going anywhere. Not that weekend. It wasn't hesitation born of fear. He knew the difference now. He was a man who had come a long way over a great period of time, and this was nothing more than a final pause, a last check, to be sure he knew what he wanted to do. Once it began, there would be no going back.

And he was right, as it turned out. Over the course of the weekend, he gradually came to the conclusion that July was too early. He'd have to wait a little longer, at least until sometime in August, before he went back to Connecticut to see Georgianne again. Yes, he decided, the first half of August would be right.

Jeff woke early on Monday morning. He drew back the drapes, opened every window, and cleaned the rooms. After a long shower, a shave, and scrubbing his teeth, he put on his favorite shirt, tie, and suit, and his best pair of shoes. He felt terrific. At the office, when Ted and Callie asked him how the hike had gone, he smiled and answered ambiguously, and they smiled back at him but didn't press for details. He looked dapper and perky, and that was good enough for them.

The days ticked by with an almost sensual rhythm that gave Jeff great pleasure. He was a sleepwalker who had finally been awakened, a zombie restored miraculously to life, and now that he was learning how to live again, the simplest things were astonishingly delicious to him—the morning air, the play of light at dusk, the buzz of an insect, or the sensation of speed when he accelerated sharply on the freeway. Even if none of his plans worked out, he had gained this much, thanks to Georgianne.

He blocked out the second weekend in August. It might not be necessary, but he felt he should cover his bases with Ted and Callie. It would be a long weekend. He finished work on Thursday evening and flew out of Los Angeles early Friday morning, paying cash for his ticket and traveling as Philip Headley. At La Guardia he had to show the phony driver's license for the first time, when he hired a car—from a different rental agency than the one he had used on his trip in May. He felt a slight tingle of nervousness, but there was no trouble with the license.

He drove to Bridgeport and parked the car in a downtown municipal lot, telling the attendant it would be there for one or two nights. Carrying one light suitcase, he walked around the center of the city until he found another car-hire outfit, from which he rented another vehicle, which had Connecticut plates.

It's like a game, he thought as he drove out of Bridgeport—the secret transcontinental mission, the false identity, paying cash all the way—all slightly unreal, but with nothing less than real love at stake. If he failed, would it be Philip Headley's failure? Would he be able to return home and go back to living as Jeff Lisker? Well, yes, but never again as the old Jeff Lisker. He was dead, for sure. No matter what happened, the new life would not be aborted. Besides, he had various fall-back positions. . . .

The run from Bridgeport to Danbury was not a great distance, but it was all country road. Jeff reached the outskirts of the city sometime after six in the evening. He got a room at the first motel he came across, the Brook Green, apparently named after the trickle of water out back and the golf course beyond it.

He couldn't eat or drink anything, he felt so excited and nervous. He thought about calling Georgianne, but he wasn't quite ready for that, and he was afraid Sean might answer. Oh yeah, Sean. Jeff seldom wasted mental energy on the subject of Georgianne's husband, but obviously he would be around. He was the problem, after all.

Jeff waited until darkness before he left the motel and drove to Foxrock. This was the crucial test, on which the rest of the weekend depended. He had not been able to figure out any way of determining in advance whether the Corcorans would be home. In another month, Bonnie would be at Harvard, and Sean would be back teaching kids at the middle school, but they could all be on vacation now, out on Cape Cod or somewhere up in Maine. He could have called from California and carefully steered the conversation around to the question of summer vacation, but he had ruled out the idea of any advance contact. The three-month gap had come to seem too important to interrupt, as if even a postcard would somehow diminish the advantage of surprise he wanted for the coming encounter. But he was prepared for their absence: he'd be back next weekend, and the one after, if need be, until he found the Corcorans at home.

By the time he reached Indian Hill Road, a warm, happy feeling had begun to come over him, and he knew his luck had held. He could sense the proximity of Georgianne even before he saw the lights on in the house. One car in the open garage, the other in the driveway. Oh yes, oh yes . . . Jeff eased up the road, turned the car around, and drove back slowly. Should he stop and see them now?

Say: Hello, yeah, it's me . . . back on business . . . thought I'd drop in and surprise you . . . listen, one thing, rather important . . . Georgianne, can I talk to you . . . alone . . . you see, I was in love with you twenty years ago . . . all this time . . . I never knew how to tell you . . . afraid . . . and I still am, yes, I do love you now . . . more than ever . . . I don't know what to do about it . . . there's Sean . . . this fucking house . . .

Or: Hello, et cetera . . . Sean, I have to talk to you . . . just you for now . . . look here, I'm sorry but I'm afraid there's been a terrible mistake . . . well, I'm glad you see it that way too . . . I didn't think you'd be so reasonable . . . oh, you could tell the first day . . . love . . . I do . . . she does . . .

To hell with it. Jeff had never especially liked that part of the plan, and now he decided it wouldn't work. It was getting on toward ten, and they went to bed early. Wrong time, wrong approach. But that was okay, because he had something better in mind. This little bit of reconnaissance had achieved its purpose. Tomorrow was the day.

Before he left Indian Hill Road, Jeff took his foot off the gas pedal and let the car slow to a crawl. He was tempted to park and sneak up to the Corcoran house. The notion of peeking in on Georgianne had an undeniable charm. It would be a playful adolescent thrill, innocent really. He thought she would understand, and would probably find it amusing. But he quickly came to his senses. The bedrooms were on the upper floor. It would be no fun to see the three of them just sitting around watching television. Besides, there were bound to be dogs in a neighborhood like this, ready to bark up a storm at any intruder. Sadly, he abandoned the idea and drove back to the Brook Green Motel.

He was tired from flying and driving all day, but he was still on California time and felt too tense to sleep. He wanted a drink, but alcohol was out of the question; he had to be sharp tomorrow. He would drink all the way back to Los Angeles. Finally, he dozed off for a few hours and awoke at five in the morning.

He had to talk to Sean. He was ready to talk to Sean. That was the next step. The Gorge. The man would be caught off guard, surprised. He would make him walk, not run, and talk. There was a great deal to talk about. And if that didn't work, there were other moves to be played. It was like a chess game, which would be over as soon as Jeff won his opponent's queen.

He put on his new jogging suit and shoes, and drove through the gray light to Foxrock. It was an overcast morning, warm and muggy already. The town was asleep, the streets empty. He parked about a quarter of a mile from the entrance to the Gorge, well away from any houses, and took the path he and Sean had followed in May. When he judged that he had gone far enough in from the street, he left the trail. Several yards into the woods, he perched on a low, flat rock, and waited. It was a good spot. Not much chance he'd be noticed where he was, but he could see anyone passing on the path. He looked at his watch. Be early, he commanded, and be alone.

Look here, I know this is going to be hard for you to take, even to grasp, all at once, but, well, the fact is, a mistake has been made. . . .

Jeff's feet felt as if they were baking in his new running shoes. Ridiculous, especially at that price. And the running duds felt like glorified pajamas, okay for lazing around the house but not to wear out on the street. He couldn't help but feel a certain contempt for people who dressed like this and ran so obsessively. It seemed to indicate that there was something wrong with their lives. They were like Shiite flagellants, suburban American style. Doing penance for their prosperity and lifestyle.

Sean probably thinks of me every day, Jeff realized. A dodging step, a smile, a chuckle, a moment of smug pleasure as he passes the spot—here's where that Lisker guy barfed. Not after today, though.

Now that he was here and waiting, Jeff felt remarkably calm. He had come so far, he knew he would see it through. A lunatic mission, doomed to failure? No. He saw it as a pilgrimage that proved the validity of his feelings for Georgianne. Their time was at hand. He had put in twenty years or more of unrequited, half-realized, platonic love. He'd paid his dues.

Things happen because they have to. It was extraordinary, when he thought about it. His father had picked the right time to die. Georgianne was at a turning point in her life. Bonnie, a year early, was about to go off to college. Sean and Georgianne would be entering a new stage in their married life, alone in that house, child-rearing finished, for the most part. It was the best possible time for something like this. Georgianne would now be more receptive, both to Jeff and to a change in her life. She would no longer have to fear the disruptive effect it might have on her daughter, who was now a young adult. And it would be an attractive alternative to the impending boredom and loneliness she faced—husband working, no Bonnie coming home from school every afternoon.

It would be a big change for Jeff, too. He would have to alter his work habits dramatically. But he could afford to do that now. With Georgianne, it would be easy. They had a lot of time to make up together. There were all kinds of possibilities. Jeff was beginning to see Lisker-Benedictus Future Systems in a fresh light.

He checked his watch again. Jesus, man, come on. Maybe he had missed Sean already. Maybe he had taken another path, or wasn't even coming this morning. It would mean a trip back to the motel and a phone call to Georgianne to arrange a meeting with her alone. They would have a serious, heart-to-heart talk. That was inevitable sooner or later anyhow.

But a moment after Jeff had worked out his next move, Sean came bouncing along the rough path. Jeff followed him at once, his whole body charged with the sudden shock of fear and excitement. He stumbled out of the woods onto the trail. Sean was already ten yards ahead. Jeff ran to catch up. When he had gained some ground, he stopped and called out.

"Sean. Hey, Sean."

Georgianne's husband halted and wheeled around with athletic grace. He started to walk back toward Jeff, at first unsure, but soon registering surprised recognition.

"Jeff? I'll be damned, it *is* you."

He came forward to shake hands, but Jeff ignored the gesture.

"Hello, Sean."

"What are you doing here? Back to see Union Carbide again?"

"Yeah, I'm back," Jeff replied coolly. "Got in last night and thought I'd surprise you."

"Well, you sure did," Sean said. "I never thought I'd see you at this place again." Now he looked Jeff over. "I see you've got yourself a new running outfit. Very nice."

He's smirking, Jeff thought. He's actually smirking at me in these clothes. How fucking typical of the man!

"You must come back to the house for breakfast," Sean was saying. "Want to run a bit? I have to do my laps. Boy, will the girls be surprised to see you!"

Not *happy* to see me? No, you wouldn't want to say that, admit that, would you, Mr. Corcoran.

"I don't want to run," Jeff said. "We ran the last time. This time we'll walk. There's something I have to talk to you about, if you don't mind."

"Okay, sure."

They walked deeper into the Gorge. Jeff was pleased with himself. Right from the first he had dictated the tempo, set the correct tone.

"What's up?" Sean asked when they had gone a short distance. "Is there some problem?"

Look here, I'm sorry, but—no, that sort of approach just wouldn't work. The lines Jeff had run through his head many times earlier now seemed too stiff and cumbersome. He couldn't get them out; it was as if his throat and vocal cords were giving him a message by refusing to function. Okay, this wasn't the kind of thing you could rehearse. You had to let it out the way it wanted to come.

"Anything I can help you with?" Sean asked. "If I can do anything, I will."

You can, you will, Jeff thought. The words were brimming up within him now.

"Yeah, yeah. It's about Georgianne and me," he said harshly. "I have to be honest with you—that's the way I am. You have to know."

"Oh?"

Sean blinked and appeared to be confused. But the situation transformed and clarified itself for him quickly as he absorbed Jeff's words and tone of voice. Then he was almost amused, and it showed on his face.

He must think I'm a fool, Jeff decided, some silly twerp who feels compelled to confess that he and Georgianne had misbehaved twenty years ago. Yes, that would be how Sean Corcoran's mind worked. He should only be so lucky. Hold on, pal, the best is yet to come.

"Yeah, you see, the thing is," Jeff continued in a rush, "I know this will be a shock to you, but the fact is I'm very serious about Georgianne. And she's just as serious about me. That's the reality of it."

"What?" A surprised, half-laugh of exclamation.

"I'm telling you the truth," Jeff followed up promptly. "There's really nothing you can do about it, except make it a little more painful and messy, and I hope you won't go in for that. I don't care about myself, it wouldn't bother me, but it would hurt Georgianne, and she doesn't deserve that kind of treatment after all she's given you."

Jeff stood there, rigid as a stone gargoyle out of the Middle Ages, but his heart thundered, and he thought he could feel the blood surging through every part of his body.

Sean put his hands on his hips. "Are you kidding?"

Jeff snapped back, "Not at all."

"This isn't a joke," Sean stated calmly. "You're really serious about this."

"Of course I am," Jeff said angrily. "I didn't have to come here at this time of day and talk to you reasonably like this. We could have taken another route, but no, I've made this effort. I want you to understand. I want you to see the whole picture."

"You *do* mean it," Sean said quietly, almost to

himself. "All right, what is the picture? Go ahead, tell me."

"Ha, that's good. What the fuck do you think it is, for Chrissake? You're finished, Sean, you're through. It's all over. It was a mistake in the first place. It never should have happened. But you've had your time, you've had *her,* and for way too long. Now I'm telling you it's over, finished, done. Ended." Jeff felt serene, steady as a pure white flame, and it was the best feeling he'd ever known.

"Jeff, you're . . ." Sean made an effort to suppress the anger he was beginning to feel. "Look," he said gently, "you've got a problem and—"

"Don't talk to me like that," Jeff responded hotly. "You're the one with the problem, man, and there's nothing you can do about it. Listen to what I'm telling you."

"Jeff, what did Georgianne say to you?"

"That's between her and me."

"Jeff, I don't know . . ." Sean looked embarrassed as well as disconcerted now. "You must have misunderstood." Then, hesitantly, he added, "Georgianne doesn't care about you—I mean, not that way."

"You're full of shit," Jeff answered, his voice low and furious. "It's a waste of time even trying to talk sense to you."

"I mean, she cares about you, of course," Sean went on soothingly. "Very much. You're a very dear friend to her. But, really, Jeff, she doesn't love you, if that's what you think." His manner was soft and patient, like a parent's trying to explain to one child why he couldn't have another child's toy.

"She doesn't love me? That's funny coming from you. What would you know about it? All you've done is bury her here for twenty years. Let me tell you something, Sean. You don't understand your own wife. You don't even come close. And you treat her like a piece of shit."

"She's my wife, and I know her far better than you do." Sean's face tightened as he spoke, and his cheeks burned. "You're imagining all this. It's just some—"

"You'd be funny if you weren't so pathetic," Jeff cut in. "You insult her all the time. I couldn't believe it. You know, I wanted to like you, because you were married to Georgianne, and I hoped she had a good life, a good husband. I tried to like you, but it isn't possible. You're a weak, sarcastic little man, and you don't have the slightest idea how to treat a woman like Georgianne. And if I were wrong about all this, she wouldn't have responded to me the way she did." His smile became a sneer.

"I don't believe you," Sean said flatly. He was fed up now. There was no point in arguing like this.

"You don't want to believe me. That's what it is," Jeff taunted insistently. "You're afraid of the truth."

One short, sharp punch to the temple would put an end to this nonsense, Sean thought. He could do it, But he knew he would regret it later, and so would Georgianne. Besides, Lisker wasn't worth the risk of a broken finger. Better to treat him like a disturbed person, which he obviously was, someone who was unbalanced rather than merely mean and nasty.

"Jeff, I don't know what to say. Maybe you need

professional help. I think you're off the deep end. But
if you're sure you're right, let's go back to the house
and see what Georgianne has to say about it. If she
tells me that she does love you . . . well, all right, then
I'll know there's something to it and I'll have to deal
with it. That's more than reasonable. We're not going
to settle anything here."

"Have to deal with it? Ha, I like that." Jeff shook
his head slightly, as if amused, but his eyes remained
fixed on Sean with cold fury. "No, no, no. I don't want
you to create a scene, upsetting Georgianne and putting her on the spot like that."

Sean returned his gaze. Jeff didn't want to confront
Georgianne because he was afraid to hear the truth
from her. He had reached a dead end: he had come
here and aired his warped fantasy, but now he had
nowhere to go. Sean felt sorry for him, but it was time
for a change of scene. Standing here and arguing was
too bizarre, and probably only made matters worse.

"Okay, Jeff. You don't want to discuss it at home
with Georgianne, and I can understand that. But I
don't see what I can do for you. We're wasting each
other's time here. I'm going to try to forget all about
this, and I hope you will too. But whether you do or
not, I don't want to see you again. Stay away from my
house, stay away from Georgianne, don't even try to
get through on the phone—and I'll let it go. But do
yourself a favor, Jeff, and get some help. You need it."

Jeff was amazed. Sean positively demanded to be
hated. It wasn't just the irrelevant ultimatum, but the
way his tiny mind worked.

139

"Oh, you put your house first, then Georgianne," Jeff said. "Is that the way it is? I might have known. You're a dumb fuck, Sean. You think you can tell me—"

"You heard me," Sean interrupted, jabbing a finger at Jeff's heart with enough force to push him back on his heels. *"You heard me."*

He turned and began to walk away, back toward the street. It was too much for Jeff, who rushed after him, grabbed a handful of his hair, and yanked his head back violently. At the same time, he reached behind his back, up under his sweatshirt, and pulled out the .22, which finally seemed to have a use. He put the gun barrel right up to Sean's eye, so that he could see the weapon clearly. It worked. Sean stopped resisting immediately. Jeff drove him off the path, into the woods, until they came to a dark, heavily shaded spot.

"Jeff," Sean said carefully, "think what you're doing. That gun won't solve anything. You can hurt me, if that's what you want to do, but you'll only end up making a mess of your own life."

"Shut up." Jeff loved the way his voice edged lower as his rage increased. It seemed to prove that he was fully in control of himself and the situation. "Just shut up, do you understand?" he added, almost intoxicated by the way he sounded. For the first time he was hearing, witnessing, the new and real Jeff Lisker. "You're so incredibly smug and arrogant. You think I'd just let you walk away from me while I'm talking to you, let you go back and take it out on Georgianne? That's your way, isn't it? Walk away from me, don't face me, then abuse Georgianne. Jesus, you make me sick, Sean, you really do. And I tried to like you. I tried to talk to you. Man to man. Let's be reasonable. Waste of fucking time."

"Jeff, they'll pick you up before the day's over," Sean said, afraid now but still trying to speak sensibly. He should have clipped Jeff when he had the chance. His only hope was in talk. He couldn't try anything else now, not with the end of that gun barrel kissing his right eyeball. "Think, man, think," he urged delicately. "Is this going to make Georgianne feel any—"

"Shut up," Jeff snarled in Sean's ear. Then he hit him in the face with the gun, and a second time, drawing blood from a couple of small cuts. It felt good—this whole course of violent action—astonishingly good. It was like a miraculous cure for blindness. The truth was dazzling, and Jeff loved it. This was what he had been trying to find for so long, a clarity of vision and purpose and self that could only be achieved by *doing something*. It was right and natural, and above all it was the one thing that succeeded in making sense of the past. Twenty, no, twenty-four years of Jeff's life came into sharp focus, like the smallest print on an eye chart seen through new lenses. "You're the problem, Sean. Maybe if you'd been more realistic about this, if you'd accepted the situation . . . but it's too late for that now. You're my problem, you're Georgianne's problem."

"It's not too late," Sean gasped anxiously. "I want to accept the situation. Just tell me what to do."

"What to do?" Jeff laughed. Sean had shriveled into something less than human. He was like a worm, cringing beneath the radiance of the noonday sun. "Sean, I want you to do the only thing you can do. I want you to go away."

He put the gun to the side of Sean's head and eased the trigger. The .22 made a noise like one hand lightly slapping another. There wasn't much blood at all, just a neat round hole in Sean's temple. Again. Again. Three holes, forming a nice tight triangle. No shuddering. No spastic, jerking movements. Sean died neatly, and Jeff appreciated it.

He let the body slide to the ground, and he stood over it for a few moments. All the anger was gone, as if it had been scorched and vaporized out of every cell in his body. He felt as clean and light and free as the spirit of the wind. Then he began to sing very softly but happily. "Heaven, I'm in Heaven . . . Heaven, I'm in Heaven . . ." He didn't know any of the other words to the song, but they weren't necessary.

He unzipped the back hip pocket of his running pants and took out the plastic bag. He tucked the gun away and then sprinkled the mixture of flour and cocaine all over Sean's face, covering it with the fine white powder. That'll give them something to think about. . . . Jeff shoved the empty plastic bag back into his pocket and studied the scene until he was satisfied he'd left nothing, not even a footprint.

What hurt was that he wouldn't be able to see Georgianne on this trip. Not even a glimpse of her from a distance. He'd give anything to see her, if only for a minute, but it was out of the question. Later, he told himself, later there would be plenty of time.

"Heaven . . . I'm in Heaven . . ."

Jeff's luck held again, and he didn't encounter anyone as he left the Gorge. He jogged all the way back to the car. It seemed appropriate.

PART III

Lateral Movement

CHAPTER FOURTEEN

Jeff checked out of the Brook Green Motel shortly after eight that morning and dropped the car off in Bridgeport within the hour. He returned the second car to the agency at La Guardia and then bought a seat on a noon flight to Los Angeles. By the end of the afternoon, local time, he was sitting on his balcony with a cigarette and an enormous glass of Scotch and ice. He was naked beneath the black robe wrapped loosely around his body. Only then, finally, did he allow himself the luxury of considering what had taken place at the Gorge.

He had to admit it was brilliant. He had treated the whole thing like a problem at work. You don't solve anything by talking about it off the top of your head. You let it simmer in the depths of your brain, and sooner or later the answer will come to the surface. It was, he reckoned, an essentially creative process. The world was full of people with stunted imaginations, poor souls who were incapable of something like this. He belonged to the select handful of individuals who had the courage, imagination, and sheer will to create their own destinies.

It had all come together so well! He felt like an architect who, seeing for the first time a construction he had designed, is overwhelmed by his own genius. The phony driver's license. The two cars. The cut cocaine, which undoubtedly would make the police think Sean had been involved in a deal that went wrong. And, best of all, the sudden inspiration that had come to Jeff only at the last moment: the tight triangle of bullet holes in Sean's skull. Didn't the Mafia go in for that sort of thing, symbolic, ritual executions? It couldn't be perfect, he knew, because nothing ever is; all the same, he thought it was pretty damn close to perfect.

There were still things to do, weak points to be covered. The Philip Headley license would be easy enough to destroy. Too many people knew that Jeff was not a jogger, so the new running suit and shoes had to go. They were brand-name products, and he had kept them in plastic bags to minimize the risk of fiber contamination, but there were brownish pinprick blood spots on the right sleeve. He had intended simply to dump the clothes in a Goodwill box, but the more he thought about it, the less he liked that idea. Expensive new duds . . . hardly used at all . . . blood spots . . . probably some of Jeff's body hairs on them. The chances that the clothes would ever be connected with a killing three thousand miles away were very slight, but why take the chance? Then there was the gun. Funny, Jeff thought, how the most trivial things can suddenly become so important. He had often regretted buying the .22. He had never needed it, and over the years had come to regard it as more of a nuisance than anything else. But he had kept it, if only because he couldn't be bothered to sell it. Now it was much more than just another cheap handgun. Jeff had made it the instrument of Georgianne's liberation. And if that were not enough to convict him, the gun was also legally registered in his name with the police. No question, he had to get rid of it quickly. Not to forget the plastic bag that had held the cocaine and flour. Things to do, important things, but no real problems. Jeff sat happily on the balcony, sipping Scotch and marveling at his accomplishment.

That evening he burned the plastic bag and the false driver's license, and washed the ashes down the kitchen sink with Liquid Drano.

The next day he packed the jogging clothes in the middle of a trash bag full of garbage and drove around until he spotted a dumpster containing similar trash bags outside a Valley mall. He added his to the collection.

On Monday, at lunchtime, he went to a hardware store and bought several small screwdrivers and a hacksaw. That night he patiently spent almost three hours dismantling the gun and cutting it into smaller pieces. On Tuesday, at lunchtime, he completed the disposal of the gun by scattering the pieces over a radius of several square miles. He threw them into ponds, reservoirs, and streams. He dropped them through sewer grates. He even put a few in various litter baskets. That evening he called the police to report the gun missing. He said he thought he'd lost it the previous weekend while hiking, alone, in Los Padres.

Jeff bought the *New York Times* every day for a week. The murder was reported in the Metro section. Sean's body had been discovered late in the morning, and the police were said to have no clues to the person or persons responsible. But it did appear to be a drug-related crime, according to an unidentified source. Family, friends, and colleagues of the dead man were shocked . . . etc. By the third day, the story had disappeared. Jeff was pleased, confident that events were taking precisely the course he'd intended.

It would be hard on Georgianne and Bonnie, but that couldn't be avoided. They would simply have to suffer through it. They were strong enough, Jeff reasoned, they'd make it. No one could blame them for Sean's transgressions. Later, they would find it easier to move away from Foxrock. A clean, fresh start somewhere else . . . like Santa Susana.

Jeff regretted the necessary cruelty to Georgianne and Bonnie, but he felt nothing for Sean. Why should he? You either experienced a sense of guilt and wrongdoing over something or you didn't, and he did not. He was enough of a scientist to know that the universe was random, arbitrary, and remorseless. It was a romantic exaggeration to call Sean's death a crime. He could just as easily have had a fatal heart attack while jogging, or been run down by a drunk teenager. Those things happened every day. And people killed other people every day, probably by the thousands world-wide. You might not like it, but there it was. Jeff would not indulge in any theatrical, hypocritical guilt. He was happy. From now on everything would be easier.

He slashed his work hours to about forty-five a week, and at the end of the first week he was startled to find that he hadn't fallen behind on anything, as he had expected to. It made him wonder how much of his life he had squandered, obsessively making work for himself. Every minute spent getting the company off the ground and keeping it alive was justified, certainly, but a few years ago some big contracts had come their way. The company had become an established fact, safe, solid, successful. Even so Jeff had continued putting in long hours, compulsively, and unnecessarily. It was a bitter thought, but he didn't linger over it. When you do gain your freedom, pain and a sense of loss tend to fade away. And he had no doubt that this was what Georgianne would experience in due course.

He spent more time socializing with his colleagues now. He ate, drank, and even took in a couple of Dodger games with them, and enjoyed all of it. He stayed away from Diane though. She was a whore, and he no longer liked the idea of having his dreams serviced by a whore. It seemed wrong, now that the way to Georgianne was clear. Diane was good at her job, one of the best, but he didn't need her any more.

All this time, too, he waited. He watched the days

go by, one after another, a week, two, a month. He was patient, and sure of himself. He found that it was even possible to savor the slow but relentless passage of time, the exquisite delay, the smoldering anticipation. It was a kind of mental foreplay.

He waited until the third week of September. That was time enough, he judged, for Georgianne and Bonnie to recover. Georgianne would be getting back to the business of coping with everyday life. Bonnie would be at Harvard, most likely trying to lose herself in her studies. That was as it should be. Jeff held back a few days more and then, on a Tuesday evening, picked up the telephone to call Georgianne. He had a large drink and a fresh pack of cigarettes at hand. It would be nine-thirty at night back in Connecticut.

Third ring. "Hello." Voice subdued.

"Hi, Georgianne." Cheerful, carefree. "This is Jeff." Pause, no response. Nearly five months since he'd last spoken with her. The shock. Understandable. "Jeff Lisker."

"Oh . . . Jeff." A slight laugh. "Sorry. I wasn't thinking. How are you? Where are you?"

"I'm fine and I'm home, in California."

"Oh. I thought you might be in Danbury on business."

"Well, that's one of the reasons I'm calling. I *am* going to be in Danbury soon."

"Oh. That's nice." Another pause. She sounded friendly, but vague and distracted. A pendulum swinging back and forth, in and out of the conversation. "Jeff, I have to tell you something," Georgianne said reluctantly.

"Oh yeah, what's that?"

"I should have called you. . . ."

Her voice, tiny and strangled now, faded again. She should be over it by now, Jeff thought anxiously. But raw grief billowed out of the telephone in his hand like some noxious gas.

"Georgianne, are you all right? What's wrong?"

"I'm sorry. I should have called you, Jeff, but I haven't been very efficient about anything lately." She spoke quietly, but she sounded more composed. "Jeff, I lost my husband. Sean is dead." A definite waver in the voice, followed by a brief gasp.

Jeff waited a couple of seconds. Then: *"What?"*

"It's true. Someone killed him last month."

Again the proper shocked pause. "Georgianne, no. I don't believe it. What on earth . . . ?"

"I don't know, I really don't know. Someone shot him one morning while he was out jogging, and . . . it's . . . I still don't understand any of it."

"My God, that's terrible. Who did it?" Jeff demanded.

"I don't know. No one knows, except . . ."

"Jesus, it's unbelievable. It must have been an absolute nightmare for you and Bonnie. You should have called me, Georgianne. I'd have come back right away."

"Thanks, Jeff, I know you would. But I didn't think . . . Anyhow, my family was here, and Sean's of course. . . ."

"And you say the police haven't found the bastard who did it? What are they doing?"

"No, they haven't, and I don't know what they're doing." Almost a whisper, but as cold and dry as a night wind coming out of the desert. "I'll tell you about it sometime, Jeff, but I really don't feel like talking about it now. Not on the phone."

"Of course, of course," Jeff said soothingly. "But tell me how you are *now*, and Bonnie."

"We're all right, I guess. Bonnie's at Harvard—she went last week. I think she's starting, just starting, to get over it. I hope her classes will help. Keep her busy."

"Sure."

"I call her every night. I have to; I'm so terrified of her being alone up there. I have to hear her voice before I can get any sleep . . . not that I'm getting much anyway."

"She'll be all right," Jeff said authoritatively. "It may take her awhile, but I got the impression that she's a strong person, with a lot of character as well as intelligence."

"Yes . . ."

"And you. How are you now?"

"Functioning, more or less. It's hard, Jeff, it's . . . so damned . . . hard."

"I can imagine. Listen, is there anything I can do for you? Anything at all? Don't ask, just tell me, and it'll be done at once."

"No, not really. But thanks, Jeff. Everyone's been very kind to us . . . well, most people. And there are no real problems about money or the house, or anything like that."

"Good. You don't need any extra headaches."

Jeff wanted very much to cheer her up, but he

couldn't find the right words, and it annoyed him. She was still deeply caught up in Sean's death. Time was the only thing that would haul her out of it. Jeff felt helpless, concerned.

"So, I just have to get myself back together," Georgianne said wanly. "I'm not as tough as Bonnie, you know. It devastated her, of course, both of us, but she was terrific all through the wake and the funeral. So good and strong and brave . . ."

"That's good," Jeff said.

"Sean and I used to ask, Where did we get her from? You know? She's so much brighter than either of us, and so adult for her age. We were so . . . lucky. . . ."

There were muffled sounds as Georgianne tried to hold on to her composure. Jeff knew the telephone conversation wasn't doing her any good, and he decided to wrap it up briskly but gently. He couldn't bear to hear her this way.

"It'll get better, Georgianne, it will," he promised. "I don't want to give you the usual baloney about life going on and all that jazz. You know that, but it won't mean anything until you get over your loss—and you will, you will."

"I know," she said distantly.

"Listen. I'm going to be in Danbury soon."

"It'll be nice to see you again."

"You're going to be around?"

"My mother wants me to go down to Florida to spend some time with her, but I think I'll wait until Christmas, when Bonnie and I can go together."

"That's a good idea."

"And my brother wants me to go out to Chicago, but I'll think about that next spring or summer. Right now I'm just seeing how I feel a day at a time."

"That's perfectly natural. Anyhow, you will be there for the next few weeks."

"Oh. Yes."

"Okay, good. I'll call you again as soon as I've got my dates worked out. We'll get together, go out for dinner . . . and talk."

"I'll look forward to it, Jeff."

"Me too."

When Jeff hung up, he lit another cigarette and paced the living-room floor. He couldn't sit still. He hated to think of Georgianne suffering this way. It was worse than he had expected. He might have to wait another two or three weeks for her to get over it.

CHAPTER FIFTEEN

It added up. The Los Angeles–New York round trip was about fifty-six hundred miles. The first time was for his father's funeral, but Jeff reckoned the real reason was to find Georgianne. The second trip was exclusively for her, and this one was the third time in less than six months. It came to a little over seventeen thousand miles when you threw in the car trips between Danbury and the airport. It added up to an impressive amount of time, money, and distance, and Jeff wished he could tell Georgianne. A small matter, but another sign of the effort he was willing to invest for her.

And she wasn't even home.

Jeff couldn't believe it. He had checked in at the Ramada Inn and called her immediately. No answer. It was just before seven, Friday evening. Where could she be? He fidgeted over a large glass of Scotch and several cigarettes, and then tried her number again. Still no reply.

Georgianne knew he would be arriving in Danbury that evening. He had phoned her from Santa Susana earlier in the week to tell her his plans. It had been a short and practical conversation, with neither of them much in a mood to chat. Georgianne had sounded as vague and absent as she had in their previous talk, but she was still glad to hear that she would see him soon. Now where was she?

Jeff showered and shaved, both for the second time that day. He remained confident that he could begin to pull Georgianne together, once he was with her in person. He had plans, ideas. He would take her out day and night. Movies, restaurants, galleries, antique shops. Relaxed, easy drives through the countryside. If all went well, he might even persuade her to spend a few days away—Massachusetts, New Hampshire, Vermont. It was the season for picking apples, drinking fresh cider, and enjoying the autumn colors. If he needed a sweetener, he would dangle the possibility of going by way of Cambridge to see Bonnie, an idea that was as attractive to Jeff as he was sure it would be to Georgianne. He had no doubt that Bonnie was his natural ally.

There were a couple of minor problems, but he thought he would be able to handle them without too much difficulty. Georgianne had not yet renewed her invitation to him to stay at her house. He would remain at the Ramada as long as necessary, for the entire two weeks if it came to that. He didn't want to press her. It was obviously a very sensitive and different situation now, with Sean dead and Bonnie away at college. Even if Georgianne did offer him a room, he might be wiser to turn it down gracefully. But would he be able to resist the temptation?

Then there was the matter of Union Carbide. He had to get out from under that millstone. He had decided to tell Georgianne that the deal had fallen through, but that he had come east anyway for a much-needed vacation. After all, it was pretty much the truth.

Georgianne finally answered the telephone shortly after nine. She sounded breathless, as if she had just come in.

"I've been calling for a couple of hours," Jeff said, simply to let her know.

"Oh. I was next door. Having dinner with the neighbors. They're very nice. I've been saying no to everything since the funeral, but today I just thought, Yeah, I want to walk across the lawn and eat with the neighbors."

"Good for you," Jeff said, taking it as a healthy sign. He was encouraged. "How are you now?"

"Better, I think. I'm not sure, but I feel better."

"Great. You do sound better." A little perkier, a little brighter. He wanted to reinforce and enhance any positive note with Georgianne. "Is it too late to take you out for a drink?" he asked, thinking surely it wasn't, not at nine o'clock on a Friday night.

But Georgianne said, "Oh, thanks, Jeff, but could we make it tomorrow?"

"Well . . ." Unwilling to concede.

"I've had a long day."

She said it as an explanation rather than an excuse, but Jeff was not pleased. A longer day than his? He had come 2,800 miles and three time zones—was it too much to ask that she go out for a nightcap with him?

"Okay. No problem," he said unhappily.

"Thanks. I hope you don't mind. I just want to have a cup of tea and go to bed."

"That's okay," he repeated. "I understand. But I hope you can spend a few minutes on the phone." He tried to keep the edge out of his voice.

"Sure," Georgianne replied. "How long are you here for?"

"Two weeks," he said, "and it's all vacation. I don't have any business to do this time."

"That's terrific, Jeff. You know, when you were here the last time, in June—"

"May," he corrected instantly.

"May, yeah. Well, you did look tired then. A vacation is probably the best thing for you!"

"So everybody at work kept telling me." Jeff laughed. "How about lunch tomorrow?"

"That'd be nice," Georgianne said. "Do you want to come here? I can make something."

"No. Let me take you out. You don't want to sit around the house. We'll go for a drive and find a restaurant."

"If you want. That would be lovely."

Jeff was pleased. He didn't want to rush in like an eager puppy. But at the same time, her offer to prepare lunch for him was a good sign. Evidently she had no hang-up about entertaining a single man alone in her home. Sean's ghost might haunt the Gorge, but not the house on Indian Hill Road. The possibility of getting her away for a few days looked better already.

The sight of Georgianne the next morning made a deep impression on Jeff. Her beauty was unchanged. He had expected some mark of trauma in her appearance—newly formed lines, a surrender in the flesh or a loss of tone in the skin. It would be natural, and he had prepared himself for it, but Georgianne had weathered the storm and come out looking as she had in May. Jeff felt a new rush of warmth and love for this woman. He kissed her on the cheek, then held her close and patted her back affectionately.

They drove north from Foxrock, into the countryside, making idle conversation. Bonnie liked it at Harvard and was working hard. Jeff had just missed the autumn colors at their best. The Union Carbide deal had fizzled, but he didn't mind; they had enough to do with Star Wars. He did his best to keep the chatter going, certain that they would settle into a rhythm and that more substantial talk would come later, over lunch and drinks. But already he had noticed what he took to be new strength and determination in Georgianne's eyes. She looked good, remarkably good. He especially liked her plaid skirt, white sweater, and tweed jacket. Most of the leaves had fallen, but Georgianne was a glorious October vision.

They stopped in New Milford and spent some time walking around looking at window displays before going into a restaurant just off the green. They drank Bloody Marys while waiting for lunch to be served.

"I *am* better," Georgianne declared, and Jeff thought her expression was nothing less than fierce. He was awed and thrilled, and he felt he was seeing for the first time a glimpse of the woman he had set free. "Bonnie and I sort of pulled each other through. I couldn't have managed it by myself. It was hard again when she went off to school, and I almost had—I don't know—a relapse, I guess. But then I thought, God, she's only seventeen, she's lost her father, she's coping somehow, she's so brave, and she's gone away alone. And all that shamed me out of the black mood I was in."

"That's good," Jeff said. "No matter what, you have to pick yourself up sooner or later, and carry on. But I still find it hard to fathom what happened. If you don't want to—"

"No, it's all right. I can talk about it—now."

"Did the police ever . . . ?"

Georgianne shook her head. "No. They don't seem to have accomplished much at all." Her face was a clash of sadness and cold anger. She told him about the supposed drug aspect of the case and, apparently referring to the triangular pattern of bullet holes, said that there were other signs the police took to indicate that Sean had criminal connections. "But it's not true," Georgianne said bitterly. "I don't care how it looked, I know that Sean hated drugs and would never, ever, have anything to do with them."

"Of course not," Jeff said.

"I lived with him long enough to know him, and to know that I'm not just kidding myself."

"I'm sure you're right."

"That's what's so lousy about it, Jeff. Not just the pain Bonnie and I suffered, which was bad enough. Whoever did it took Sean away from us forever, and we'll never be the same two people we were. But they also stole Sean's good name, and that's really lousy. It hurts to admit it, but I know there are people, and not just the police, who believe Sean was dealing in drugs. It's so—unfair."

"Of course it is," Jeff agreed. "But you know Sean, and that's all that matters, that's what you'll remember."

"It must have been a case of mistaken identity," Georgianne went on. "Whoever did it was looking for someone else and got Sean, without realizing he was the wrong person. You see, he always left his wallet locked in the car when he ran, and with no identification, well, a killer wouldn't take his word for it, would he?"

"No. You could be right." Jeff almost smiled. He hadn't noticed Sean's leaving his wallet in the car, but then, Jeff had stared straight ahead most of the way to and from the Gorge. It was beautiful. A little extra help from Sean. Georgianne had it worked out so that she could live with it. It wouldn't become an obsession.

"Even the police agree that it could have been mistaken identity. They won't say yes, but . . . maybe."

"What you know is what counts."

Their steaks were served then, and Jeff was grateful

for the interruption. He had learned enough to reassure himself that he was quite safe, and now all he wanted was to steer the conversation away from the subject of Sean. Sean was dead. Forget Sean.

"Have you thought about whether you want to stay on at the house, or is it too soon . . . ?"

"Oh, yes," Georgianne replied promptly. "I'm keeping the house, at least until next summer. Where would I go? Besides, I want it for Bonnie to come home to."

"Of course." Said tonelessly.

"It's bad enough, what she's been through, without suddenly seeing the house go too."

"There's no rush," he agreed.

"Right, and—oh, did I tell you? I don't remember if I did. I have a job now. Only part time, but it's a job."

Jeff blinked at his plate. The piece of meat in his mouth turned dry and tasteless. He chewed mechanically for a few seconds before looking up at Georgianne.

"You have a job, did you say?"

"Yes. Carole Richards, a neighbor up the street, talked me into it. I work mornings, until twelve-thirty, at a nursery school. The kids are three and four, and they're a real handful, but you know what? I love it. It's just what I needed."

"That's great," he said vacantly. "Where is it?"

"In Foxrock."

"Well. I'm very happy for you, Georgianne." His voice was straining ever so slightly. "I did tell you that you should get out and do something with yourself."

"Right. So, I'll see how it goes. I did think about moving to Boston and trying to find something to do in the city. I'd be close to Bonnie; we could even live together, share an apartment. But then I thought if I rushed away, it would look bad, you know—like I was admitting that Sean was involved in something criminal. And besides, it would be unfair to Bonnie. She's entitled to the experience of being away at college on her own, without her mother breathing down her neck."

"That's true."

"I'll stick it out here until next summer, and see how we both feel about things then."

"You're making some wise decisions," Jeff said, feeling as if he were talking by rote. His mind was in disarray, but he couldn't reorganize his thoughts and plans now. "It's all too easy easy to go off in the wrong direction after a major upset in your life. You've got to stay active, see people, do things. And work is good. But take your time before jumping into any big change."

"Right." Georgianne nodded.

Jeff forced himself to smile, but he hated this whole line of talk. It was worse than discussing Sean. He felt he was saying things that ran precisely contrary to what he hoped to accomplish.

Back in the hotel room late that afternoon, he tried to view it all in a constructive light. He had come here knowing that he couldn't rush Georgianne, knowing that it would take time. They had passed several hours easily, pleasantly, comfortably. The lunch had confirmed that he was safe and that Georgianne was well along the road to full recovery—at the very least, she was no longer deep in the pit of mourning. All of this was to the good.

Her job messed things up somewhat. Getting her away for a few days on a drive north was probably out of the question now, but it was too late for the autumn colors anyway. He would adjust. Mornings were gone, but the rest of the days and nights still belonged to him. He had the inside track. He had the time. But whatever it took, he would get her all the way into his life, where she belonged.

CHAPTER SIXTEEN

"Georgie tells me you're doing business with Union Carbide," Burt Maddox said.

"No, not really," Jeff replied. "We were talking about working on something together, but it didn't come off."

"Oh, that's too bad," Burt said. "So this is just a pleasure trip for you then."

"A vacation, yes." Then Jeff added defensively, "My first in about five years."

In less than a minute he had taken a dislike to Burt Maddox. The man had a forced gregariousness that did nothing to hide the fact that he was sizing Jeff up. But the worst thing was his habit of referring to Georgianne as Georgie. Jeff hated it, and he could hardly keep from wincing whenever he heard it.

At the last minute, Georgianne had almost balked, and Jeff wished she had. A few of her friends had persuaded her to come to the Maddox house that evening. No party, no special occasion, just a handful of friends and neighbors getting together for a drink. Georgianne hadn't wanted to go, but she had finally given in, and Jeff had agreed to accompany her. Then, in the car on the way there, she had begun to worry about it again. It would look wrong. It was too soon. Sean had been dead less than three months. Jeff sympathized, but didn't want to argue the case one way or the other. He did point out to her that she had no reason to feel guilty. She would simply be stopping by a friend's house for a short visit. Georgianne looked pale and nervous when they arrived at the Maddox house, but she decided to go through with it, intending to stay for only an hour or so.

"I've been with them for nine years now," Burt was saying.

"Oh . . . uh . . . Union Carbide?"

Jeff could feel the blood leaving his face in a rush, and he bent over to take a hideous-looking hors d'oeuvre from a tray on a side table. It tasted awful, but the maneuver gained him a few seconds, and he hoped his cheeks had regained some color. His heart was pounding.

"That's right," Burt continued smoothly. "Didn't Georgie tell you? I'm a marketing manager." Then, with mock chagrin, "One of many."

"I see," Jeff said aimlessly. "It's quite an outfit."

Maddox *would* be a salesman, he thought contemptuously. He could tell the type: large, florid, incapable of tolerating two seconds of silence in a conversation, pursuing a rendezvous with a coronary—which in this case wouldn't come a day too soon, as far as Jeff was concerned.

Maddox tried to stick to the subject of Union Carbide, but Jeff killed it easily, and his host was too polite to persist. Jeff wished he had known ahead of time that he would be meeting someone from Union Carbide. It wasn't that he couldn't handle such an encounter, especially with someone as transparent as Maddox. But he didn't like surprises. For some time now, weeks, months, he'd felt as if he were walking a tightrope—a very long tightrope—to Georgianne. It had the effect of magnifying everything else in his daily life, and the most trivial vibrations could turn suddenly into tremors and quakes. How much easier it would be if he could simply whisk Georgianne away to some remote mountain cabin for a month or two, where he could win her over by sheer undistracted force of character and love. Instead, the tightrope stretched ahead indefinitely.

There were fewer than a dozen people scattered about the capacious, L-shaped Maddox living room. They all looked prosperous and satisfied, a little too much so for Jeff's liking. He wanted to see an edge in someone, but this crowd was round and soft. It was impossible to think of them as Georgianne's friends, even if, inexplicably, they were.

"Oh, I think Georgianne wants me," Jeff said, creating a flimsy opportunity to edge away from his host. "Excuse me."

"Catch you later," Maddox said, turning in the other direction to mingle.

Jeff drifted across the room and perched on the end

of the sofa next to Georgianne. He lit a cigarette, acutely aware that all eyes were on him. Cool and professional, he told himself, that's the best stance to maintain.

"Georgie tells me you're doing some very exciting work with computers," Carole Richards said, leaning forward to rope Jeff into the conversation.

"Some of it is," Jeff allowed. He didn't like Carole Richards, because she had arranged the job for Georgianne. And because she called her Georgie too. It was appalling.

"And you two were in high school together?"

Everytime she spoke, Carole arranged her face in an expression of intense seriousness, which was utterly disproportionate to what she actually said. She was frizzy-haired and forty, Jeff figured, and trying to keep a young and intelligent look—and missing by a wide margin.

"That's right."

"It's so nice that you got in touch again. . . ."

And on and on. Jeff went to get fresh drinks, and Carole was still nattering on when he returned. It was definitely worrying. Georgianne seemed relaxed and at home with these people. But who were they? Maddox and his bouffant wife with the eyes of an appraiser. Carole Richards, a self-styled progressive teacher, and her husband, a financial adviser. The others, with names Jeff had already forgotten, included a local lawyer, a "publisher" of advertising supplements, an Audi dealer, and their spouses. There was a certain sameness about them, he thought, an enforced healthiness, an endless capacity for small talk,

GET UP TO 4 FREE BOOKS!

You can have the best fiction delivered to your door for less than what you'd pay in a bookstore or online—only $4.25 a book! Sign up for our book clubs today, and we'll send you FREE* BOOKS just for trying it out...**with no obligation to buy, ever!**

LEISURE HORROR BOOK CLUB

With more award-winning horror authors than any other publisher, it's easy to see why CNN.com says "Leisure Books has been leading the way in paperback horror novels." Your shipments will include authors such as RICHARD LAYMON, DOUGLAS CLEGG, JACK KETCHUM, MARY ANN MITCHELL, and many more.

LEISURE THRILLER BOOK CLUB

If you love fast-paced page-turners, you won't want to miss any of the books in Leisure's thriller line. Filled with gripping tension and edge-of-your-seat excitement, these titles feature everything from psychological suspense to legal thrillers to police procedurals and more!

As a book club member you also receive the following special benefits:

- **30% OFF** all orders through our website & telecenter!
- **Exclusive access to** special discounts!
- **Convenient** home delivery **and 10 days to return any books you don't want to keep.**

There is no minimum number of books to buy, and you may cancel membership at any time. See back to sign up!

*Please include $2.00 for shipping and handling.

YES! ☐

Sign me up for the Leisure Horror Book Club and send my TWO FREE BOOKS! If I choose to stay in the club, I will pay only $8.50* each month, a savings of $5.48!

YES! ☐

Sign me up for the Leisure Thriller Book Club and send my TWO FREE BOOKS! If I choose to stay in the club, I will pay only $8.50* each month, a savings of $5.48!

NAME: _____

ADDRESS: _____

_____

TELEPHONE: _____

E-MAIL: _____

☐ **I WANT TO PAY BY CREDIT CARD.**

☐ VISA   ☐ MasterCard   ☐ DISCOVER

ACCOUNT #: _____

EXPIRATION DATE: _____

SIGNATURE: _____

Send this card along with $2.00 shipping & handling for each club you wish to join, to:

Horror/Thriller Book Clubs
20 Academy Street
Norwalk, CT 06850-4032

Or fax (must include credit card information!) to: 610.995.9274. You can also sign up online at www.dorchesterpub.com.

*Plus $2.00 for shipping. Offer open to residents of the U.S. and Canada only. Canadian residents please call 1.800.481.9191 for pricing information. If under 18, a parent or guardian must sign. Terms, prices and conditions subject to change. Subscription subject to acceptance. Dorchester Publishing reserves the right to reject any order or cancel any subscription.

JOIN NOW!

and a way of standing or sitting that seemed somehow practiced.

They were all apparently normal, but Jeff couldn't imagine himself knowing these people, seeing them regularly—much less ever think of an evening like this as fun. Were they enjoying themselves? Perhaps, but he couldn't help thinking of it as the shared jollity of people stuck in the same boat—one that he had no desire to board.

And there in the middle was Georgianne. She seemed the most natural in the whole crowd. One of the things he found so attractive in her was her down-to-earth acceptance of her own life, her lack of airs and pretensions. But he could see that she and Sean might fit in with these people: Georgianne with her daily swim at the Fitness Center and her pen-and-ink sketches, Sean with his wood-burning stove and his do-it-yourself approach to suburbia. It made a certain kind of sense.

But would Georgianne want to go on living like this? Jeff knew that these people would find his lifestyle far too severe. But this, the way they lived, was boring and empty. He was beginning to feel glad he and Georgianne had come to the Maddox house. It was tedious and uncomfortable, but it confirmed the rightness of his mission to open Georgianne to change, to help her grow and become the kind of person she was meant to be. They would grow together.

First, he would have to get her away from Foxrock, which was nothing more than a well-upholstered enclave of phony, self-preoccupied people. Then, he had to do something daring with his own life, something that was still almost inconceivable. When he and Georgianne were finally alone together, their love would blossom.

He sat back to let Georgianne and Carole continue their conversation. Bobbie Maddox saw her chance and moved in. She pulled a large hassock next to him at the end of the sofa and sat down on it. She wore a white jumpsuit, open to an unexciting cleavage, and a pair of gaudy earrings that looked like surrealistic cornucopias. She put a hand on Jeff's arm, as if to make sure he wouldn't bolt for the door.

"I'm so glad you brought Georgie tonight," she said in a conspiratorial hush. "It's time she began to get out again and see her friends, don't you think?"

"Yes," Jeff agreed. "She's doing pretty well, but something like this can only help."

"I hope so. Of course, she is so much better now, thank God." She paused theatrically. "And you have your own company . . . ?"

Subtle as a billboard, Jeff thought. "That's right."

"How nice. California's the place, isn't it?"

"It's where I work," he replied, reluctant to follow her obscure train of thought. A minute later, he finished his drink and used the empty glass as an excuse to escape the company of this Maddox. At the makeshift bar on the kitchen table, he wondered if it was possible that these people were secretly hoping, even plotting, that he and Georgianne would get together. It seemed a wild, fantastic notion, but maybe there was a grain of truth in it. If they were her friends, they'd surely want to see her happily married again in due course. I should be making more of an effort to cultivate this crowd, he reminded himself. They could help me, they might even want to help me.

"How are you bearing up?"

It was another wife. Jeff tried to remember her name. Mandy, he thought. Yes, Mandy, and the reason he remembered was because, after Georgianne, she was the best-looking woman there. She was conservatively dressed, which seemed to enhance her voluptuous sexiness.

"Pardon?"

"I asked how you were bearing up, surrounded by strangers. Don't worry," she continued before he could reply, "we're not all as stuffy as you might think."

"I'm having a fine time," Jeff said, smiling. "Everyone has been very nice to me."

"That's good," she said with a sly smile. "And what's going on with you and Georgianne?"

At last, someone who didn't call her Georgie. Jeff hadn't expected such a blunt question, but he was more amused than surprised. It couldn't be a bad thing that these people were thinking of him as a potential mate for Georgianne.

"Oh, we're just old school friends, you know. . . ."

"Uh-huh." Mandy looked as if she didn't believe that was all there was to it, but would let it pass for now. "She's such a sweet kid."

"Yes."

"A good, old-fashioned kind of girl. And there aren't too many of those around any more."

"I know," Jeff said. She had put her finger on exactly what made Georgianne so special. But he couldn't understand why she was talking to him this way. Was she trying to sell Georgianne to him, or warning him not to hurt her? "I'm glad to see she has so many friends here, especially at a time like this."

"Yeah, but I'm afraid we might lose her."

"Why?"

"I might be wrong," Mandy said with a shrug, "but I think a town like this can be hard on a woman alone, a widow. It's kind of isolated, and there's not much going on, even in Danbury. It may get to her after a while."

"You could be right," he said hopefully.

"Unless she remarries, and I'd be surprised if she didn't, sooner or later."

"She's too young to stay a widow," he agreed.

Jeff and Georgianne were at the Maddox house for nearly two hours. He chatted with most of the people there, and they all revealed a certain curiosity about him along with a general concern for Georgianne. It wasn't as uncomfortable as it might have been, but he didn't like Georgianne's friends and he hoped he wouldn't have to meet any of them again.

When he dropped Georgianne off at her house, he accepted her invitation to come in for a nightcap. The place felt cold and empty, and he wondered how much worse it must seem to her. When she looked ahead, what would she see? Night after night in an empty bed, an empty house, winter chills, and the air dry as dust and dead flowers. But tonight she was in a good mood. Jeff sat on the couch, and Georgianne took the armchair facing him, a few feet away.

"I like your friends," he said.

"I'm glad." She looked at her drink. "They've been very kind to me through . . . all this."

The house seemed too quiet, and Jeff suddenly felt a responsibility to keep the mood upbeat. It was as if the large gambrel wanted to wrap them in its own forlorn atmosphere. The sensation of death was almost physical. She would have to move out, he thought, and the sooner the better. He forced a slight laugh.

"One thing, though," he said. "I never heard anyone call you Georgie before tonight. Everyone calls you Georgie. Oh, except for Mandy."

Georgianne smiled mischievously. "I saw that you found Mandy."

"She found me." He guessed there was probably a bit of history to Mandy. "Actually, they all did. One after another."

"They were just being friendly, and trying to make you feel welcome."

"I know. I wasn't complaining." Then, "All the same, I couldn't help feeling that I was being sized up, somehow."

"Oh?" Georgianne was still smiling, but she cocked her head to one side and gave him a quizzical look. "For what?"

He shrugged. "I don't know. Nothing, probably. I imagine they were just being protective on your behalf. But, you know, they're all wondering what you're going to do."

"About what?"

"The house, Foxrock. Whether you'll stay here or not. That kind of thing."

"I'm not moving. It's my house, and I live here," she said firmly. But then her voice faltered as she concluded, "At least for the next year or so."

"Sure, of course, and they all want you to stay," he assured her. "I did get the impression that the women would love to see you married off again." He laughed in an attempt to keep the tone light. "So you'd better watch out, kid. By Christmas they'll be fixing you up with likely candidates."

"I know," Georgianne said with a bittersweet smile.

"But you're lucky to have friends nearby."

"What's it like where you live?"

The question shocked and thrilled him. It didn't matter whether she was simply changing the subject or if there was indeed something more to it. He took it as an important signal from Georgianne's subconscious. She was beginning to look beyond her own grief—to him.

"Santa Susana? It's beautiful out there," he said enthusiastically. "I love it. . . ."

He told Georgianne more about Santa Susana, the valley, the coast, Los Angeles, and his condominium. He described his rooms and the simple but elegant way he had furnished them. He told her how he had framed and hung her sketch of the dilapidated barn, and he asked if she would let him have another one for his office. That led him to Lisker-Benedictus, and he gave Georgianne a brief history of the company, how he and Ted had gotten together, the building they had constructed—a combination office, computer plant, and research center in the canyon. He avoided going into too much unnecessary detail, but Georgianne listened intently.

Something is different, Jeff realized as he talked. In May, she had listened and expressed a certain interest, but this was different. Now, he felt she really wanted to learn about him, what he did and how he lived. It was because Sean was dead and fading into a memory. Her mind was no longer complicated by the presence of Sean. Georgianne doesn't know it yet, he thought, but she's already beginning to see me in a new light.

When it came time to leave, Georgianne thanked Jeff for being such good company and for taking her to the gathering at the Maddox house.

"My return to society, I guess," she joked, but there was a measure of sadness in her eyes.

"It'll get better. You'll see."

"I know," she said wearily. "I know."

Jeff hugged her and held her close to him for several long minutes. He stroked her hair and kissed her lightly on the forehead, but was afraid to do anything else. Although Georgianne didn't break away, he could feel the same hesitancy in her.

"It's all right," he whispered. It's just a line in the sand. We'll cross it soon, and then I'll hold you safe all through the night, every night. "It's all right."

CHAPTER SEVENTEEN

On the last Saturday of his trip Jeff had an early lunch
with Georgianne at her house. She made steak sandwiches, and after the meal they got into his rental car
and drove east on I-84. It was to be a day out, one
that Jeff hoped would serve as a brief swing through
the past and on into the future.

"I haven't been to Millville since Mom closed the
house and moved down to Tampa," Georgianne said.

Two pleasant long weeks had passed, and Jeff
didn't know what they added up to as far as he and
Georgianne were concerned. He'd been through a
lot. He felt drained, mentally, emotionally, and even
physically, and, although he had enjoyed all his time
with Georgianne, he wondered if he shouldn't have
more than nice memories and continued hope to
show for it.

He had seen her every single day. She worked five

mornings a week at the nursery school, so he would meet her in the afternoon or evening, or both. They would go out to eat, or stop somewhere for a few drinks, or she would cook something at home for him. They took drives through the countryside of northwestern Connecticut. They visited an antique shop owned by a friend of Georgianne, and they looked in at a gallery, where Jeff compared the art on exhibit unfavorably with her sketches. They looked at the lovely old houses in villages like Roxbury, Washington, Bridgewater, Gaylordsville, Kent, and Cornwall. Most of all, they talked—and it was good. There was no question in Jeff's mind that Georgianne was making a real effort to put her personal tragedy behind her. Every day he thought he saw some small sign that she was getting better.

He knew he had a lot to do with it, simply by being there, keeping her busy and drawing her out. But it was a strain in many ways, and he thought, ironically, that getting back to work in California would be like taking a rest.

One of the strains he had to cope with was the need to rein himself in when he was with Georgianne. His instinct was to be more aggressive about burying the past and Sean, and to be more open about his feelings for Georgianne. But he was terrified of upsetting everything he was working for with her, and so he was constantly on guard against himself. He had the pleasure of being with her, but not the full pleasure. He had her to himself for large chunks of time, but always within carefully drawn limits.

Georgianne liked being with Jeff. She felt safe with him, and it was a time when she needed more than anything else to feel safe. He was a distraction, an old friend and good company. In his own somewhat awkward, glancing way, he made her think about things she knew she had to deal with, and he did so inoffensively.

After they'd been to Burt and Bobbie's house, for instance, Jeff had mentioned widowhood and remarriage. He probably didn't even know what he'd done, but he'd made her think for the first time since Sean's death about her sex life. Georgianne had been forced to admit to herself that a significant part of the awful loneliness she felt, missing Sean, was purely sexual. She had no idea what she would do about it in the coming weeks and months, but at least she had a better understanding of the problem now, and that represented progress. The funny part about Jeff's helping her to see this was that her feelings for him were not at all sexual.

Jeff, in idle moments, occupied himself with the ever-changing numbers that testified to his love for Georgianne. She had never mentioned the subject of his staying at her house, so he kept his room at the Ramada and watched the bill accumulate. When he added in the car-rental charges, the round-trip air fares, all the meals and miles, it came to an impressive sum of money. He was pleased. Numbers were symbols, and the larger they became, the happier he felt. Movie stars and rock singers lived like this, falling in love in Honolulu, breaking up in Vail, reconciling in Saint Tropez. Jeff knew that he and Georgianne would never live that recklessly, but they would enjoy the same freedom—it was part of the new life he was creating for both of them.

He turned off I-84 a few miles before Waterbury and drove the back roads into Millville. They swung by the high school, where a crowd of cars in the parking lot suggested a football game in progress, although the field wasn't visible from the road. They circled the green, another place where many hours had been idled away, and they passed the town library, one of Jeff's favorite refuges in adolescence. The library was freighted with erotic history for him. It was where he'd first started looking up girl's skirts. Two of his former girlfriends had worked part time at the library. The long dark aisles of books, especially the upstairs stacks, were wonderful places for useful peeking, fast kisses, and an occasional grope.

After a quick run through the center of Millville, they headed south on the New Haven Road. When they were approaching the Brewer house, Jeff asked Georgianne if she wanted to stop and say hello.

"No, don't bother," she replied definitely.

He took it as a good sign: Georgianne didn't want to go through the inevitable explanations of Sean's death.

"Miss the old homestead?" he asked as the Slaton driveway appeared ahead on the left.

"No . . . not really." A moment later, she continued. "It was a good house and I loved growing up there, but you can't live in the past."

He said nothing, but he felt a shiver of excitement.

She was looking to the future. If she could say that about her family home . . . But it didn't occur to him that her words might have any bearing on his own life.

They reached New Haven thirty minutes later, and Jeff went to the parking lot in the center of Broadway. He and Georgianne spent a while browsing through the Yale Co-op and looking in the windows of some of the fancy clothing stores nearby.

Jeff still had a certain fondness for New Haven. In high school, it had had a vague prestige value: if you could take your date thirty miles to New Haven, find your way to some worthwhile joint—a jazzy coffee bar, a folk club, a shady head shop that sold nitrous oxide—you were a cut above the jerks who couldn't find their way beyond the creature-feature drive-in. It wasn't New York or Boston, but in those days and at that age New Haven had been the first step toward some imaginary sophistication.

And this, Jeff thought as he and Georgianne strolled along York Street, is the date we should have had back then. . . .

The air was crisp and sweet, the light sharp, the afternoon purely October. They walked through Yale courtyards and side streets. They said little, but seemed content to enjoy the day in each other's presence. Later, they went to a Truffaut double bill, *Stolen Kisses* and *The Man Who Loved Women*, and then had a white clam sauce pizza and cold beer at Pepe's. It was all as effortless as a dream, a dream of the future by way of the past, and if it was the best day of the entire two weeks, Jeff attributed that to the fact that they'd come a distance from Foxrock. When

Georgianne moved away from there permanently, every day would be like this one.

That morning he had worked out a quicker, alternate route back to Danbury, by way of Shelton and Newtown, but it was still a fair drive. Georgianne dozed off on the way. Jeff found some quiet jazz on the FM band and pulled her gently closer to him. She settled comfortably, resting her head on his shoulder. As soon as that happened, he eased up on the gas pedal. No need to rush. He wanted to enjoy every second of the drive. He was taking Georgianne home after a date. She was nestled against him, and he could smell her hair. A moment he had dreamed of and waited for, and now that it had finally arrived he didn't want it to end. He would have been happy to drive around the back roads of Connecticut like this all night.

When he did park the car on Indian Hill Road, Georgianne stirred and looked up at him. She smiled sleepily. Perfect, he thought, just perfect. And he smiled back at her.

"Sorry . . . I hope I didn't bother you."

"Of course you didn't."

"Do you want some coffee, or a drink?"

"Not coffee, but a nightcap would be nice." He was flying back to Los Angeles the next day. He had no intention of saying good-bye to her at this point.

The house was chilly again. Jeff went to mix the drinks in the kitchen while Georgianne turned up the heat. He knew what it was—she wasn't yet used to looking after every little thing about the house by herself. One winter alone here would do it for her, he

181

thought. A house required a good deal of regular maintenance. As Sean had said, there were always chores and repairs to be done. And the snow— Connecticut winters were no fun. He was convinced that by spring Georgianne would feel different about this house.

"Thanks for a wonderful day," she said after he'd brought the drinks into the living room.

"It was nice, wasn't it."

"I shouldn't have fallen asleep like that."

"Why not? It was a long day, and we did quite a bit of walking. Besides, I enjoyed driving you home that way."

They were sitting together on the couch.

"Do you want anything?" she asked. "If you're hungry . . ."

Jeff shook his head. "No thanks. Tomorrow I have to fly back to California and my job. So right now all I want is to sit here and get quietly drunk with you."

"I haven't been drunk in ages." Georgianne smiled at the thought, but then became very still. A moment later she asked, "What was your wife like, Jeff?"

"I don't remember," he answered. Her question didn't surprise him, but seemed a natural expression of her growing interest in his life. "I know that sounds strange," he went on, "but I can remember people I haven't seen in twenty years better than I can Audrey. She was just a brief period in my life that's now a blank spot, more or less."

"Oh, but you know what she looked like."

"Well, yeah, I guess," he said. "Her hair was dirty

blond, about medium length, like yours. After we got married, she went from being the right weight for her build to being fashionably skinny. And she cut her hair short, so that she looked more like a boy. Maybe that was part of the problem."

"Did she remarry?"

"Yes, thank God." He laughed. "Saved me a lot of money. Best thing she ever did for me."

"But you never did. Marry again."

A couple of small statements, like coins clicking faintly in an empty pocket.

"No," Jeff replied. She seemed to be waiting for more, but he had anticipated this question many times. He couldn't be flip. It was important. Yet he still didn't have a good answer. "I just buried myself in my work, and it was probably the right thing to do at the time. But I'm getting away from that now. I can see that I let work become a kind of mania for me, and I don't want to live that way now. I let it go on for far too long. There are more important things in life." Then, softly, "I would, you know. Marry again. If it was right . . ."

"You should," Georgianne said distantly. She had been listening to him and taking in his words, but she was lost in her own thoughts as well. He'd been through a bad marriage; he was entitled to a good one, and he could still look and hope for it. But she'd had a good marriage already, a very good one, and now she thought she had no right to hope for anything.

Jeff took their glasses into the kitchen for refilling. He made Georgianne's drink a little stronger, his own weaker. She wasn't yet thinking in terms of a possible relationship between the two of them—he understood that. And he knew it wasn't something he could rush. But he felt disconcerted. He thought about all the time and effort and energy he had expended, the months of planning and work, the extraordinary risks he had taken—all culminating in these two weeks alone with her. Now he was about to return to California, a separation that would only make things harder. At the very least, he had to make sure he had planted the idea in her mind, even if he had to jolt her a little bit to do so. He wouldn't be able to live with himself if he left here thinking he'd been too hesitant and fearful again.

When he returned to the living room, he found Georgianne looking more cheerful. She was standing, smiling at him, and she held something behind her back.

"Uh . . . would you just sit down there, please," she said.

"Yes, ma'am."

He set their drinks on the coasters on the coffee table, and then took his place on the couch.

"This is for you," she said. She handed him a large, framed pen-and-ink sketch. As he took it and looked at it, she came around to sit beside him.

"It's—beautiful." His throat was constricted with emotion. "Thank you. I love it."

It was a drawing of an old country stone wall. There were weeds and field grass along the foot of it, some brambles curling over the top at one side, a few stones missing or fallen off, but the wall itself was the overwhelming heart of the picture, an immense and powerful presence.

"You told me you especially liked the wall in the other sketch I gave you. . . ."

"Yes, I did." He gasped. "But this is so much better. It's fantastic . . . the amount of detail." He turned to her. "Thank you. Very much. This will go up as soon as I get back. God, I love it."

"It's like you," she said. "Solid and strong."

He kissed her on the cheek and squeezed her hand while he continued to admire the drawing. Although he had asked for another sketch, he hadn't expected anything like this, and he was deeply moved.

"I've got a carton for it," Georgianne said. "So you can carry it easily on the plane."

He set the picture on the armchair, on the other side of the coffee table, and then sat down next to her again.

"It's . . . fantastic."

"Do you really like it?"

"I sure do. Can't you tell?"

"Good, I'm glad." She smiled with pleasure. "I don't know what I'd have done if you didn't." She laughed, but then her face became serious. "You've been so kind and good to me these last two weeks, Jeff . . . I just want to tell you how grateful I am to you."

"I've enjoyed every minute of it."

"I really mean it," she continued. "You gave me a lot of your time, and I appreciate it. I enjoyed it too, and you came at a time when I didn't think I could ever enjoy anything again. There are lots of more exciting ways you could have spent your vacation than looking after someone coming out of . . ."

"Hey, forget it," he hushed her. "I've been here because I wanted to be, not because it was something I was obliged to do. You know, when I was here in May, I said I'd stay in touch, but I never did and I felt bad about it."

"I didn't either."

"Yeah, well, it was different for you. But I should have and I didn't, and I'm not going to let that happen again. There aren't that many good friendships in the course of a lifetime, and now that we've found ours again I don't want to lose it."

"Neither do I."

"I'll be on the phone to you every week."

"Oh, Jeff, that's not—"

"Never mind. I want to. What's a telephone for? And I hope you'll give some thought to visiting L.A. Bring Bonnie. I'd love to show you around; there's a lot to see and do out there. I know you want to go to Florida and Chicago, but think about L.A. too. You have a friend there. One who cares about you."

"Maybe we will. Sometime."

A silence overtook them. Jeff wondered if he'd said too much too quickly, his words creating a vacuum in their wake. But then, he didn't care. He felt instinctively that the right moment had come.

He put an arm around Georgianne's shoulders and turned her face to his. They looked at each other for just a second or two, and then he kissed her on the lips. For him, it was a moment of great fear, and greater excitement. He was crossing an important line. He was kissing her the way a man kisses a woman, seriously, not like a brother or an old friend. She would remember it and think about it, and that, he hoped, would be enough.

Georgianne didn't respond. She felt a tiny flicker within herself, but it died instantly. Her sexual orientation was still to Sean. Her body was numb to any other man. It was too soon. And there, in that house which was hers and Sean's, it was wrong; it seemed, irrationally, almost incestuous. She felt confused and sad. She didn't want this to be happening, not now and especially not there. But she could hardly move—the situation had turned her into dead weight. Finally she moved her face slightly and rested her forehead on Jeff's shoulder.

The only thing he could do was sit there and hold her for as long as was necessary. He knew that the moment had passed. No, that wasn't it. The moment had never really been there except in his imagination. All the same, he had at last kissed Georgianne properly, and he was happy about that. Twenty years overdue, and all the sweeter for it.

"I'm sorry I'm not better company," Georgianne said weakly after a while. She reached for her drink, disengaging herself a little from Jeff in the process. "It still gets to me, you know. It still gets to me."

It: Sean, Jeff thought. The man was slow to die, but die he would, and his hold on Georgianne would disappear with him. It was just a matter of time. Meanwhile, Jeff had given her something to remember and think about. . . .

The next morning, before he checked out of the hotel, Jeff called Georgianne, and they had an easy, cheerful conversation for nearly half an hour. No harm had been done, it seemed, although neither of them alluded to that moment the night before. By tacit agreement, it had been placed in a special container and set aside for an indefinite period.

CHAPTER EIGHTEEN

Jeff's long-distance pursuit of Georgianne began the following week. He fell into a routine of calling her on Tuesdays and Fridays. His preparations for each telephone encounter were as ritualistic as those of a baseball player setting himself in the batter's box before the next pitch. He would come home from work early in the evening, remove his shoes, unknot his tie, and unbutton his shirt. He would pour a large measure of malt Scotch into a crystal tumbler and add a splash of bottled water. The drink would be placed on a tweed coaster on the coffee table, next to a clean crystal ashtray, a fresh pack of cigarettes, and a book of matches. Then he would stretch out on the couch, propping himself up at one end with a pillow. He would light the first smoke, take a sip of whiskey, and pick up the telephone. He even developed a certain rhythm for tapping out the sequence of numbers that would bring him Georgianne's voice.

Once in a while, she had something planned for a

Friday night, and would tell Jeff on the Tuesday before; then he would call on Thursday or Saturday, and the routine went on.

He liked to think of her taking all his calls in her bedroom: half-dressed, in a pajama top perhaps, or some girlish nightie. The mental image was sometimes so distracting that he lost the thread of the conversation. But it was always easy, reminding him of the many hours he had spent on the phone with his various girlfriends in high school. Two people could often say more to each other on the phone than they ever did face to face. And the connection was usually so clear Jeff had no difficulty imagining that he and Georgianne were in the same town.

At first, he had to make the greater effort. Georgianne found it hard to accept the fact that Jeff really didn't mind piling up large telephone bills. She felt uncomfortable, as if she could hear the meter ticking, but after a couple of weeks she relaxed about it. The telephone had become an important part of her life since Sean's death. She talked to Bonnie every night, her mother once a week, and now she had Jeff on the line every Tuesday and Friday night.

He talked about anything that came to mind. He knew that, for a while at least, the mere fact that they were in constant communication was more important than what they actually said. So he told her about all sorts of things—Los Angeles, the weather, systems analysis, the people he worked with, his aquarium of tropical fish, the bars and restaurants he knew in the area, even defense spending. He managed to give her a better idea of some of the things being done in molecular biology, and how Bonnie's field of interest might interface with the work he did. The whole high-tech future was a minor but recurrent motif in his conversation.

Georgianne was a good listener. At appropriate moments she always came up with a reasonable question or comment. There were no awkward pauses or stifled yawns.

For her part, Georgianne talked about Bonnie most frequently. She was still doing well at Harvard and she liked the school and the whole Cambridge environment. Jeff was also given odd bits of news about Georgianne's mother, and her two brothers and their families. It was boring, and Jeff couldn't have cared less, but he always listened patiently. She also told him regularly about her job at the nursery school. She liked working there. The kids were endlessly energetic, and she always went home feeling worn out, but she thought that was good for her and she hadn't regretted a day of it yet. Besides, some of the children were really wonderful. Jeff had to agree that it was a good thing for Georgianne to be doing.

The house soon became a factor. This pleased Jeff. Every time he called, it seemed, he heard about one thing or another Georgianne had to take care of—the storm windows, leaves clogging a gutter pipe, a leak in the dishwasher, loose tiles in the bathroom—never anything serious, just the usual household nuisances. Georgianne was far from helpless, and she coped well. She paid a neighbor's son to mow the lawn, rake the leaves, and when it snowed, to clear the driveway. She was proud of the fact that she could handle problems one way or another, but as the weeks went by, Jeff was sure that the whole business of maintaining a house was beginning to get to her.

With time, too, he and Georgianne were able to talk about more personal matters. The telephone seemed to make it safer and easier. She hinted at, then admitted to, being lonely, as if she were somehow to blame for it. He told her it was the most natural thing in the world. She told him about the increasingly open advice she was getting from her friends—she should start to date, she couldn't deny herself that right, she couldn't hide herself away and become old before her time, and so on. She found this predictable and even a little amusing, but it was clear she was also considering it seriously. Jeff tried to remain neutral. If, one evening, she told him that she was going out to dinner or to a movie with another man, he would deal with it then. But he sensed that Georgianne had real reservations about becoming a dating woman again after all these years, and he believed that his reassuring presence on the phone twice a week helped somewhat to lessen her need for male companionship.

Jeff was carefully ambiguous about his personal life. He let Georgianne know that he socialized to a certain extent, insofar as it went with the job, but that he could take it or leave it. Once, she asked him if he was dating anyone special, and he replied immediately, "Yes—you, every Tuesday and Friday." Georgianne laughed at this, but warmly, like a confirmation, and he felt good about it. He always tried to strike a light tone. He didn't want to make any intense declarations over the telephone, at such a distance. If she clammed up or otherwise failed to respond, everything would be in jeopardy. So he would kid her, joke with her, and sympathize with her when necessary. His role was to be there, safe, solid, reassuring, the complete friend. They were, thanks to the telephone, two disembodied souls moving slowly closer together. One day, Jeff was sure, Georgianne would answer his call and he would hear something new in her voice. Understanding. She would realize that he was *the* man in her life and she would be ecstatic about it. . . .

Late in November, she told Jeff that Bobbie Maddox had introduced her to a single man at a cocktail party. It had been a terrifying experience. Georgianne still felt too close to Sean, and she had hardly been able to talk coherently to the stranger. The man didn't interest her in any way, but she was disturbed by her reactions, her inability to handle a perfectly ordinary situation.

Jeff soothed her and told her that she hadn't done anything wrong, that she had no social obligation to feel comfortable with any stranger who happened to cross her path. The only timetable she had to follow was the one dictated by her own feelings; nothing else mattered. Georgianne sounded much better after talking to Jeff about that incident. Secretly, he was quite pleased. It was still too early for her to have real feelings for another man, but she had never felt the least bit uncomfortable with him; just the opposite. It was a message to Jeff that he had the inside track and was far ahead of anyone else.

The only worry, and it did bother him when he thought about it, was that Georgianne regarded him a little too casually. Sometimes he got the impression that she talked to him the same way she would to a close girlfriend. His greatest fear was that their relationship would solidify at a certain superficial level that included confiding, sharing, and affection, but nothing more. A sanitized, platonic, brotherly load of nonsense. But all he could safely do was to hint at his true feelings and occasionally, lightly, call her "my girlfriend."

Georgianne spent the long Thanksgiving weekend in Boston. She stayed at a hotel and took Bonnie out to a restaurant for a turkey dinner. They went to a football game, a play, a couple of films, and a punk gig at a Cambridge club. They had a great time together, Georgianne said. Jeff wished he could have been there with them. It was just the kind of weekend away he wanted with Georgianne. But it would have been wrong to intrude, and he knew there would be many more Thanksgivings for them.

Georgianne and Bonnie spent the Christmas holidays in Tampa, where the rest of the Slaton family had gathered. Georgianne later admitted feeling miserable, thinking of Sean on Christmas Eve. In a way, Jeff was glad to hear that. The holidays were drab and lonely for him in Santa Susana. He went to a couple of parties but was unable to get in the mood. In the past he had just continued working, but now he couldn't be bothered. He stayed in and drank or went out and drank, mostly alone. He called Georgianne in Tampa on Christmas morning, but their conversation was brief and limited to the usual season's greetings and best wishes. He could hear music and laughter in the background, and he knew it was the wrong time for a longer talk, so he got off the phone. He called her mother's number again on New Year's Eve, but Georgianne was out with her brothers and their wives, celebrating at some restaurant. That night he drove to Triffids and got drunk. He danced with, kissed, and groped a number of merry women. He woke up early the following afternoon, fully dressed but with his pants around his knees. Whoever had returned with him was gone. Considering the amount of liquor he had put away and the blank spot of twelve hours or so in his memory, he decided that unzipping his pants was all he had accomplished. He sat up and let his monster headache do its worst while he stared uncomprehendingly at Georgianne's drawing of the stone wall.

The turning point came in January. Connecticut was experiencing particularly bad weather that month, and Georgianne was growing restless. She complained about the cold, the house, and the loneliness. She still liked her work, and she was happy about Bonnie's progress at Harvard, but otherwise she was coming to dislike the way she lived. Her friends were well intentioned, but she hated being their special project. She was tired of gratuitous advice and she had no stomach for the ritual of being introduced to single men, none of whom aroused any response in her. She wasn't at all sure she was capable of responding to anyone, but at night, alone, she began to want someone in her life. Georgianne didn't say these things to Jeff in so many words, but he was certain that he understood her meaning perfectly.

His time was coming, and he knew it. He started to plan another trip to Danbury. February, he thought, would be right. It was usually as bad as January in terms of the weather, and even worse psychologically. February was the bottom of the pit of winter, when spring still seems still seems impossibly far away. Georgianne would feel low and blue. He would arrive at exactly the right moment, in the nick of time, and convince her to come out to Los Angeles for a visit. At his expense, of course, unless she absolutely insisted on paying her own way. There wasn't the slightest doubt in his mind that if he could just get her to California, she would want to stay. She *would* stay.

Jeff was certain that his elaborate, grand scenario had reached its final phase. He thought of it as a very natural progression geared to the seasons of the earth, and he felt he was on the verge of a remarkable achievement. When it is complete, he told himself, I will have plucked Georgianne from the past, transformed her life utterly and mine as well, and saved two people who were going nowhere without even realizing it. And all because he had finally learned how to read and follow his deepest instincts. It was extraordinary how the whole thing had started and grown. A whim had taken over the personal destinies of several people. A gesture of curiosity and half-buried longing had snowballed, gaining the momentum of an irresistible force. It gave Jeff a feeling of almost godlike power. The only thing that bothered him was the fact that he couldn't share this knowledge with anyone—for who else on this planet had gone to such lengths for the love of a woman? Jeff was now unique in his own eyes. At the center of this transformation was Sean's killing, which he regarded as the one true act of his life. Even now, months later, it had a magical, religious significance: it was an act of transubstantiation.

Late in January, before Jeff could announce his plans for another trip east, the change in Georgianne became more pronounced. She wouldn't stay on the phone talking as long as she had previously. She always sounded tired, and sometimes his calls actually woke her from sleep. She worked full time at the nursery school now, came home dead tired, and went to bed early. Jeff didn't know how to deal with this new development. It was just until June, Georgianne told him. She liked the work, she wanted the extra money, and, besides, it kept her mind off other things. He saw that she was doing what he had done years before—she was deliberately losing herself in her job. But he didn't know how to talk her out of it, or even if it was a good idea to try.

On the plus side, it seemed to show that Georgianne was taking charge of her life, finding a new strength and sense of purpose. Work was a way of buying time to heal. But there were negative aspects too. The long telephone talks with Jeff were no longer quite so important to her. She didn't need them the way she had earlier. Now they were friendly, brief chats—nothing more. They left Jeff feeling increasingly removed from her.

Georgianne was still vague about her plans. She was saving money. She was thinking seriously of selling the house in the summer, but then again, she might not. A condominium in the Danbury area was a possibility, but only if she decided she really wanted to stay on at the nursery school. Boston was the other alternative, and one that she admitted was attractive. She could go back to school there, take some night courses, and also find a job. Bonnie would be nearby. A city offered social and cultural distractions, and many opportunities to find a new direction for her life. There were a lot of things to be weighed and considered, and she was still far from sure what to do.

This was what Jeff had expected, in a way. Georgianne was beginning to see the various possibilities that lay before her, and she was taking a healthy interest in them. But it was happening *quite apart from him*, which was not what he had intended. He was disturbed and frightened at the prospect of somehow losing control.

Now that the right moment seemed to be at hand, he felt tense and nervous. Twice he couldn't bring himself to say what he wanted to say to Georgianne. He felt intimidated by the new sense of self-assurance that radiated through the telephone. She was on a positive upswing, and that threatened to disarm him completely.

On the first Tuesday in February, Jeff had to force himself to say something explicit to Georgianne. Get it out in the open. He planned to fly to New York the next week, or the week after at the latest, and she had to be told. This wasn't going to be another vacation, nor would he try to revive the spurious Union Carbide connection. He wanted Georgianne to know that he was making the long journey for the sole purpose of seeing her and being with her.

It felt like the most important day in his life. He came home from work and had two cold beers to take the edge off and settle himself. He went about his ritual preparations and then sat staring at the fish in the aquarium, as if they could help him plan his words. His mind had a way of going blank at important moments, and this was one of them. You can't rehearse real life, he thought glumly. Feeling heavy and slow, he picked up the telephone. The rhythm wasn't there. He disconnected, got a new dial tone, and then tapped out the sacred numbers correctly. He and Georgianne chatted for a few minutes, and when she mentioned Bonnie, he took it as his opening.

"What about L.A.?"

Bread on the water. A slight pause.

"Los Angeles? What do you mean?"

"Well, you know. You've been thinking of selling the house and moving to Boston this summer."

"Yes, it's an idea," Georgianne said as if it were more than just an idea. And then she confirmed this. "I've just been looking through some study programs."

"Well, good. But, as I said, what about L.A.? Anything you can do in Boston you can do here, and the weather is a lot better."

Hesitation.

"Oh, Jeff, I'd love to come out and see L.A. and visit you sometime, but—"

"No, I mean why don't you think about living out here?"

"I couldn't possibly." Quick, definite.

"Why not?"

"Jeff, it's so far away."

"No it's not. It's just down the road from here."

It was such a feeble attempt at lightness that Jeff was oddly annoyed when Georgianne laughed. She was taking it as a joke, ignoring the very clear implication of his remark.

"It's the other side of the country," she said. "If I do move, it'll be to some place where I'm still close to Bonnie."

"Anywhere in the country is only a few hours' flying time," he pointed out lamely.

"That's not the same thing," she replied.

"No, really. Stop and think about it for a minute," he urged reasonably. "How often do you see her now? At Thanksgiving and Christmas and Easter, and then in the summer. If you were in California, you'd still see her at those times. When a kid is away at college, the distance, the exact mileage, doesn't make a whole lot of difference."

"I guess that's true," Georgianne said dubiously. "But if I moved to Boston I'd be able to see her much more often. Every weekend, at least."

Jeff couldn't argue with that. It was a mistake, a digression. He had the nasty feeling that things were quickly slipping away from him now. The whole point of her moving to L.A. was that he loved her, and if she still didn't have a clue about that, he wouldn't get anywhere. Perhaps it had been a blunder to put himself in this position on the damn telephone.

"Oh, I wanted to tell you," he started over, "I'm coming to Danbury again."

"How nice. It'll be good to see you. When are you coming?"

She did seem pleased, he thought hopefully. "Pretty soon," he said. "Next week, or the week after, maybe. Which would suit you better?"

Silence. A sickening sensation. He could almost see the puzzlement on her face.

"Uh . . . doesn't it depend on your work, Jeff? You *are* coming to see the people at Union Carbide, aren't you?"

"No, that's all over. I told you about that the last time I was there."

"Oh, yeah, I guess you did." Pause. "Well . . ."

"This time I was planning to come back . . . just to take a few days off and . . . see you."

"Oh."

"Is there anything wrong with that?"

"No, of course not. But I am working full time now, and I get home pretty beat at night. I mean, it would be great to see you again, but I just don't have much time during the week. Not time when I'm fit company for anybody."

"So? How about if I turn it into a long weekend? That's easy enough to arrange."

"Yeah . . . but I'm just waiting for the weatherman to say we're going to have a halfway decent weekend so that I can go up to see Bonnie again."

"Fine. I'll come on the next lousy weekend. We can sit around the fire, have a few drinks, and watch the snow drift."

"Jeff, you don't have to."

"What if I want to?"

"Yeah, but I'm just saying you don't have to."

"I don't understand."

"You were very kind to me, Jeff. You were really very good to me, and it meant a lot. But I'm better now. I feel like I've finally gotten up off the floor and—"

"I wasn't planning to come just because I thought you needed help or sympathetic company."

"I know, I know. You're very sweet, but—"

"I love you, Georgianne." *Fuck sweet!*

"I love you too, Jeff."

She means friendship, he thought bitterly. A black thundercloud was swallowing his mind.

"No, really, I mean—"

"I know," Georgianne interrupted. "It's just that I don't want you to come all this way for . . . oh, I wish I knew what to say."

Jeff recognized this as the vacant, pseudo-innocent tone of voice a woman uses when she wants you to figure out what she can't bring herself to tell you. He was no longer aware of his whiskey, his cigarette, his room, or even the telephone in his hand. He was floating in darkness, high above the earth, and a voice was broadcasting a message to his brain: Stay there, don't come back.

"Say it's okay," he begged.

"It's okay, of course. But it's not necessary, Jeff. You don't have to. Really, I mean it. I wish you'd just . . . understand that. . . ."

He did. That was the trouble. When he hung up the telephone a few moments later, he kicked the coffee table over in a rage, spilling whiskey and scattering ashes. Then he buried his face in the couch and pounded his head with the heels of his hands. It took more than an hour for the fury and trembling to subside, and then, still in a daze, he noticed that he had bitten clean through one of the seat cushions.

On the following Friday, he called Georgianne at the usual time. No answer. She hadn't told him beforehand that she wouldn't be there, and this single disruption of the routine, the only one to occur in four months, dealt their relationship another mortal blow. He waited grimly until the next Tuesday. Georgianne was there, but the conversation was brief and trivial. She seemed distracted, as if she wouldn't mind getting off the phone because she was busy with something else. He tried to raise serious matters, but it was impossible. Georgianne seemed to have erected an invisible barrier that he couldn't penetrate. Anything he said was either deflected or ignored. Her only news was that she felt fine and was going to Boston the next weekend to see Bonnie. He got the message: she wouldn't be there to take a Friday call.

Jeff knew it was all over before he hung up the phone. His grand scenario had been washed away like a sand castle at high tide. He could hardly believe it, but no other conclusion was possible. Ten months had elapsed since he had re-established contact with Georgianne. He had zeroed in on her, pierced the heart of her life, isolated her, consoled her, pursued her, and opened himself to her. But now, astonishingly, he had apparently passed right through and come out on the other side, as insignificant and transitory as a stray atomic particle. He was back in the vacuum.

After that second Tuesday in February, Jeff abandoned his ritual. He wouldn't call her again. The next time, she would come to him. And there would be a next time—of that he had no doubt.

PART IV

Rendezvous with an Echo

CHAPTER NINETEEN

Au Bon Pain.

He knew *Bon: Bon* was good, as in Bon Ami household cleaner, or as in *Bonjour*, one of the three or four French words he did know. *Bonjour, monsieur, merci, oui.* He'd been a student of German, not French. *Bon* was good.

Bonnie, as they say in Scotland.

Au was a mystery. *Pain* was a mystery.

But were they so difficult? Let *Au* be Oh. Let *Pain* be Pain. Oh Good Pain! It sounded like something out of Shakespeare, or a toast by the Marquis de Sade. He smiled. The line went perfectly with the jingle on a television beer commercial. "Here's to good pain, tonight is kind of special . . ." With good pain. Through good pain. By good pain. Toward the good pain. Pain à la mode. Pie, that was it. *Pain* had to mean pie. For Good Pie. Disappointing, but then, the solution of a mystery often is. For Good Pain. He liked that much more. For Good Pain, stop here. It sounded punk, and he was feeling punk.

At the next table a small crowd had gathered around two young men locked in a five-minute game of lightning chess. Fingers flew, pieces banged about the board, and the clock was hammered continuously. The challenger lost his dollar. The winner looked philosophical. He was mediocre, a club-strength player, but he could keep his cool for five minutes, which was more than many others could do in the face of a reckless, unsound attack. If you say A, you must . . .

It was a mistake to be sitting there, he knew. He could be seen first, at any time, and that was the opposite of what he wanted. The coffee at the bottom of his cup was too little and too cold to bother finishing. He crushed his cigarette in the plastic ashtray, stood up, and left the outdoor terrace of the Café Au Bon Pain.

He walked past the newsstand and on up the street as far as the Old Burying Ground. He carried a paperback of Katz's *Life After Nuclear War*, which he had purchased that same morning. It was the first of May, and his first full day there. The sun was shining brilliantly on Harvard Square.

Early afternoon now. He resumed his post on the concrete bench outside the Science Center. It was the easiest way. She had to take at least one course in that ugly building, and even if she didn't, she was bound to pass by sooner or later. He had patience, and plenty of time. He waited and watched, glancing up through mirrored sunglasses whenever a female came along. Otherwise he stared at the book open on his lap. Apparently it would take only 335 warheads to set the Soviet Union back a thousand years. But was that far enough?

He looked like someone else, not Jeff Lisker. Not Phil Headley, nor even the equally mythical Jonathan Tate, which was the name he currently used for purposes of airline tickets, hotel registrations, and traveler's checks. He had let his hair grow for most of April. It wasn't really long, but longer and fuller. Then he'd gone to a unisex salon in West Hollywood, not so much for a cut as to have the color and style changed. Gone was the dull brown, gone, too, the part that had been with him since childhood. Now his hair was a kind of muddy cream color, and it was swept back on his head. Ted and Callie hadn't liked the change but Jeff didn't care. He had to use mousse every morning to keep the part from reasserting itself. He had also applied peroxide to his eyebrows, with mixed results. He wore a pair of scuffed loafers, corduroy jeans, a Dodgers T-shirt, and an old, comfortable tweed jacket he'd been surprised to find he still had in his closet. He hoped he looked like a graduate student or a member of the faculty.

Another fool's errand? Possibly. Probably. What would he say to Bonnie when he did see her? He didn't have the slightest idea. But he had already decided that it was pointless to sit around in Ventura County and try to figure these things out in his head. Now that he was on the scene, something would happen, or it wouldn't. All it would cost was time and money, and he had those to burn.

Jeff's feelings for Georgianne were no less intense than they had been the last time he'd spoken with her, nearly three months ago. It had to be love—there was nothing else to call it, and he couldn't begin to consider the alternatives. Say love, then. But why did he feel as if he were being victimized? It shouldn't be happening this way. What did he have to do, how far did he have to go to demonstrate his love? Didn't she understand how strong her hold on him was? Obviously not. Georgianne was one of those women who go through life scarcely realizing the effect they have on some men.

There was nothing he could do but go along with the situation and hope it would take a turn in his favor at some point. He had tried to forget about her back in February, when he'd stopped calling her. Ten months of remarkable effort had come to nothing, and his instinct had been to cut his losses. But it hadn't worked out that way. Georgianne still dominated his thoughts, like a river of lost opportunity flowing through his life. The desire to pursue and possess that one woman refused to fade away. She never called or wrote, but that didn't matter. Georgianne never let Jeff go.

He had found himself returning to Diane. She became Georgianne in a bikini, or in a slip and bra, or in a teddy, or in black patterned stockings with her skirt riding up while she sat and read a book and Jeff watched. But the satisfaction he got with Diane was diminishing, the illusion more difficult to maintain. Georgianne was under his skin, in his blood, and no substitute would do. Diane's hair didn't smell the same as Georgianne's, her body didn't feel quite the same in an embrace. Even when they both had their clothes on, Diane's breasts lightly touching his chest somehow felt wrong. Jeff had two Georgiannes locked in his head—the one from high school and the one who lived now—and Diane couldn't fully translate into either of them.

Jeff liked to regard Georgianne as a special project. He couldn't give up on her. As an intellectual puzzle, he thought she might still be solved, that he would finally figure out what it took to win her. And on an emotional level, the idea of abandoning her never had a chance.

It hurt him that she never called. She hadn't lifted a finger to contact him at any time since they'd met on the street in Danbury almost exactly a year ago. During the period when he was calling her twice a week it was understandable, perhaps. But in February, March, and April it wasn't. Their last conversation, after all, hadn't ended on a sour note, not openly, not really. By then, he thought, she owed him at least one damn phone call. She had the three numbers at which he could be reached, Lisker-Benedictus, his private line at work, and his home telephone, but the call never came. She just let him go.

Through the rest of February and into March, Jeff had experienced a growing sense of disbelief. Could she really forget about him so easily? Was that how she regarded their friendship—if he called or was there in person, fine; otherwise, she didn't give him a thought? It was a shocking conclusion, one that he refused to accept. Hadn't she told him she felt bad about not staying in touch with Mrs. Brewer, her long-time neighbor in Millville? Perhaps it was just Georgianne's way, a fact of no particular significance. Besides, she had more than enough to keep her busy. Her life was in a state of uncertainty. She had to decide about her job, her house, her whole future, and all of this coming in the aftermath of her husband's death and her daughter's going away to college.

By April, Jeff was actively planning how to get himself back into Georgianne's life. A telephone call. A long letter. A surprise visit. He considered these ideas among others, but nothing appealed to him. Points of access were limited. He blamed himself for the failure in February and he knew that a rerun would be disastrous beyond words.

It was around the middle of April when he began to think about Bonnie. He had met her only a couple of times, almost a year ago now, but whenever she came to mind it was as a potential ally. The girl had seemed to like him well enough, but beyond that superficial impression was the fact that she wanted to be a scientist. Jeff was a computer scientist. Bonnie would understand him and respect him for what he was and what he did. Her way of looking at things, he reasoned, could not be so very different from his. There had to be a meeting point, a common ground between them, and that in turn might provide the key to Georgianne.

Knobs, the fellow who had sold Jeff the coke and the phony driver's license, was taking a short but mandatory sabbatical at a state facility. His soul mate, a petite Brazilian transsexual known as Creamy, was looking after the family business and had provided Jeff with the Jonathan Tate identification. The fee was higher this time, adjusted apparently to take account of the inflation rate in Brazil. Jeff paid, but he shook his head all the way back to Santa Susana, wondering why he had bothered with this pointless charade. His meeting with Bonnie would be friendly. There was no hostility or rivalry involved, as there had been with Sean. There would be no unpleasant confrontation—over what? Either Bonnie could help him or she couldn't, that's all there was to it. But if he didn't need to cover his tracks, the urge to do so proved irresistible. It was as if he had to take that one little step away from himself before he could act. And to act was everything.

He spotted her that first afternoon. It was nearly half past two when Jeff looked up and recognized Bonnie. How easy it proves to be, he thought, suppressing a grin and turning his head down to the book. She clicked past, a glimpse of boots, black jeans, and a high fanny. Jeff trailed casually after her. Bonnie's hair had become a full, flowing mane. She went into the Science Center and took a seat in Lecture Hall C. Jeff thought about sitting a few rows behind her, but decided it was a bad idea. It would be a poor setting if she happened to recognize him there. He bought coffee instead and waited at one of the Cinzano tables down the hall, next to the Cabot Science Library. If Bonnie left the building the same way she had come in, she'd pass him again.

He was reluctant to approach her and introduce himself on campus. He was afraid she wouldn't be able to give him more than a few minutes before she had to hurry off to another class, a meeting with her adviser, or some other scheduled appointment. He wanted time alone with her, and he thought his best chance would come if he caught up with her out on the street. He waited and read. Apparently a one-megaton warhead could wipe out greater Waterbury. Ah, but there were at least two contradictions in that theory.

Bonnie reappeared an hour later. Jeff followed her outside. She was strolling now, rather than walking purposefully. He adjusted his sunglasses, lit a cigarette, and trudged slowly a safe distance behind. She passed Memorial Church, the Widener, came out on Quincy Street, then turned up Massachusetts Avenue toward the Square. At the newsstand, she bought *Interview* and *Elle*. Jeff was ready to intercept her if it looked like she was heading back to campus, but she crossed to Au Bon Pain, where she bought iced tea and sat at a table by herself. Jeff smiled. If he had stayed there, she would have come to him. But he didn't mind, he was pleased. It was still the first day, after all, and he'd wasted very little time. He kept his sunglasses on and sat down across the table from her.

"Hello, Bonnie."

She looked up, a blank expression on her face.

"I said: Hello, Bonnie."

Now she sat back and smiled.

"Hi, Jeff. What took you so long?"

CHAPTER TWENTY

The sunglasses didn't help. They might even be what Bonnie was smirking at, so Jeff took them off. She must have spotted him earlier, at the Science Center. He found it hard to believe, but why else would she look so unsurprised and act as if she had been expecting him?

"So you do recognize me?"

"Sure. Who else could you be?"

Jeff was trying to figure out the expression on Bonnie's face. A smile, a residual smirk, a look of curiosity and interest. It had something of the arrogance of youth about it too, as if she were thinking, I know this guy, I know what's going on here. Jeff didn't fear this, but he didn't like it either.

"I thought I would surprise you," he said, trying to smile sheepishly. "But you've surprised me instead. Did you know I was here?"

"I had no idea you were within a thousand miles of

Cambridge, but I always thought we'd meet again sooner or later. Funny, isn't it? You don't look like you did last year, but I knew it was you the minute you sat down."

"Very sharp," Jeff conceded gracefully.

"Well, Mom has mentioned you from time to time, and I did think about you when I drew up my list."

"List?"

"Yeah, it must have been last October," Bonnie said, "after I'd been here long enough to get settled and know my way around. One night I sat down and made out a list of every person I knew, from family right down to the slightest, most casual acquaintance. Did you ever try to do that? It's scary how many people you know. Anyhow, you were on it, of course."

"What was the purpose?" Jeff tried to sound amused, as if he were listening to some odd college anecdote.

"I wanted to see if I could think of anyone who might have a reason for killing my father, and I thought a list would help. Most murder victims die at the hands of someone they already know."

"I've heard that," Jeff said. "What did you decide?"

A distant sadness appeared in Bonnie's eyes, but she blinked it away instantly. "Oh, I threw the list away a few days later. It didn't help, and I couldn't come up with any ideas that made sense . . . and I had too much to do here. It's not healthy to let yourself be obsessed with death."

"But you must have discussed it with your mother."

"Just, you know, right after it happened, and with

the police," Bonnie said. "After that, no. She wouldn't mention it, and I never wanted to bring up the subject. It's hard to talk about on the phone, and whenever I see Mom I don't want to ruin the good mood, you know?"

"Sure. It was terrible, what happened to your dad, but, as you said, you can't let it become an obsession. He'd want both of you to get on with your lives."

Bonnie nodded. "It *had* to be a case of mistaken identity. My father was the wrong person in the wrong place at the wrong time."

"I agree completely." A tightness that had been gathering in Jeff's chest began to ease somewhat. "So, what made you think we'd meet again?"

"I don't know; it was just a feeling I had." Bonnie shrugged, then smiled again. "What *are* you doing here?"

"I got in earlier this week. I had some business in Boston, but that's all taken care of now, and I have a couple of free days, so . . . I thought I'd take a look around Harvard and see if I could find you."

"Well," Bonnie said. "Did you go to my room, or try to get me on the phone?"

"No. I was just on my way to check the student directory when I noticed you crossing the street."

"I see. That's interesting. I guess it means that my mother doesn't know you're here."

"Uh . . . no, she doesn't," Jeff said. "I didn't know I was coming east until the last minute and I wasn't sure I'd have any free time, so I couldn't really make any plans."

"And you found me, just like that." Bonnie's smirk gave way to a smile of playful complicity. "Don't worry, I won't tell Mom about it."

"We can talk about that later. What's your schedule?"

"Nothing serious," Bonnie said. "Anyway, I haven't missed a class or a lecture all year. I was just going to study this weekend. But you're the visitor—what do you want to do?"

"Let's put it this way," Jeff replied with a broad smile, feeling that things were finally beginning to go his way, "I'm the one with the money. It's my treat, whatever. You tell me what you'd like to do. Anything."

"Anything?" Bonnie's eyes widened.

"Sure, why not?" Jeff made a motion to leave. He was afraid someone Bonnie knew might appear at any moment. "Come on, let's walk while we discuss it."

"Okay, fine."

Bonnie grabbed up her notebooks, and they left the café, walking down Dunster Street toward Memorial Drive and the river. Jeff put on his sunglasses again.

"Are you sure I'm not taking you away from anything important?"

"I could take the finals tomorrow," Bonnie answered nonchalantly. "My grade point average is three point five."

"Jesus," Jeff muttered.

"Who were you seeing on business?"

"Wang, and Prime," Jeff replied, smiling to himself. It was just like his first conversation with Georgianne on the street in Danbury. He had his story ready. "We're just in the process of sounding people out. We need someone to produce a special component we've designed. In quantity."

"Is it for Star Wars?"

"Hey, please." Jeff looked suitably distraught.

"Sorry. I get you," Bonnie said quickly. "Where are you staying?"

"At the Hyatt."

"That's handy," Bonnie said. She stopped and sat on the coping of a low brick wall. "Maybe not to Wang or Prime . . ."

"In Los Angeles they told me it was convenient."

"It is, to Harvard."

She had an odd look on her face, and she seemed to be appraising him in a new light. Jeff felt mildly uncomfortable, but all he could do was stick to his story.

"Why are we stopping here?" he asked, lighting another cigarette and looking around. They were still surrounded by college buildings.

"I've decided what I want to do," Bonnie said.

"What?"

"Have a drink. No, a couple of drinks. Three."

Jeff laughed. It was going to be all right.

"Let's go by the numbers, kid," he said. "One is first, then we'll see."

"Terrific. Outrageous." Forget the smirk, the grade point average, the casual arrogance; at that moment Bonnie was just another excited teenager. "I've never been out with an older man before, you know."

"Come on, let's find a bar."

"Well, that's a problem. Maybe. I'm eighteen, and the drinking age here is twenty-one."

"Aha, I see. You want me to start off by breaking the law and contributing to the delinquency of a minor."

"Jeff, come on. You're kidding, right?"

He smiled and took her arm, and they continued on toward the Charles. Yes, it was going to be just fine, he thought. She didn't even have to be told to call him by his first name. He liked that. He still wasn't sure what to say to her or what to expect from her with regard to her mother, but he felt calm and confident now. After all, if he couldn't deal successfully with Bonnie, a teen-ager, he had no business even dreaming about Georgianne.

"I have a bottle of malt Scotch back at the hotel," Jeff told her. "I could get away with buying you drinks in plenty of places, but it might not be so easy when you're dressed like that and carrying schoolbooks."

He spotted an empty taxi and flagged it down. A little while later they were in his room on the ninth floor of the Hyatt.

"Fantastic," Bonnie exclaimed while Jeff was closing the door behind them. She dropped her books on a chair and went to the large window. It was a clear, bright day, the sky a deep blue, and now the sun was just beginning its descent. Students dismantled an eight-man shell on the riverbank next to the Boston University boathouse. Across the Charles, Boston sprawled to the south and east. The view was impressive, and Bonnie was taking it all in. "It's just fantastic," she said. "I've never been in a hotel like this. When we came up for our visit last year, we stayed at—I forget the name, but it was one of those motor inns. Ugh. But this . . ."

See? It doesn't take that much to dazzle her, Jeff told himself as he tossed his jacket over her books. He got two glasses from the bathroom and poured an inch of malt in each. Take it slow: he didn't want a drunk teenager on his hands. Bonnie was at the television set. She had turned it on and was scanning the channels expertly.

"There we are," she said happily. "Do you watch MTV?"

"I don't see much television."

"Me either. This is a treat."

Bonnie increased the volume and began dancing in front of the set, her eyes following the cascade of video images. Better this than quiz shows or soaps, Jeff decided. He handed Bonnie her drink.

"Cheers," she said with a bright smile.

"Cheers."

"Wow, smooth," she said after her first sip, but then rushed into the bathroom. She reappeared a moment later, having topped up the glass with water. What had been an amber liquid was now straw-colored.

"To tell you the truth, I don't drink much."

"No kidding."

"I might have a beer in the dorm. You know, on the weekend, when there's plenty around."

Jeff nodded. There she was, precocious as hell, but still only an eighteen-year-old kid, a newcomer to a glamorous new world. This is an adventure for her, he reminded himself. A secret meeting with an older man, a friend of her mother's, drinks in a luxurious hotel room with a penthouse view of Boston. All this—and MTV! It meant nothing to Jeff but he had to remember that it amounted to a pretty bold departure from routine for Bonnie.

He crossed the room, sat in one of the armchairs by the window, and lit a cigarette. Bonnie hadn't settled yet but she was drifting his way, swinging her body lightly to the music. He looked her over carefully now. She was a good inch taller than her mother, and the boots she wore increased her height. The black jeans were tight, but the silver-gray sweater was loose, with sleeves pushed up to her elbows. She also wore a Liberty scarf around her neck and a cluster of cheap bracelets on one wrist. Georgianne would never put on such a mix of things, he thought.

The music didn't interest him at all. He used to like rock, but what he heard these days made him think of processed cheese. The videos were just fancy wrapping, dream sequences, and dark-side fantasies. A cover for bad music. On the TV screen now, shots of Duran Duran performing were intercut with shots of a young woman exciting her nipples with an ice cube. Jeff almost laughed.

"So you really came all this way just to see some people about a little computer part."

"That's business," he said, shrugging.

"Mm-hmm. But I know what you really want to do."

"What's that?"

"You want to talk about my mother."

"How is she?" he asked tonelessly.

"Pretty good."

Bonnie smiled devilishly, as if they were playing some kind of game. She took the other armchair and stretched her legs out on the coffee table. It didn't seem like the sort of gesture she would make naturally, but perhaps the whiskey was getting to her already. Jeff studied the scarred soles of her boots for a few seconds.

"I haven't talked to her in a while," he said. "It must be . . . oh, . . . a couple of months now, I guess."

"You used to call her all the time."

It was a simple statement, but one that Jeff knew demanded a response. Bonnie waited.

"Well, not all the time," he said. "But I did a better job of keeping in touch than I have lately, yes. I was very worried about her, suddenly alone there. You know. It must have been a rough time."

"Yeah." Bonnie looked out the window, fixed on something in the distance for a moment, and then turned back to Jeff. "Is that all?"

"What do you mean?"

"You were just calling her all that time because you were worried about her?"

"Sure. Why?"

"I don't know." Eyes out the window again. "I had the impression there might be more to it."

"What?"

"I don't know."

"What did your mother say?"

"Not much. She would just tell me that you called, back during the time when you were calling her regularly."

"And what has she said about me lately?" Jeff felt tense now, but he had to remain cautious. Bonnie had started this, and he wanted to get something out of it.

"Nothing," Bonnie replied. "She hasn't mentioned you in some time. Why did you stop calling her?"

Jeff ignored this by crossing the room to pour a little more Scotch into his glass. It was deeply upsetting to hear that Georgianne had not spoken of him at all since February. I'm nothing to her, he thought bitterly. I'm an object. A thing. When it turns up now and then you call it friend and act nice to it until it goes away again. A couple of drops of whiskey splashed on his thumb.

"Know what I think?" Bonnie asked.

"What?"

"The same thing I thought when I first met you last year. That you have a thing for my mother."

"A thing." Jeff laughed at the word, then shook his head dismissively. "No, Bonnie, you—"

"Don't you?" she interrupted coolly.

"Bonnie, listen." He returned to the armchair. "Your mother means a great deal to me. We're old friends, we went through school together. Of course I care about her, very much. Very much."

Bonnie nodded her head patiently, as if she were waiting for him to put his official version of things on record before they proceeded with the truth of the matter.

"Well, that's about all there is to it," he concluded weakly. It was too early to tell how far he could trust the girl, and he thought it was time to change the subject. "Has she made any decision about the house?"

"It's on the market now."

"Really," he said, absorbing the news. So things were definitely moving along. He was glad to hear it, but at the same time he felt a new sense of urgency. "What's she going to do?"

"She's coming here around the end of June to look for an apartment. That's a good time to look, because thousands of students have gone home for the summer and there are a lot of places available to choose from."

"Right."

It was all going the way he had foreseen, but, ironically, he had less ability to influence the course of events now than he'd had at any time in the previous twelve months. He felt he wasn't even on the periphery of Georgianne's life any more. It was a freezing, shattering sensation. This trip was not merely a good idea; it was crucial. He hadn't come to Boston a day too soon.

"Do you think she's doing the right thing?" Bonnie asked.

"Oh, sure. I tried to encourage her to do something like this. Not right away, but when she was ready. That town was bound to get to her sooner or later. Limited contacts, not much to do, living alone. Boston will be great for her."

His tone sounded hollow, perfunctory. When he thought about all the time, effort, and money he had invested in Georgianne, the enormous risks he'd taken on her behalf, it all seemed to add up to this: he had succeeded in moving her to Boston, a couple of hundred miles farther away from him. Absurdly, the thought came to him that if he redoubled his efforts, poured all his resources and energy into the task, Georgianne might end up in London. Still the same question haunted him: What do I do now?

CHAPTER TWENTY-ONE

"Do you think I look a lot like my mother?"

This came two drinks later. Jeff hadn't intended to let Bonnie get drunk, but now he thought it would help if he did. He wanted her to talk uninhibitedly. He wanted to find out all she knew. Bonnie would sleep it off and probably wake up the next day not remembering much of what she'd said. Jeff didn't regard this as the underhanded, base manipulation of an inexperienced youth, but as just one more necessary step along the rocky road to Georgianne. Besides, having a few drinks had been Bonnie's idea in the first place.

"Yes, you do," he told her. "Your hair is darker and you're a little taller, but those are the only differences of any significance. You have the same eyes, the same face, and the same general bone structure."

He took their glasses for refilling, turning the volume down on the television as he passed it. He liked leaving the whiskey bottle on the bureau across the room. It gave him something to do when he needed a moment to think. This time Bonnie followed him like a cat.

"I mean," she said, "I know I do look like her. Everybody has been saying so for years, and I've seen all those high-school snapshots of her and you guys, but . . ."

"You look like your mother, Bonnie," he said patiently. "Take my word for it."

"What I mean is, do I look now just like she did when she was my age? When the two of you were in your senior year of high school."

Bonnie had a look of heightened interest, and her words suddenly seemed heavy with meaning. Jeff handed her a fresh drink and sipped his own.

"Yes and no," he replied deliberately. "The similarities are there, but so are the differences. The hair, for instance. Not just the color, but the style. And the clothes too."

"Is that all?"

"No. There's something else, but I'm not sure what it is. Probably just the fact that you're a separate person, not a clone."

"I'm too thin," Bonnie said.

"Your mother was never plump."

"Yeah, but you can see in the pictures that she was always kind of voluptuous."

"Well proportioned," he said as a matter of accuracy.

"Voluptuous is back."

"For some of us, it was never gone."

"You can't tell with this, but . . ." Bonnie set her drink on top of the television and, in one swift movement, took off her sweater. All she had on above the jeans was a Harvard T-shirt and the Liberty scarf. She put her hands on her hips. "There was a little more to Mom, right?"

Jeff shrugged, wondering how he could change the direction in which the conversation seemed to be moving. He wanted information, not narcissism from her.

"Do you think I'm too small? I mean, compared with the way my Mom looked when she was my age."

Bonnie smoothed the T-shirt down over her breasts, cupping them in her fingers. She had the wide-eyed provocativeness that only a teen-age girl can carry off, the flaunting of a recently discovered sexuality and freedom. Jeff tried to look unimpressed. He wouldn't hurt his chances with Georgianne by resisting Bonnie, but he might well destroy them if he made a foolish move. It could be just what she wanted him to do, reach for her, so that she could back away at the last minute in a show of anger and righteousness. Then he would be in the shit, but good.

"You're fine, Bonnie," he said paternally. "You've got the usual equipment, but I really don't remember your mother's high-school figure that well. She wasn't my girlfriend."

That last sentence scraped its way out of his throat, but it had been necessary. He started to walk past Bonnie to the armchair, but she put a hand on his chest to stop him.

"Jeff, you wouldn't try to hit on me when I was falling-down drunk, would you?"

"Of course not. I wouldn't—"

"I didn't think so. You'd feel bad about it later, like

you'd taken advantage of me. That's why I'm asking now, when I'm standing up, feeling fine and tingly."

Jeff smiled. "I'm glad to hear you're feeling fine and tingly, but—" He gently removed her hand from his chest. Before he could say any more, Bonnie whipped off her T-shirt and tossed it aside, leaving only the bracelets on her wrist and the Liberty scarf, which trailed down between her firm young breasts. Jeff gave a little sigh, as if he thought this act merely childish, and he kept his eyes on hers by sheer will power.

"Do you think your mother would be proud of this?"

"Come on, Jeff," Bonnie said, moving closer to him, her arms reaching around his neck. "I thought this was just between the two of us. Why are you playing hard to get? You know you want to do it. You came three thousand miles for it, man. . . ." Then she kissed him, a long, hot, wet, open-mouthed, tongue-filled kiss, and she moved him back easily until they fell onto the bed. Jeff's drink splashed, and he barely managed to set the glass down on the bedside table. Bonnie was pulling his shirt out, unbuckling his belt, and continuing to kiss him energetically.

"Bonnie . . . this isn't . . . a good idea . . ."

"Oh yes, it is," she whispered urgently. "I'm eighteen, Jeff. The drink's illegal; I'm not."

"Yeah, but . . ."

She smothered his mouth again with hers. At least one part of Jeff's body, far from resisting, was ready for action, and within a few moments he no longer wanted to avoid this situation. Aside from the obvious sexual arousal, strange feelings were sweeping through him. His eyes locked on Bonnie's perfect face while they wrestled each other out of their clothes but he didn't see her. He was in bed with Georgianne. The situation that had never occurred except in his dreams was now about to become real. He lost the ability to distinguish between Bonnie and her mother. The dream took hold of him, seized him, enthralled him, and he surrendered to it gratefully.

"Jesus, you're big." Her voice was a gasping exclamation.

Bonnie was tight, but moist. Jeff's body was beyond control, and he came convulsively as soon as he entered her. He didn't stop then, but continued moving back and forth in her, at a slower pace. He remained more or less erect, and Bonnie kept responding to his movements. A while later, a second, more powerful orgasm rocked him, and finally they lay still, resting.

"I guess you like me," Bonnie said.

Jeff found this kind of talk embarrassing, and it spoiled the illusion. He tried to ignore it, burying his face in her neck.

"Well, it—"

He put his hand over her mouth to shut her up. It worked, but not the way he expected. She began to suck his fingers. He tried to think. What now? He hadn't come to Boston to hop into bed with Bonnie Corcoran. He wanted information from her, and he hoped to win the girl's help with Georgianne. To make friends with her, so that she wouldn't develop a negative attitude to his intended relationship with her mother.

He had certainly befriended Bonnie, and then

some. But he wasn't sure how it would change things. I guess she likes me, he thought, echoing her peculiar phraseology, but how will she react now to the possibility of having me for a stepfather? It seemed shocking to him—he wanted Georgianne, but he'd just screwed her daughter. Could the three of them ever get along together as a family, in the normal sense, after this? Would Bonnie be able to keep this a secret from her mother? Would she hold it over him indefinitely, threatening catastrophe at any time? Or would she find it simply too much to contain? I hate to tell you this, Mom, I feel ashamed of myself, but I went to bed with your friend. . . . .Georgianne would be horrified, that was certain. Bonnie was only eighteen, which made her completely unreliable in Jeff's eyes. Why had he given in to her?

Perhaps he should have expected something like this, but he hadn't. Far from it. He'd thought Bonnie would be polite, moderately friendly, and busy studying for her finals. He'd hoped to spend a few hours with her, impressing her with dinner at a classy restaurant. Instead, she had taken the initiative. She hadn't been surprised to see him. She'd jumped him in his hotel room. In a short period of time all his plans had become irrelevant. He needed time to think. There was no way he could get out of this now. The damage was done. He might as well make a long weekend of it. Enjoy Bonnie. Enjoy the dream. It might be the best he could hope for, and it might have to last him the rest of his life.

Bonnie wasn't quite her mother. Lying there in bed with her, Jeff felt more acutely aware of his age and the difference in years between them. Bonnie's body was taut and firm, but supple, the skin so silky, her breasts still approaching their time of ripe perfection, her face so girlish. Jeff's heart ached at all the time he'd lost. He was thirty-nine, a year away from the start of his fifth decade. His body was slackening everywhere, it seemed. A softness in the upper arms, the sides, and the buttocks. Lines appearing on his face. Steel-gray stubble when he didn't shave for a day or two. Jeff had longed for Georgianne twenty years ago, and he still did, but in all that time he'd never accomplished anything with her. Now he had reached this strange point where, effortlessly, he'd fallen into bed with her grown daughter. There *was* something perverse and disturbing about it. No matter how exquisitely pleasing it was, it only seemed to underline his failure.

Bonnie got out of bed, shook her long hair vigorously, and went toward the bathroom. She glanced back at Jeff, who smiled. He liked the way she walked in the nude, obviously proud of her fine young body. Bonnie was bolder than her mother had ever seemed, more aggressive, more adventurous, and much more willing. Wasn't that how he'd always wanted Georgianne to be? He'd never been able to find or arouse those qualities in Georgianne. He knew that he liked a certain measure of assertiveness in a woman, the ability to take the lead when necessary. That's what he had needed so long ago: for Georgianne to make the first move. He had simply turned up in Harvard Square, and Bonnie had taken charge immediately. That was fine. But Georgianne had never given the slightest signal, and as a result Jeff had remained emotionally paralyzed. When he thought about it like this, he found it impossible to avoid the conclusion that Georgianne was as much to blame as he was. It was sad. It hurt.

When Bonnie came out of the bathroom, she retrieved her drink from the television set and sat at the foot of the bed. She crossed her legs Indian-style, letting her full fluffy hair hang forward.

"Let's talk," she said.

"Okay."

Jeff sat up against the headboard. The bedcovers were a rumpled mess, but he kept the sheet over the lower half of his body. He thought that a woman's body was beautiful, meant to be looked at, but that a man's, with its ugly dangling genitals, was not, and he always felt uncomfortable with his own nakedness.

"Let's talk about us."

"Okay."

"You really came all this way to see me, didn't you?"

Bonnie smiled slyly as she said this, and Jeff could see that she was enjoying the sense of importance it gave her. But he wasn't ready to indulge it.

"As I said," he explained calmly, "I had to come to Boston on business. When I finished my business, I decided to see if I could find you. That's all there is to it."

"Uh-huh, yeah, right," Bonnie said, laughing briefly, as if she saw a joke that Jeff didn't. "I don't know why I find that hard to believe . . . but I do."

He shrugged. "If you'd gone to Yale, you'd be in New Haven now, and I'd still be here. Actually, I'd be out at Logan, getting on a plane for L.A."

"Yeah, well . . ." Bonnie's expression changed, indicating that she was back in her naughty-kids-together mood. "So, what are we going to do?"

"What do you want to do?" Keep tossing it back to her.

"Okay. I think that you and I should have a nice, torrid little three-day affair, you know? Today, tomorrow, Sunday, and then on Monday morning we say good-bye, you go back to L.A., and I go back to my books. What do you say?"

He smiled. She was too much, but he liked it. "I'd say we're already well on the way."

"Right, right. Just between the two of us. We'll make it very torrid, outrageous, and special. Right?"

Jeff found this almost endearing. It might have amused him coming from some other woman, but Bonnie's honesty and openness transformed it into something else—something indeed special. It was hard to think of someone so sexually alive as innocent, but that was the word that came to his mind.

"All right. But listen to me," he said. "It *will* be just between the two of us. I want you with me all the time, from now until Monday morning. I don't want anyone to know—not your roommates or friends, and, most of all, not your mother. You have to promise me that."

"I do."

Those two words gave Jeff a sudden, queer thrill. "And you have to keep that promise. We're adults. This is not a kids' game."

"I know. I will." Bonnie was wide-eyed with enthusiasm. "Are we going to stay in here all weekend?"

"No. We'll go out. Why?"

"Well, I should go back to my room for a change of clothes at some point."

"That's not necessary," he said firmly. "I'll buy you something to wear. Something suitable for a restaurant or night club, and . . . something else, suitable for wearing here . . . for a minute or two . . . until I tear it off."

"All right." Bonnie laughed. "Are you rich?"

"I have some money."

"A lot?"

"Enough."

"And we're going to spend some? Terrific. Oh, this is going to be fun, I just know it is. Our very own torrid weekend together. Uh . . . but there is one thing. I *will* have to call my roommate and my mother; otherwise they'll have the cops out looking for me."

"Of course. I understand. Tell them anything you want, but nothing about where you are and what you're doing. And nothing, not a word, about me."

"No problem," Bonnie said. "I can call them later."

"Good. Now . . ." Jeff lit a cigarette. "Go stand by the window . . . I want to look at you in the light of the sunset. I want to watch you there. . . . I want you to forget about me, forget I'm even in the same room with you. Good, good. Now close your eyes . . . *I want you to feel how beautiful you are.* Dip your finger in the whiskey, touch your nipples with it . . ."

CHAPTER TWENTY-TWO

Now that she had set him free by taking the first step, Jeff knew how to act. It came naturally. Everything worked, everything was right. He told her what to do, and she did it, never once giving him so much as a questioning glance. When she had pleased him, composing herself into a hundred pictures and poses, doing things to herself, he called her back to bed and made love to her with no thought for his own pleasure. He worshiped her body with his fingers and mouth. He took her through thrashing energetic responses that seemed somehow superficial, as if this was how her inexperience told her to react, and then to a deeper level where ecstasy was wide, roaring, and irresistible. When she was hardly aware of him any more, and was caught up in a series of thundering orgasms, a feeling of great joy filled him. Bonnie had a genuinely rejuvenating effect on him. With her, he had rediscovered the wonder and delight there can be in making a woman feel that good. It was a high in itself, the power to give such pleasure. He couldn't remember the last time he had done this to a woman. It was a godlike sensation, and he wondered if he could go on all night or if she would pass out first. She was helpless at his touch, and that made everything right with him. He was in a clearing, free of the past and the future.

Finally Bonnie grabbed at his shoulders and clumsily pulled him up. Her whole body was slick, her face bathed in moisture, and her hair drenched. She couldn't open her eyes yet, but her fingers moved over his face like those of a blind person trying to read a mysterious script. After they hugged and stroked each other for a few moments, Jeff rolled her over onto her belly so that he could rest his head in the small of her back. He wanted to see nothing but the perfect curve of her bottom, which he encompassed with one arm across the top of her thighs.

It was nearly eight in the evening when they stumbled into the shower and washed each other thoroughly. Jeff got out first, dried himself, brushed his damp hair back, and dressed. He took the elevator down to the ground floor, where he bought an inexpensive hair drier in the drugstore. When he returned to his room, he found Bonnie standing by the bed, combing snarls out of her hair. His first thought was how wonderful it would be to have her around the house, nude, all the time. She was an astonishing creature. He tossed the carton containing the hair drier onto the bed.

"A little present for you."

"Oh, fantastic. Thank you."

He went to her, took her in his arms, and ran his hands down her backside. It was like holding the warm, glowing fire of life itself, he thought happily.

"You look and smell and feel like heaven."

"Mmm . . ."

Bonnie went into the bathroom and dried her hair, and when she came out a few minutes later, she called her roommate. She was on the telephone for about five minutes. Jeff was pleased with the way she handled the situation. He stood right behind her, running his hands up and down the front of her body while she chatted casually, resting her head back on his shoulder. Bonnie was like some amazing toy he had picked up in a magic shop, so remarkable that even after you'd played with it for hours you still wanted to look at it and fondle it lovingly.

"What about your mother?"

"Yeah, I should do that now too."

While Bonnie talked to Georgianne, Jeff moved away and lit a cigarette. He would have loved to kiss and touch the girl at that moment, and catch the sound of Georgianne's voice, but just the thought of doing it made him tremble, and he was afraid his body would betray him in some way to Bonnie. She told her mother, as she had her roommate, that she would be out with friends for most of the weekend, not to expect to find her in, that she would call again. Bonnie kept it vague, but she sounded so casual and convincing that no serious questions were asked. Jeff, watching her from the armchair across the room, admired what he saw. She was cool, she could deal with a delicate situation, and in a few years she'd probably be able to get people to do whatever she wanted. She showed more potential than Georgianne ever had, but he knew he was looking for something else. In the long run, Bonnie might well prove to be too much to handle. Georgianne was the dream, a promise of love secure and solid.

"Are we going anywhere tonight?" she asked after hanging up.

"Sure. Let's go out and get something to eat," he replied. "I'm starved."

"Okay, great. Now let me just see what I can come up with here. Don't panic."

Jeff smiled but said nothing. He took another sip of malt and watched. Bonnie pulled on her panties and black jeans, then a clean pair of Jeff's socks and her boots. She found the one white shirt he'd bothered to bring and put it on, rolling the sleeves up over her wrists. She tucked it in her jeans and left the top four buttons unfastened. Then she took his off-white linen jacket from the closet and tried it on. The sleeves were again too long, but she carefully folded them back, forming neat cuffs. Finally she arranged her scarf so that it looked like an explosion of silk and color erupting from the breast pocket of the jacket. She grabbed her handbag and went into the bathroom to apply some make-up. When she returned, Jeff noticed the faint lavender lipstick and the blue shading around her eyes.

"Well?"

"Fantastic," he told her. "You look better in my clothes than I do."

"No offense, but I should hope so."

They took a taxi into downtown Boston and wandered around the streets for a while, enjoying the cool night air. They ate in an Italian restaurant, talking about college and Bonnie's future. Jeff painted a glamorous picture of high-tech work in Southern California, telling her of the endless possibilities, the generous pay, and how important it was to get some practical experience. He didn't want her to think she had to stay on at Harvard until she had her master's degree and doctorate.

After dinner they walked until they came upon a place called the Seafront, a night club that featured a good jazz quartet. No one questioned Bonnie's age. They drank through two sets of music. Then she tried to persuade Jeff to take her to one of the strip bars in the Combat Zone.

"I want to see what they're like," she explained over an elegant saxophone solo. "I'd be safe with you."

Safe. The word seemed to echo in the back of Jeff's mind, but he wasn't sure why. He liked Bonnie's sense of curiosity, though, and her trust in him.

"I've been in those kinds of places," he said dismissively, a man of the world. "They're full of lonely men, tourists, and other stray suckers."

Bonnie looked as if she were about to answer that, but she stifled it beneath an odd smile.

Back in the hotel room later, they took their clothes off, got under the covers, and watched a made-for-television movie about cloning. Rock Hudson created Barbara Carerra in his laboratory and then had to explain the twentieth century to her. It wasn't easy. Why bother? Jeff's mind drifted. He was trying to understand something about sex. Time was the extra, invisible ingredient. Sex was one way Bonnie forged ahead with her life, seizing her future and making it the present. But for Jeff it seemed to be all about the past, his way of driving back through the years toward some lost, incomplete version of himself. When he made love to Bonnie, wasn't he also making love to Georgianne? Or was he really just trying to penetrate a ghost that existed only in the spirit world of his own mind? Could Georgianne ever be as good as he hoped and dreamed? That was the cruelest question of all. Before he fell asleep, he tried to plan how he would talk to Bonnie about her mother. There had to be a right way. He had a crucial opportunity in the palm of his hand, but he also knew that time was working against him—and his ghost.

In the morning, Jeff and Bonnie walked to a diner for breakfast and then strolled along the Charles watching four- and eight-man shells streak downriver. She put her arm through his and they walked slowly, close together, like lovers. She mentioned her father almost accidentally, in reference to something else, and Jeff did not respond. A moment later she stopped and looked at him.

"What do you think about my father's murder, Jeff?" she asked. "What do you really think?"

It was a clear, bright morning, but there was a brisk breeze coming off the Charles. She was watching him with curiosity and interest, he thought, rather than with any real suspicion. He felt safe and unworried, and although he didn't care for the subject, he hoped he could use it to reassure Bonnie in some way. Especially about himself.

"It was mistaken identity," he said.

"Do you have any doubts about that?"

"Not really. Do you?"

"Sometimes I wonder if . . ."

"If it was someone your father knew?"

"Yes."

Jeff took his time cupping his hands and lighting a cigarette, then tossing the match aside before speaking.

"Of course that's a possibility," he allowed reasonably. "But then you have to look for a motive. Who were your father's enemies—that kind of thing. And from what I understand, your mother and you and the police couldn't think of any reason why someone would have wanted to . . . do that. It's been quite a while now. Mistaken identity isn't nice. It's absurd, when you think about it. But it also makes a kind of sense. What else could it be? I thought you said yesterday that you *did* think it was mistaken identity. But obviously you don't. Okay, what do you suggest instead?"

He hadn't expected to say so much, but now he was pleased. The words had come naturally, and he could feel the confidence growing within him as he spoke. How long would it take to bury Sean, for Chrissake? It seemed to work, because Bonnie looked less sure of herself.

"I don't know," she admitted. "I don't have anything . . . not really, I guess. It's the not knowing that hurts."

"But you do know, if you let yourself," he said obscurely. "It's hard, but it's the acceptance of death."

Too much, he thought immediately. She can't handle that yet. Still, it was good to get it said. Sooner or later she would realize he was right. For now, Bonnie had fallen silent and had a distant look on her face. She started walking again. Jeff kept up with her.

"Hey, are you all right?" he asked, patting her back gently.

"Yeah, sure." She pushed across a smile. "You know what I'd really like though? A change of clothes."

CHAPTER TWENTY-THREE

Jeff cashed a few more traveler's checks, and they spent the rest of the morning and most of the afternoon in downtown Boston. They walked from the Common to Faneuil Hall Marketplace and browsed leisurely from shop to shop, buying slices of pizza, cookies, and ice cream as they went. Jeff liked being out with Bonnie, and he felt safely anonymous in the crowds that thronged the Marketplace.

Later they toured the Computer Museum on Congress Street, near the waterfront. Bonnie seemed to enjoy it, which pleased Jeff, because it had been his idea and she'd been reluctant at first, hoping for something more exciting. As they came back past South Station, he babbled on about supercomputers, and she asked some intelligent questions. If I had the time, he thought, and I wanted to make a special project of it, I could get her out of biology and into advanced computer science for sure. Bonnie was raw talent, and a lot of it, just waiting to be developed. It was something to think about—if other things didn't work out right.

They wandered through Chinatown. Bonnie seemed to be steering them in a certain direction, and a few minutes later she stopped.

"Know where you are?" she asked.

"Sure. Chinatown."

"Anything else?"

"I give up. What?"

"Wang," Bonnie said, pointing to a large white building a block away. Yesterday's smirk was back on her face.

"Oh yeah," Jeff muttered. "So it is. Actually, that's the back of it, or the side. When I went there the other day, a taxi dropped me off in front, and I called for another cab when I was ready to leave, so . . ." He was aware that he was trying too hard to explain his lack of recognition, and shut his mouth.

"Of course," Bonnie said.

They resumed walking, and a few minutes later they came out onto Washington Street, which seemed to be lined with strip clubs, dingy bars, sex shops, and X-rated movies. The sidewalks were crowded with hustlers, pimps, hookers, tourists, the curious, the lonely, and the lost.

"The Combat Zone, I presume," Jeff said.

"That's right. Want to take in a show?"

"No thanks."

"We could, you know. We'd get away with it."

"I thought you wanted to get some clothes," he reminded her, and made a point of studying his watch.

"You're right," she said reluctantly. "I don't know how early the stores close on Saturday. We better get over to Filene's." But she dawdled a moment more in front of a window display. "Any of those girls look better than me?" she asked. "What do you think?"

"No, none of them," Jeff replied with an indulgent smile. "Come on, now."

When they got to Filene's, Jeff slipped a small wad of money into Bonnie's hand and told her to put it in her pocket discreetly.

"I'll wait out here for you," he went on, sitting down on a bench in the pedestrian walkway. "Get whatever you want, but don't wave that cash around or make a big deal about it. Don't draw attention to yourself."

"I know, I know. Secret mission. Hush hush. You sure you want to wait here?"

"Why? How long will you be—fifteen minutes?"

"Are you kidding? Come on, Jeff, give me time to look around a bit. How about an hour? You can come with me."

He sighed. "All right, I'll meet you here at four. That's almost an hour. In the meantime, I'm going to find a cold drink. Okay?"

"Four o'clock. Right here. Great."

Bonnie stood on her toes and kissed his cheek. Then she hurried into the department store while he set off in search of a quiet bar. Over two icy bottles of Stella Artois, Jeff wondered what Georgianne would think if she knew he had just given Bonnie two hundred dollars to spend on clothes. She'd be outraged.

She'd think he was treating the girl like a whore. Was he? It bothered him, now that he thought about it. A mistress, maybe, but then, what was a mistress but a glorified whore. One way or another, he was paying for Bonnie's favors—with food, drinks, a visit to a jazz club, and additions to her wardrobe. It was a hell of a situation, but he wondered if it would really be that different if they spent the entire weekend in the hotel room. The money didn't matter, ultimately, he told himself. The first time he'd fucked Bonnie he was ruined in Georgianne's eyes—if she ever heard about it. That was the main fact, and everything that had happened since was essentially irrelevant. It still came down to this: everything depended on Bonnie's discretion. Georgianne must never know about this weekend, or even that Jeff had been in touch with Bonnie at all.

The plan still held, roughly. Tonight he would take her out to dinner again. He would begin to speak frankly to her about Georgianne. Not too much, just enough to get her mind working on it. Then they'd go to a night club, drink, maybe dance some, have a good time. He'd keep her distracted and happy while her mind adjusted to the idea he'd planted. And tomorrow they'd take the discussion the rest of the way, as far as it would go.

That was about all Jeff could think to do, and it seemed reasonable enough. But he didn't look forward to it at all. He would be at Bonnie's mercy, and that prospect filled him with dread. It would be worse than falling on his knees before Georgianne herself. How on earth do you spend a dirty weekend with a teenager and at the same time tell her you really love her mother? He had no idea what kids were like today. Even after spending one night with Bonnie, he couldn't begin to guess how she would react. She might surprise him and take it in stride. Or she might not . . . In the wake of his intimacy with her, Bonnie might decide he was a pretty poor candidate for Georgianne, that his professed feelings for her mother couldn't possibly be true. If he'd go to bed with me, Bonnie might think, how reliable and faithful would he be as a husband?

Bonnie had said she thought Jeff "had a thing" for Georgianne, but that didn't necessarily count for much. She might still be surprised or even shocked to hear him admit it was true. Perhaps he should have admitted it then, when Bonnie had made that remark. If he had, she might not have taken her shirt off and jumped him, and the whole situation would be much more in his favor now. But this was tricky ground to explore, because he was far from sure that he hadn't hoped all along to get Bonnie into bed at some point. In any case, it's all futile speculation, he decided as he left the bar. He had no real choice but to carry on, take his chances with Bonnie, and hope for the best.

If Jeff was subdued when he met her outside Filene's, Bonnie didn't appear to notice. She was carrying a large shopping bag containing two or three parcels and she looked very happy. She grabbed Jeff's arm and gave him a half-hug.

"Do you know how much money you put in my hand?" she asked in a conspiratorial whisper.

"Sure."

"And did you mean I could spend it all?"

"Sure."

Bonnie shook her head as if she found it hard to believe. "Well, I didn't," she said. "Not quite. But I did get a couple of nice things."

"Good."

Back in the hotel lobby, Bonnie asked Jeff for the room key and told him to wait downstairs for about twenty minutes—she had bought something special to wear just for him. Jeff got a newspaper and sipped a Scotch-and-water in the cocktail lounge. He gave her half an hour and then went up to the room.

Bonnie had drawn the drapes. The place was only dimly illuminated by the little bit of late-afternoon light that filtered in around the edges. She sat on the bed waiting for him, one leg dangling toward the floor, the other curled under her. She wore some kind of corset affair and thigh-high stockings. She had a ribbon tied around her throat. There was something about the way she held herself there, the way her hair was brushed or the way she looked up at him, like a child hoping for approval, that reminded him of a picture pose in a Combat Zone window display or . . . something about Diane. It was how Bonnie thought she should look to appear sexy and sinful. The effect wasn't as natural or as exciting as the day before, when she'd simply peeled off her T-shirt, but he liked it, and he appreciated the effort. He started to say something, but the words wouldn't come, and he had to clear his throat, which pleased Bonnie, who thought she'd knocked him speechless.

"It's called crystal gray," she said softly, running a hand across her outfit. "Do you like it?"

"You're beautiful, very beautiful," he told her as he went and stood beside the bed. "Undress me . . ."

They were in the middle of coitus when Jeff opened his eyes and saw Bonnie watching him. She was smiling sweetly, but beyond that was a look of curious, almost detached interest. It confused him momentarily, and he slowed the rhythm of his movements.

"Are you thinking of my mother?"

Her voice was a ghost of a whisper. He couldn't answer, nor could he control the emotions that transformed his face and froze his body.

"It's all right," she murmured gently. "It's all right."

CHAPTER TWENTY-FOUR

The sea was crusted with whitecaps, the sand was still hard-packed from winter, and the sky was uniformly gray. A sharp breeze licked in off the water, swept along the shore, and then died, only to reappear a few minutes later. It was Sunday afternoon, and the weather had turned. It wasn't really cold, but brisk and invigorating or chilly and raw, according to taste.

"When I was back in Connecticut just about a year ago," Jeff said, "there was a tremendous heat wave the whole time."

"That was the exception," Bonnie told him. "This is normal for the beginning of May."

"I guess."

He took a slug of malt Scotch. There was about a third of the bottle left, and he passed it to Bonnie. She hoisted it like a veteran drinker, but pursed her lips tightly and took only a small amount of the whiskey.

"This stuff numbs my lips," she said. "You know that?"

He smiled. "It's actually very smooth."

"But it does give you a nice warm feeling inside," she added, completing her thought.

There wasn't a boat to be seen on Cape Cod Bay, weather threats apparently having prevailed. The shore was equally deserted in both directions. Jeff and Bonnie had come to this place more or less by accident. Boston had looked dreary and uninviting from the ninth floor of the Hyatt that morning, but neither of them had wanted to hang around the hotel room all day.

"We could do this every year," Bonnie said.

"What?"

"What we've been doing. Three days and nights of sinful sex and fun. We could get together once a year, every May, just for a long delicious weekend, and then not see or talk to each other at all until the next year."

"Why?"

"I don't know. Wouldn't it be kind of adventurous and romantic?"

"A reunion," Jeff said, and the word reverberated through his mind.

"Right. I bet it would be fun."

"I'm not sure reunions are such a great idea."

"I think there was a movie about two people who did that," Bonnie continued. "They'd meet once a year, and they kept the affair going for about twenty years."

"There's a movie about everything, but that doesn't mean it would work."

"Oh, Jeff." She poked him playfully. "You're getting tired of me already."

"No, it isn't that. I wouldn't mind taking you back to L.A. with me tomorrow. But a year is a very long time in some ways, and you'll be a different person next May."

"Yeah, but I might still like the idea of spending a dirty weekend with you."

"Bonnie . . ."

But she knelt forward and put a finger to his lips while she tried to keep herself from giggling.

"Never mind, Jeff. I was only kidding. Honest to God, you take things so seriously, sometimes it's impossible not to put you on."

Jeff made a face at her and then busied himself taking another gulp of whiskey and lighting a cigarette. The trouble was, she had a point, even if she didn't fully realize it. The weekend was disappearing fast, and he'd hardly begun to come to terms with this girl. He knew much more about her, he *knew her* intimately—but that didn't seem to matter. He hadn't found a way to use that knowledge and, if anything, he felt less sure of himself than he had before he'd come to Boston. Bonnie always seemed to be a step ahead of him, or she'd say something that would stop him in his tracks and make him wonder. He was the older, the one with the experience and the money, but in some way Bonnie had taken control of the situation, and never relinquished it.

The previous night had been a nonevent as far as Jeff was concerned. He'd wanted to begin talking about Georgianne, but with that one simple stabbing question in the middle of their love-making, she'd made it impossible for him to speak seriously. For someone essentially so innocent, she seemed to know him, and understand him, all too well. That was starting to frighten him.

They'd gone to a steakhouse for dinner and talked about sex—Jeff reluctantly, Bonnie enthusiastically. She informed him that she wasn't wearing panties under the dress she'd bought at Filene's. It was something she'd wanted to try doing once, since she'd read *The Story of O*. Jeff didn't know the book.

"So how does it feel?"

"Put your hand up in there, and I'll tell you."

"Here? No thanks."

Then she told him about an associate professor who'd called her into his office one day to discuss a course. He mumbled vaguely for five or ten minutes and then casually asked her if she'd sit on his face. According to Bonnie, she had done it, but by then Jeff didn't believe a word she said. She was trying too hard, he thought, to make fact out of fantasy— something he had enough experience of to recognize.

"Does your mother know how you . . . live at college?"

"What do you mean—how I live?"

"Well, you know. Does she know you sleep with men?"

"As opposed to women?"

"You don't sleep with women."

"And how do *you* know that?"

"Does your mother know?"

"What do parents ever know about their kids? Mom and I haven't really discussed it since she sent me off last year with all the usual warnings and advice. I love my mother, but she lives in her world and I live in mine. If I need to talk to her about something, she's always there. But she respects me, and my privacy."

"She trusts you."

"Right. Besides, you make it sound like I sleep around all the time. Actually, I'm very choosy."

"Uh-huh, like the associate professor."

"He was an exception, and so are you, for that matter. But then, I'm an exception for you too, right?"

"What do you mean?"

"Oh, I could tell right away, Jeff. You don't sleep around much at all, do you? We're really very alike in that regard. You sleep alone nearly all the time. . . ."

Sometime early Sunday morning Jeff's sleep had been disturbed by a strange voice. "One and two and three and four . . . One and two and three and four . . ." He rolled over in bed and opened his eyes. Bonnie was doing something on the floor. The television set was turned on, the volume low but clear. "One and two and . . ." Jeff blinked a couple of times and sat up. Now Bonnie was wearing only a pair of panties. She was doing exercises, along with the two girls in brightly colored, geometrically patterned leotards on the TV screen. A few minutes later, the television clicked off, and Bonnie slipped back into bed with him. She had worked up a light sweat, and her body was warm and arousing.

"Rise and shine," she whispered.

At that moment the thought had come to him that

it might be the last of their love-making, but now, as they relaxed and passed the Scotch back and forth in the shelter of the dunes, he realized he'd been mistaken. They still had tonight, and tomorrow morning, unless he botched it. But he had to talk about Georgianne and run that risk, because Georgianne was far more important than screwing Bonnie one more time.

"What do you think your mother is doing this afternoon?" he asked idly. "Right now."

"I don't know." Bonnie shrugged, and then said, "But what if she tried to call you? Your phone could be ringing in California right now, and you'd never know you missed her."

"I doubt it," he replied, turning his face away. Did she know what she was doing to him when she said things like that, or was she completely, innocently oblivious? He wasn't sure which was worse. All he knew was that when she got too close, little flares of pain or anguish went off inside him and he couldn't do anything about it.

"Are you a very lonely person?" Bonnie asked quietly. "I think you must be."

"Oh boy." Jeff tried to force a laugh, but it sounded weak. Triffids came to mind, the few times he had gone there in search of someone or something, the driven people he had met, the whole depressing scene. But Bonnie had kicked away the last block that held him back, and Jeff found that the words finally began to come easily to him. "Yes, I guess I am, or I have been. For a long time I never thought about whether I was lonely or not. After the divorce, I just worked and worked, and worked some more. Loneliness is something you have to sit down and think about—you have to notice it one way or another. If you stay busy enough, you can get by for quite a while. But that doesn't mean it goes away. It does catch up with you sooner or later, like an illness that doesn't have any symptoms until it develops to a certain point. . . ."

"Critical mass," Bonnie said.

"Yes. Exactly."

And what's beyond critical mass, Bonnie wondered. She had seen enough of Jeff over the past forty-eight hours, in bed and out, to get a clear impression of the man. He was more than lonely; he seemed to be possessed of strange demons. She had seen it in the stiffness of his manner, in his hunger for physical contact, in the way his eyes moved and his skin tightened across his face when he didn't know what to say. She had seen it immediately in the mirrored sunglasses and what he'd done to his hair, and in his willingness to go along with whatever she wanted to do (which was probably because he couldn't think of anything to do himself; he had very little spontaneity). And she had seen it again this morning. He'd gone out by himself for a few minutes and then returned to announce that he'd rented a car and they were going for a drive. That was fine, but as soon as they were on the highway heading south, it became clear he didn't know what to do next. Get off at Quincy? Braintree? Weymouth? Assinippi? He wanted to be the man, the one in charge, but he just didn't do a very good job of it—a fact that seemed to haunt him all the time.

Finally they had stopped in Plymouth for lunch at a fish shack and then a look at the Rock. They had proceeded on as far as Sagamore, where Jeff had decided abruptly that he didn't want to drive to the end of the Cape after all. So they meandered back north along the old coast road until they'd come across this neglected, unprepossessing patch of sea front. It wasn't much of a beach and it wasn't pretty, but they were near Manomet Point, and there would be people around if the weather were better.

"I think I reached that point when I met your mother again last year," Jeff said nervously. "Critical mass, or whatever you want to call it."

"Really?" Bonnie sat up, brushed some sand off her sweater, and dug her boot heels into the hard ground. "What did Mom say or do to . . . ?"

"Nothing, really. But seeing her old family house for sale, and then meeting her after so many years, well, it made me sit back and think. I'd been rushing through my life, but like a zombie, blind to everything but the work in front of me. When I got back to California, I was still thinking about it, and I realized what I had been missing. All those years, I hadn't really been enjoying life at all. I decided that it wasn't too late and that I could change my life; it didn't even matter if I made mistakes or it didn't work out—because the important thing was that I try, that I make the effort."

"That's good," Bonnie told him. "That's healthy."

He gave a short, bitter laugh. "And the funny part is, as soon as I started changing my habits I discovered that I had a lot more freedom than I would have guessed. It came as a shock to me, but at the same time I liked what I was doing. I knew immediately I was right."

"You were Rip Van Winkle," Bonnie said.

"In a way, yes. That's right."

"Were you in love with my mother?" Bonnie thought she knew the answer to the question already, but it was time to make Jeff talk about it. They had skirted around it all weekend, but he could hardly bring himself to get it out in the open and face it with her.

"Was I . . ." Jeff echoed. He didn't seem to understand what she was asking.

"When you were in high school together."

"Oh, well. Maybe I was," he replied vaguely, shaking his head and smiling oddly. He should have expected a blunt question like that from Bonnie sooner or later. In fact, he *had* seen it coming after yesterday's question. But he still felt an enormous dread, even with the moment at hand, and he wasn't sure what to say. "That was a long time ago. I was a teenager, and who knows what teenagers think and feel? I've spent a weekend with you, but I can't pretend I really know or understand you."

Bonnie absently nudged a piece of broken shell, but she was not to be diverted. "Are you now?" she asked. "Are you still in love with her now?"

Jeff lit a cigarette, turning his face away from her. He stared at the bay, at his feet; he brushed his hair back with his hand. Finally he faced the girl again.

"Yes," he said simply, quietly.

Bonnie nodded slightly to herself. The look on her face seemed so neutral it was almost scientific. Jeff had the unpleasant sensation that she was looking right through him at something else. But then she glanced at the sky.

"It must be getting late," she said. "Don't you think we should start back to Boston?"

"Hey, wait a minute," he said anxiously, sitting up. "I want to talk about it."

"Yeah, but I'm getting cold here, Jeff, even with the Scotch. Can't we talk while we're driving?"

"Sure, we'll talk in the car, but"—Jeff put his hand on her arm—"I want to get something clear first. Are you mad at me?"

"No. Why should I be?"

"Because I've been to bed with you several times this weekend and now I've told you I love your mother."

"Well, that's the way it goes."

"That's the way it goes?" Jeff was astounded. "That's all you have to say about it?"

"I told you I'm not mad at you. I don't know what else to say."

"Say what you think."

"Give me a few minutes to get used to it," Bonnie said. "In the car I'll tell you what I think. Okay?"

"Hang on a sec. Was it very obvious to you?"

"I had an idea," she admitted. "I wondered about it."

"Since when?"

"Last year. The first time I met you."

"You're kidding." Jeff felt his face reddening.

"No. You hardly ever took your eyes off Mom. It kind of reminded me of the way a kid in my class used to look at me, and I thought: Hmm, I wonder."

"Was it that obvious to your mother and father?"

"They didn't talk to me about it," Bonnie answered with a deliberate shrug. "Maybe Dad was a little uncomfortable, but then you went back to California and that was the end of it, so . . ."

"Yeah, right."

"Shall we go now?" Bonnie suggested brightly.

"No, wait a minute."

His hand was on her arm again. He's not going to let me go, Bonnie thought. He wants to have it all out right here. She was aware of being a little frightened, but she still had a lot of confidence as well. She should have waited until they were in the car and back out on the road before asking Jeff if he loved her mother, but even then, at that last moment, she hadn't really believed it was true, or that he would admit it. Everything added up exactly as it had each time she'd looked at the situation—and yet she'd still been reluctant to accept it. It was a fact the mind naturally wanted to resist. And could she be sure . . . ? Or was she simply overreacting?

Bonnie had given a great deal of thought to Jeff Lisker the previous autumn, when she'd drawn up her list of names. He became more interesting when she learned that he'd been back to visit her mother again, and that he was calling her on the phone twice a week. But that was all there was to it. The move from Jeff's interest in Georgianne to Sean's murder was simply too big a leap. Bonnie had thought then that if Jeff ever turned up in Cambridge looking for her, she'd know. That would be it, that would tell her everything. But she'd thrown away the list and tried to forget about it all.

Until Friday. Jeff's sudden appearance had shocked and frightened her, but she hadn't been entirely unprepared, and she thought she'd handled it well. What he'd done to his hair was interesting. The fact that she hadn't seen any computer components or business papers in his hotel room was also noteworthy. But the real questions were whether he'd come to Boston because he wanted Georgianne or because he wanted her daughter, and whether he really was capable of killing. She had taken him to bed to find out what kind of man he was.

Bonnie soon had no doubt that he was in love with her mother, but she was also surprised that he let himself be seduced so easily. And the more time she spent with him, the less she thought it likely he could hurt anyone. He acted like he'd learned to live by following instructions in a manual. Killing Sean for the love of Georgianne would be insane, but it would also require courage and romantic heroism, however twisted, and Bonnie had seen nothing of those qualities in Jeff. He might love her mother, but he had too much of the spinster aunt in him to do anything drastic about it.

Bonnie didn't actually feel threatened—just now Jeff looked puzzled more than anything else—but she did want to get away from that empty beach. He wasn't ready to go. But she had persuaded him to do whatever she wanted all weekend, and there was no reason for that to stop now. She simply had to talk to him and reassure him until they were in the car and moving.

"What are you going to do?" she asked softly, squeezing his hand affectionately.

"About what?" He sounded confused but wary.

"Well, you haven't talked about this with Mom, have you? Are you going to?"

"I don't know. I guess so, but that's what I wanted to talk to you about. Are you sure you're not upset?"

"Because we've slept together? No, I told you. Why should I be upset? I wanted it as much as you did, maybe more. It doesn't have anything to do with my mother. Besides, you're better in bed than you think, and if you and Mom get together, well, that's nice to know."

Jeff liked what she said, but something was wrong. It didn't quite ring true. Bonnie was clever, but she'd also been open and frank all the time he'd been with her. Now she was just saying whatever she thought would sound right to him.

"You wouldn't tell her," he said.

"Christ, no. Why would I do that? Imagine how it would hurt her. And even if I didn't care what she thought about you, I do care what she thinks about me."

That made sense. "The thing is," he said, "I did try to let Georgianne know how I felt about her, but it didn't seem to get through to her. Uh . . . this was some time after your father's death, of course."

"Sure, well . . ."

"And it's depressing, very depressing. Back in February, she more or less told me not to come for a visit. And I thought that if I didn't call for a while, it might . . . she might . . . well, nothing came of it. Nothing happened at all."

"I see."

"I guess I probably didn't do a very good job of making myself clear to her," he went on.

"Maybe you did," she told him.

"What do you mean?" he asked. Her remark threw him off stride for a moment, but then he understood. "You mean I did get through to her but she isn't interested in me?"

"No. I mean maybe she isn't interested in *any* man right now. Maybe it's still too soon for her. It hasn't even been a year since my father's murder, and my mother is not the kind of woman to start looking around for a replacement in a hurry."

Her tone was still maddeningly detached. Jeff felt he was losing ground, a foot a minute.

"Yeah, okay, that could certainly be true," he said. "But why did she cut me off? That wasn't necessary." He could barely conceal the bitterness he felt.

"Well, I know what you're saying," Bonnie replied calmly. "But you've got to remember that you stopped calling her, you broke the routine. More important, maybe she was afraid to let things go too far. The thought of your coming to visit at that time, maybe it scared her. Maybe she knew she wasn't ready to commit herself to anyone, and she didn't want you to get your hopes up and then be hurt. Telling you not to come last February might have been her way of protecting you, as much as herself."

"So what do you think I should do? Just leave her alone? Am I supposed to wait another month? Six months? A year? What do *you* think I should do? You know your mother, and now you know the situation."

"I don't know what to tell you, Jeff. I can't lie to you; I don't think she's ready for a serious relationship at this time. She's got a lot on her mind, with the sale of the house, the move to Boston, and all that. But it sure wouldn't hurt if you called her up again, just to say, Hi, how are you, what's new. That kind of thing."

Bonnie had to remind herself that she was talking like this to a man more than twice her age.

"Hi, how are you, what's new," Jeff echoed sullenly.

"How come you never made a play for her back when you were in school together?"

"I don't know, I don't know," he said, rubbing his forehead. "That was then and that's the way it happened. All I'm concerned about now is—now."

He was getting into a mood, and Bonnie knew she had to pull him out of it.

"Look, you know I'll do what I can for you, Jeff. On top of everything else, though, there is the problem of distance. You've got to admit it's not going to be easy to develop a relationship when you're in L.A. and she's in Boston. But let's try to—"

"You mean you don't think it's a bad idea?" he asked, looking up sharply.

"What?"

"Your mother and me. I mean, when she's ready for

an involvement with another man. Would you think she'd be making a mistake if it was me?"

"No. Of course not." Bonnie tried to think of something more to say, but couldn't. "No."

"I think you should tell me the truth," Jeff said.

"About what? I have been—"

"There's something you're not telling me."

"What?"

"I want to know what Georgianne has said to you about me. What does she feel about me? You have to have a better idea than what you've told me so far, and I think it's only fair that you let me know. I'm sick of . . . hanging like this."

Bonnie frowned. Clasping her arms around her knees, she rocked her body slightly while she began forming the words in her mind.

"Well, I guess she knew how you felt about her."

It was a vindication of sorts. Jeff hadn't completely failed; he *had* gotten through to Georgianne. But that only seemed to make matters worse. Georgianne had known, but she deliberately hadn't responded.

"But I don't think she knew how to handle it," Bonnie went on. "As I said, it's too soon, or—"

"What else? Come on, there's more to it."

Bonnie glanced sideways at Jeff. His face was a wreck; he was all torn up emotionally. She had never seen an adult like this. It was a little frightening, but also fascinating. She discovered that she felt he deserved it, somehow, and that she really didn't want to make it any easier for him.

"The worst that can happen is that the two of you don't click, right?" Bonnie said. "Maybe you will, but

266

maybe you won't. My mother hasn't said anything about it to me, one way or the other, but you have to consider the possibilities. She married my father, and he was a different kind of guy from you. Maybe you're not my mother's type."

"Why shouldn't I be?" Jeff asked petulantly. "We were always friends, we always got along together really well."

"Yeah, maybe. But that's not the same thing—is it?"

"Is that what she told you about me? That I'm not her type. Did she say that?"

"Well, no, not in those words, but . . ."

"But what? What *did* she say?"

"She has a very high opinion of you, Jeff," Bonnie replied, trying not to sound exasperated. "She said you're a good person. But it's not what she said; it's what she didn't say. I just didn't get the impression that there was any real romantic . . . well, you know . . . that she didn't think of you in those terms. At least not yet," she added quickly. "That doesn't mean something couldn't build up, in time, when she's in the right frame of mind for it."

Bonnie had the uneasy feeling that she was letting it get away from her. Jeff didn't seem to be listening. What would he do if she stood up and started to walk toward the road? She decided that would be too abrupt a move and that there wasn't any need for it at the moment.

"Going nowhere," Jeff muttered, "going nowhere."

"What?" Bonnie snuggled down beside him, resting her head on his chest. "What is it?"

"Just the feeling that I'm getting nowhere . . . and going nowhere."

"Ah, Jeff, Jeff . . ." She stroked his face gently. "It really means a lot to you, doesn't it."

"Everything."

"Everything?"

"Yes."

"Then it'll work out. Somehow. Don't worry."

What does she have on me, Jeff wondered. The fact that Bonnie had once put his name on a list bothered him, although he knew it shouldn't. Everyone she knew even slightly was on that list; he hadn't been singled out for special consideration. But then he'd begun to pursue Georgianne. Yesterday Bonnie had asked him about her father's death. Was she putting it all together? She didn't appear to be particularly suspicious of him, but she was so clever and precocious it was impossible to know what was going on in her mind. And if she did think about it seriously, if she did come to believe that he might have been involved in her father's death, then surely she would get around to discussing it with Georgianne. Legally, Jeff was convinced he had no worries. There was no weapon, and nearly a year had passed. No one could put him in the Gorge on that morning. But life would be terribly complicated if they decided to investigate further and started to ask questions.

"I'd like to make love right now," Bonnie whispered, caressing his thigh. "But someone might come along and spoil it for us. . . ."

How could he have any doubts about a girl who would lie in his arms and behave with him the way she did? It didn't make sense, but at the same time he knew that the only person he could trust absolutely was himself. There were things that could be checked out and verified or disproved. Union Carbide, for instance. Georgianne would never do that herself, but if Bonnie ever admitted that Jeff had been to Boston to see her, it might come to mind. His visit to Boston just didn't look right, he knew, and it would be the easiest thing for a cop to determine that neither he nor anyone else at Lisker-Benedictus had ever had any business dealings with Union Carbide, Wang, or Prime. So why did you lie about these things, Mr. Lisker? What *were* you doing there?

"Come on, Jeff," Bonnie suggested. "Let's get back to the hotel and jump into bed." In spite of her roving hand, he showed no signs of interest or arousal. "It's getting cold, honey. Please."

Jeff ignored her. The real problem was Georgianne, who was sooner or later going to move to Boston. He was just beginning to understand what that would mean to him. She would be farther away, she would have many new distractions, and she would come into contact with countless new men, one of whom, surely, would take an active interest in her. Boston would change everything about Georgianne's life. It was only a matter of time, but the result was inevitable. He, on the other side of the country, wouldn't have a chance.

Bonnie got up, brushed sand off her jeans, looked around, and shivered. Jeff was still lying on his back, staring at her. His face was expressionless.

"Well, you can stay there a while longer if you want," Bonnie said nonchalantly. "But I think I'll wait in the car. I'm getting a chill out here and I don't want to come down with a cold just when I'm about to take my finals." She picked up her handbag and rummaged through it, looking for something.

"Bonnie."

"Hm?"

"I want to ask you something."

"What?"

He raised himself on one elbow. "When you drew up that list of names last year, did you really think I could have had anything to do with your father's death?"

Bonnie froze, her hand still in the leather bag. "No, of course not."

"Why not?"

"Jeff." A protest. "I told you. Listen, I wrote my uncles' names down too. It didn't mean anything. It was just something I did to ease my mind at the time."

"But then you didn't know that I loved your mother."

"So what?"

"People do kill for love."

"Yeah, but in the heat of the moment, on impulse, a sudden explosion, that kind of thing."

"So you don't think someone would travel clear across the country and calmly kill another person out of love?"

"No." Bonnie found what she wanted in the handbag. "No, that doesn't make any more sense than my father being a drug dealer."

"Really?" He could see she was nervous and lying. "But you wouldn't think someone would try to impress Jodie Foster by shooting the President either, would you?"

"That was insanity."

"Isn't love a form of insanity?" He wanted to say, *And something, maybe your mother, has made me crazy, has made me do things I wouldn't have believed possible. . . .*

"No, I don't think that," Bonnie said. "And you don't believe it either, Jeff, I know you don't."

"How can you be so sure?"

"What are you trying to tell me, Jeff? Are you trying to say that you *did* kill my father?" She tried to sound hard and skeptical, but there was a tremor in her voice.

"Haven't you been thinking about that all weekend?"

"No."

"Don't lie to me. You started thinking about it the minute I sat down in the café in Harvard Square, and it's been on your mind ever since. You're too intelligent not to consider the possibility, now that you know how I feel about your mother."

"If this is some sort of mind game you're playing, it's in very poor taste."

"Sick?"

Bonnie knew she couldn't answer that, because to do so would play right into his hands. She didn't like the situation, but she still felt she could take care of herself. If only her options weren't so limited. Perhaps she could outrun him back to the car, lock herself inside, and then sit on the horn until someone came. It wasn't pretty, but it might be the best alternative.

"Why are you acting like this, Jeff? It's just nasty and pointless. I didn't want the weekend to end like this. We've had such a good time together. . . ."

"I wanted to know what you think about it," he replied simply, with a thin smile.

"Well, I don't like it, and I haven't thought about it."

But you are now, Jeff thought.

"Bonnie, Bonnie. What am I going to do?"

"You're going to drive us back to the hotel, and we're going to get in bed and see if we can't put all this nonsense behind us and finish the weekend on a real high."

But Bonnie knew she didn't sound convincing. She knew Jeff figured, correctly, that once they got back to Boston she'd ditch him in a hurry. There was nothing left to say or do but to get out of this place. Now. Bonnie started to walk away, but Jeff grabbed her hand and pulled her down.

"I'm sorry," he said. Then he took the front of her sweater and maneuvered her on top of him. "Kiss me."

She obeyed mechanically, closing her eyes because he kept his open. It was a cool, asexual kiss, and while their lips were together, Jeff started to do something peculiar with his fingers on her neck. She tried to pull back slightly, but he wouldn't let her. Bonnie's body was stiffening with fear, and she knew she had to act immediately, before he had her completely paralyzed. She let herself lie on him, one hand stroking his hair while she continued to kiss him. Her other hand came out of the leather handbag with the knife, and she held the point of the blade against his throat.

It was a small hunting and camping knife, with a three-inch blade, but it was quite sharp. She had bought it shortly after her father's murder and she carried it with her at all times. Jeff's eyes widened a little when he felt the cold metal on his vulnerable flesh.

"Listen carefully," Bonnie said, her voice shaky but very serious. "I'm sorry I have to do this, Jeff, but you give me no choice. Please don't move, not even a fraction of an inch. Put your hands down and slide them slowly under your back, but don't do anything else. If you try to get up, you'll just stab yourself on this knife, and it's very, very sharp. Believe me."

Jeff let go of her and moved his hands slightly under his body. Bonnie tightened her grip on his hair, holding his head to the ground. She had surprised him, and she had him in a pretty good position—he couldn't move without hurting himself, perhaps fatally. But to his amazement, Jeff felt utterly serene. It was beautiful. He had to admire the girl. What courage and presence of mind she had, for an eighteen year old child. She was truly worthy of him, and he loved her for it. He wasn't afraid of death. In a way, it would make sense to die here at Bonnie's hands. He had no desire to escape this sudden new situation. He felt light and airy, as if freedom were finally at hand. None of the many scenarios he had dreamed up for his own triumph could equal the abrupt possibility of his tragic demise. A man who had taken life and then given his own—for love. All for love. It was as close as he had ever come to making a hero and a myth out of himself. He smiled at Bonnie, with love and real gratitude. The two of them were growing enormously with each passing second.

But she looked terrified now that she had gained a positional advantage. Her face was pale, and her body trembled on his. She slid off carefully, kneeling beside him, not for an instant loosening her grip on his hair or the knife. Jeff could imagine what an extraordinary effort of nerve and will it took for her to do this. It was like finding out she was *his* daughter.

"Sex isn't like this, is it?" he asked. "Sex isn't nearly this good. I'll bet you've never felt more alive than you do right now."

"Please," Bonnie said. "Just listen to me and answer me and do what I say. I'm sorry about this. I didn't want it, but I have to protect myself."

"Of course." It was difficult to speak with the knife point jabbing his throat, but he ignored the discomfort.

"I want an honest answer from you," Bonnie said. "And I'll know if you're lying. I'll know."

"What if I did?"

"What, lie?"

"No. What if I did kill your father?"

"My God," she gasped.

"That's what you wanted to ask, isn't it?"

"You did. I can't believe it. You really did."

"I didn't *say that*," Jeff replied pedantically.

But Bonnie looked at him as if she no longer had any doubt. She had considered the possibility many times before, but it still came as a shock to her. It was real now, and she had to adjust to it.

"I knew it," she murmured. "I knew it."

"Knew what?"

"Last year, when you first stopped in Danbury," she said. "You called my number the night before you met my mother. You asked for Harry or somebody, a wrong number—right? When I met you a day or two later, I recognized your voice. You did a lousy job of disguising it on the phone, Jeff."

"I don't know what you're talking about," he said. "I didn't call you; I didn't even know you had your own phone."

"And you never had any business with Union Carbide, or Wang, or Prime, right? It was all just an act, an excuse to be where you wanted to be."

"Call them and ask."

"Why did you come to Boston?" she asked. "To get me, to fuck me because you couldn't have Mom? Or to kill me?"

Both, maybe, Jeff thought. To fuck you, yes, sure. To kill you, maybe that too. Because he had been slowly drifting to the point where he realized that he had to isolate Georgianne completely, to strip her life of any ties and trappings that kept her from him. Yes, even to keep her from moving to Boston.

"Tell me," Bonnie went on. "Tell me the truth."

"What truth?"

"I'm asking you if you killed my father. I'm asking you if you can deny it to my face."

Jeff looked at her calmly and smiled.

"What are you going to do, Bonnie? You've got me where you want me now, but what are you going to do? Kill me? Go ahead. I won't resist. You can do it, you know. You're really a lot like me."

"Don't say that," she responded angrily. "I'm not like you, *not at all*."

"Oh yes, oh yes."

"When my father was murdered, I bought this knife for my own protection. I thought that whoever did it might come after me next and I wanted to be prepared. But even when you came along the other day, I was surprised and I found it hard to believe. I have to believe it now, though. I have no choice. I'm sorry for you, Jeff, I really am. Obviously my mother reaches deep, deep inside you, and you can't help it. I guess that's not your fault, but it's not hers either. I hope to God I never have that kind of effect on any man. But you didn't have any right to kill my father, and you did. I know you did. *Tell me*."

Jeff didn't flinch or show any reaction.

"You have your mind made up," he told her. "I just wish you'd do whatever you're going to do. Go on, do it. Now."

"I wonder," Bonnie said. "Would you be so eager to die if you hadn't killed my father? Somehow I doubt it. You're not brave enough to come right out and admit it, but the way you're acting is as much as a confession."

"Think what you want. You will anyway."

"But I'm not going to kill you," Bonnie said. "Because *I'm not like you*, Jeff."

That's not right, he thought. One of us has to die here.

He was ready for it to be him. His death would be an exclamation mark at the end of a sentence practically no one had heard. It would transform Bonnie's and Georgianne's lives forever. The whole story would come out and make news all around the country. They would never escape the importance he would have achieved in their lives. In death, at least, he would have them both, and they would spend the rest of their days haunted by the memory of him. It was a sweet and profoundly satisfying thought, and Jeff smiled at Bonnie again.

"You *are* like me," he repeated, "and you'd better kill me while you have the chance."

"Listen to me," Bonnie ordered, painfully aware of the cramps developing in her hands. "With that hand, reach into your pocket and take out the car keys. Very slowly, and make no other moves. Then put the keys on your stomach and your hand back under you."

When he did that, Bonnie intended to release his hair, put the keys between her teeth, and then pour some sand in his open eyes so that he couldn't race right after her when she broke for the car. It wasn't a great plan, but it was the best she could devise. She didn't want to hurt him, she just wanted to get away. Filling his eyes with sand would slow him down enough . . . but Jeff refused to cooperate.

"No," he was saying, "no. You listen to me for a second. I'm not going through that rigmarole with you, Bonnie. You can kill me if you want, but I'm going to stand up. And you should think what you'll say if you do kill me. Are you going to tell the police that I killed your father? What proof will you show them?

You don't have a weapon, you don't have a confession, you don't have anything to tie me to your father's death. And what'll you say when the police come up with witnesses who'll testify that I was at home in California when your father actually died? Kill me if you think you have to, but you'll destroy your mother and ruin your own life in the process."

"Don't move," Bonnie demanded, but it came out more as a plea than a command. Her eyes were wide with terror. Her resolve had crumbled away in the few moments it had taken Jeff to speak, and she no longer knew what to do. As long as he had been willing, eager to die, she'd had no doubt that she was right about him. But now everything he'd just said rang true, and she realized how flimsy her case was. Regardless of what had transpired between them, she didn't have a single concrete piece of evidence against him.

"I am moving," Jeff said, and he started to take his hands out from beneath his body. "I'm getting up right now."

Bonnie twisted his head away sharply and shoved him. Then she jumped up and bolted for the car. Annoyed but smiling, Jeff caught up with her before she'd gone twenty yards. He knocked her to the ground, and when she started to roll over, he stepped on her hand and pulled the knife from her grip. Then he positioned himself so that Bonnie would have to pass him to get to the car and, beyond it, the road. He glanced around, but they were the only two people in sight. Bonnie got to her feet slowly, rubbing her wrist and looking confused. She looked at Jeff, and it all came back into focus. A fine mist, so light it was nearly invisible, floated on the air.

"You can understand, can't you?" she asked anxiously. "You can see why I might have thought—"

"Bonnie."

"If you had nothing to do with what happened to my father, what you'd do now is drive me back to Boston."

"And?" It was Jeff's turn to smirk.

"And we'd say good-bye, and that would be the end of it."

"Oh, really? You'd decide you had been wrong about me and that I was really all right, is that it? And you'd never say a word about me to your mother, you'd never tell her anything about—this?"

Bonnie couldn't answer. She kept thinking she should have stabbed him, cut him somehow, not fatally but enough to slow him down. But how could she do that to someone who hadn't raised a hand to her and who might not have had anything to do with her father's killing? Jeff had toyed with her, he had let her appear to get the upper hand, and then, when he was ready, he'd pulled the rug out from under her as if it was the easiest thing in the world. And the worst part of it—what had rendered her helpless—was that he was right: she had no proof, no evidence, not a single hard fact to justify her suspicions.

"You have to understand what it's been like for my mother and me," she said, because she knew she had to talk to him. "I'm sorry, very sorry, I acted like that, but . . . I didn't want to think you were involved, but so many crazy things have been going through my mind since Dad died. It really fucked me up. You can understand that, Jeff, can't you? I'm sorry I put you through that whole scene. I was wrong, and I'm sorry. I was scared, and—"

"Yeah, well."

Jeff pursed his lips and looked up and down the chilly gray beach with its lumpy dunes and thickening mist. The whitecaps were like razor cuts in the slate sea. The air was quiet and damp but charged with risks and chances, impossible choices.

"You're very bright and very brave," he told Bonnie, "but you fall short in your knowledge of human nature."

"It's been such a great weekend, until now," she said, trying to find a positive note. "Think about how I made love to you, Jeff. I wasn't just going through the motions. You know I made love to you like I cared about you and wanted you, like it meant something to me. Because that's the truth—I did care about you, I did want you, and it did mean something to me. Do you really think I could have done that if I thought you were the one who shot my father?"

She was good, she was making an effort, but she was out of her depth, Jeff thought. She was a precocious child, nothing more.

"So you don't think I killed him?"

"Well, no. I think you would have said so before, when I had the . . ." She couldn't bring herself to mention the knife. Then, a final inspiration. "You love my mother. You wouldn't ever hurt her like that."

Jeff put his arm around Bonnie's shoulders and walked her into the shelter of the dunes. They sat down together. He stuck the knife into the sand beside him and held her close, embraced and kissed her. He stroked her hair and face. Bonnie responded eagerly, like a person reaching for a life line. It took him a minute or two to find the carotid artery in her neck. The security chief at Lisker-Benedictus had taught him this maneuver a few years ago. He gently increased the pressure until she sagged against him and passed out. He held her for a few more moments, thinking how beautiful she looked. What a waste! But it seemed to be the only way.

He took the knife, tested the blade, and found it very sharp. She hadn't lied about that. He pulled his shirttail out and used it to wipe the knife clean of fingerprints and transfer it to Bonnie's right hand, carefully wrapping her fingers around the handle. Then he opened her left wrist and watched the warm blood jet out of her onto the cold sand. A thin vapor rose from the growing pool. The red was almost too bright, but it quickly dulled and blackened as it spread and soaked into the sand.

Bonnie stirred two or three times, but Jeff applied his fingers to her neck and put her under again. After a while she became too weak to resist. She didn't seem to know what was happening, which pleased him. Such a strong young heart, mightily pumping the life out of her. He was awed and fascinated by the sight of it, and a little sad. But then he reminded himself that Bonnie had never been more than a diversion. Close but not the real thing. She had nearly won his heart, he thought, but in the final analysis that was impossible.

When the flow of blood was no more than a bare trickle and Jeff couldn't detect a heartbeat, he left, taking the Scotch bottle with him. He didn't try to cover his tracks completely, but obscured them enough so that no particular shoe print remained. They would know someone had been with her—a friendly accomplice, he hoped they would think. After he pulled the car out onto the road, he ran back to blur the tire tracks in the sand. It was the best he could do in an unfortunate situation. Let them make of it what they could.

He was thinking of Georgianne. She didn't know it yet, but she was alone now. She was about to endure another terrible shock. Jeff thought of it as somehow purifying. She'd come out of it eventually, and in a way she'd be back to where she was twenty-one years ago, alone, on her own. That was what he had achieved for her, and for himself. This time he wouldn't falter. Georgianne would need him, more than ever. And he would be there.

PART V

The Land of Lost Content

CHAPTER TWENTY-FIVE

Jeff couldn't sleep that night at the Cambridge Hyatt. Not guilt, but attention to detail kept him awake. He could have checked out immediately and caught a late flight to the West Coast, but he didn't want to draw attention to himself by leaving in a rush. You make mistakes that way. Besides, he didn't think Bonnie would be found that quickly.

He reserved a seat on a Monday-morning plane and asked the front desk for an early wake-up call. Then he very carefully packed his luggage. It wasn't easy, because he had to take with him everything Bonnie had left in the hotel room, including the several items of clothing she'd bought at Filene's, as well as the notebooks, texts, and magazines she'd been carrying on Friday. They were dangerous, incriminating things to have, but he could think of no sure, safe way to dispose of them there. In California, it would be a cinch—drop the clothes in a trash barrel somewhere and burn all the paper. The only things he felt comfortable about leaving in the hotel room wastebasket were the whiskey bottle, empty and wiped, and the crumpled shopping bags.

Using one of his T-shirts, he cleaned every surface Bonnie might have touched while she had been in the room. It was a long and tedious chore, but he didn't mind at all, and when it was finally done, he felt a measure of pride. The chances were incredibly slight that anyone would ever search this room with the idea of connecting it with Bonnie Corcoran, but you have to do these things right, and he had.

Jonathan Tate checked out of the Hyatt the next morning and drove to Logan Airport. He caught the news on the radio twice, in the hotel room and again in the car, and neither time was there any mention of a body being discovered on the south shore. He turned in the rental car and boarded a flight to San Francisco, where he retrieved his own car and cruised down 101 at a leisurely speed to L.A.

Was it just another case of overkill, these ridiculous and perhaps unnecessary precautions he took to cover his tracks? Probably, Jeff admitted to himself. But he liked it. There was, he thought, something almost sacramental about it.

Back in Santa Susana, he read the *Boston Globe* for a week. There were only two news items about Bonnie. The first reported the discovery of her body, stating that she was an "apparent suicide" and that the police were questioning her friends and classmates at Harvard about her recent activities and state of mind. The second article mentioned that the girl's father had been a murder victim the previous year in an "apparent drug-related case" in Connecticut that remained unsolved. Police interviews in Cambridge had turned up no new information or leads of any significance. An unnamed police source speculated that, although she had appeared to be in generally good spirits and was regarded as an outstanding student, the girl might never have recovered psychologically from the loss of her father and, unable to cope any longer with a persistent and growing depression, had taken her own life with the assistance of a sympathetic friend, as yet unidentified. The investigation continued, but no new developments were expected.

It was true: Bonnie's death, however unfortunate, however necessary, didn't change the fact that Jeff thought of himself as her friend.

Georgianne was shocked by her own lack of surprise. When the words came, they were words she had feared but half-expected many times previously, words from a bad dream that had never stopped playing in the depths of her mind. The last of her borrowed time had run out. Life had condemned her in its absurd, arbitrary, undeniable way, and Bonnie's death was the completion of the sentence. Georgianne tried briefly to resist the fact, but it was like scratching at granite. Suicide? Bonnie? Never. But what did Georgianne know? She knew nothing any more, nothing about anything.

Had Bonnie been on drugs? Could they test the blood or find out somehow without resorting to a complete autopsy? Georgianne couldn't bear the thought of her daughter's body being dissected and then cobbled together again for the funeral.

When she told them the details of Sean's death, as she had to, the two polite officers who interviewed her looked at each other as if to say, There you are.

Georgianne went ahead with the sale of the house. It seemed inevitable, so why turn down a good offer? She had less reason than ever to stay on at Indian Hill Road. Her husband and daughter were buried in Foxrock, and Georgianne wasn't sure she wanted to leave, but the house was like a tomb, and she could no longer live in it. There were no apartments in the village, but if she decided to remain in the area, she would probably be able to find a place in Danbury.

She packed up everything she wanted to keep and had the load put in storage. It didn't amount to much, because she found she was becoming ruthless about sentiment and possessions. She had lost the strength and courage to attach emotional value to anything. She went through the days like some minimally functional creature, semihuman, semirobot. Everything else, the furniture, the tools, the unneeded clothes and miscellaneous household items, she left behind, and Burt Maddox kindly agreed to sell them for her.

Then she flew down to Tampa to spend time with her mother and brother while the horrible business was concluded.

"Of course I remember you! How are you?"

"Fine, thanks. I—"

"Looking good, yes, looking very good. But I can

tell you haven't used your mousse today, have you?
Tsk tsk tsk."

"Well, that's the thing. I—"

"The *thing*? What *thing*, dear boy?"

"I'd like it back the way it was," Jeff said.

"What!"

"The color and the style."

"*Not* the way it *was*."

"Yes. Please."

"Color *and* style?"

"That's right."

"Are you sure you wouldn't like to think it over?
Have a nice glass of iced Red Zinger and give it another little think. Hmm?"

"No, thanks. My mind's made up."

"You're sure you're sure?"

"Positive."

"All right, one Steve Garvey coming up."

After four weeks, Georgianne was ready to leave
Florida. It was summer, the wrong time of the year,
and the heat was even worse than she had expected.
It felt far more oppressive than any heat wave she had
ever experienced in New England.

Her mother lived in a "permanent mobile home" in
a protected, self-contained community just outside
Tampa. It looked like a real house, but smaller, and it
was built with prefabricated sections on a concrete
slab. Mrs. Slaton had her own little social set among
the other older people who lived in similar houses on
the "estate."

THOMAS TESSIER

Georgianne's brother Donnie lived about eight miles away with his wife and two children. A teacher, he had the summer free, and Georgianne spent more time at his house than with her mother. The company of her family was a great help, not just in comforting her, but in restoring some sense of equilibrium.

After four weeks Georgianne wasn't ready to stop mourning, but she did want to take herself somewhere else. She thought of herself as morbid and depressed, and that was too much to continue to inflict on her family. They never complained, but she was sensitive to the likelihood that she was a disruption in the daily pattern of their lives. And they had done more than enough for her already.

One question plagued her: could she really have failed to notice the warning signs? She still wasn't sure, however much she scoured her memory, that Bonnie had shown *any* warning signs, but perhaps she had. It was a bitter, demoralizing thought that Georgianne must not have paid attention to her daughter's every word, phrase, and gesture. When depression got the upper hand, as it so often did, Georgianne could barely stand herself. She should have been perpetually vigilant; instead, she'd begun to relax just a little in the spring months. She couldn't have anticipated her husband's murder; nor could she have done anything to prevent it. But Bonnie was different, and now she had to live with the terrible thought that she had failed her daughter in the most important test of all.

* * *

"I misunderstood you, all that time. I really underestimated you. I always liked you, but I never took you as seriously as I should have, and that was a mistake. We missed out on a lot—I can see that now, and it was my fault, not yours. You were always the quiet one, and I guess I thought that meant you weren't interested or that you were kind of dull. I should have seen it for what it really was—a sign of maturity and intelligence. It didn't mean you weren't capable of having fun. You did have fun, and so did I, but we should have been together, sharing it. I always knew you were a solid guy, safe to be with and dependable. But there's more to you, and I'm sorry I missed it for so long. It was my fault, really. But thank God it's not too late. There's plenty of time left, we're still young, and we won't waste a minute of it. I'm yours now, only yours. Do anything you want to me, Jeff. I love you,"

Diane told him.

"Why don't you stay on here for a while?" Jack asked. "There are plenty of worse places in the world than Chicago. You don't like Florida enough to want to live there, and is there really anything for you back in Connecticut? You're going to carry a lot of memories around with you for the rest of your life—there's no need to live in a place that'll make it even harder to forget."

"I know," Georgianne admitted quietly.

"You can find work here. You can take courses here if you want. And there are a lot of beautiful old buildings in the city. Have you taken a look at the architecture? Chicago is an interesting city, and if you started drawing it, I bet you'd never want to stop."

"Maybe."

"Winter's a bitch—I have to tell you that. But it's not much worse here than in Connecticut, and, like Connecticut, you do get four definite, real seasons."

Georgianne smiled. "I get the idea, Mr. Weatherman."

"You know you can stay here with us for as long as you want," he went on. "Take your time and find an apartment or a condo that you really like, in a good neighborhood. Anyhow, give it some thought, Sis, and don't be in any hurry to make up your mind. There's no need for that."

No there isn't, Georgianne agreed silently. Just as well, too. She didn't want to stay in Chicago, or anywhere, but neither did she want to leave. She had nowhere to go, nowhere else to be. She didn't want to do anything but drift along with the days, bother no one, and sleep as much as possible. She would stay until she began to feel awkward and then, perhaps, she would move on or try to make some definite plan for herself.

"Yes," she said finally. "I am thinking about it."

The day Georgianne returned to the cemetery was bright, clear, and crisp, the picture of early autumn. The grass was still a rich green but it wore a scattering of leaves, the first to mark the season's change. In less than a year, she had buried a husband and a daughter there. It seemed impossible. A family had ceased to exist. As simple as that. Both stones were in place now. The names and dates told everything, and nothing. Georgianne imagined someone stopping there a hundred years in the future. Would that person notice that the man had died young? That the woman had died still a girl, less than a year later? Would that person even wonder about it? A mystery. A story lost in time. The names would mean nothing, but would merely indicate two more human beings restored to the anonymity of the earth. Maybe that is the story, the only story. It hurt to think that if she lived out a normal life span, Georgianne would eventually be the odd one of the three buried there, and sometimes she wondered if it wouldn't be better to join them now. Get it over with, accept the last portion of an abrupt fate. But they wouldn't want her like that. She could almost see Sean and Bonnie shaking their heads, saying, *No, stay away, live.* Georgianne arranged the flowers she had brought and sat for a while on the grass, thinking about all the good days and nights, the years she'd had with Sean and Bonnie, telling herself that in spite of what had happened she had for a long time been very lucky.

Georgianne sipped the hot drink carefully. Exquisite. The glass held Irish whiskey, a slice of lemon, sugar, cloves, a silver spoon, and water that had just boiled. She wanted to let the liquor take hold of her and make her feel better. But it was like drinking after a funeral—it didn't quite work. She'd been trying, with Bobbie Maddox's help, for several days now. They'd gotten tipsy, they'd even fallen asleep drunk a couple of times, but it still didn't quite work. Nothing did, nothing ever would. Georgianne was beginning to reconcile herself to that. But drinking with a friend was a distraction at least, sometimes fun and occasionally enough to diffuse the pain a little.

She had concluded all her business in Foxrock that day. She'd kept a few trunks of personal items in storage in Danbury, but everything else that had been in her home on Indian Hill Road was sold and gone. The last of the bills were paid, the papers signed and filed away.

Georgianne had more money in her checking account than ever before, and much larger sums secure in certificates of deposit. Burt wanted her to see a friend of his about investment planning. Money, money, money—not a cent of which she wanted or knew how to spend. It gave her nothing but a spurious, meaningless freedom.

Burt and Bobbie, like almost everyone else, had been more than kind. Georgianne stayed with them for five days, taking care of her personal business but mostly just talking, joking, and reminiscing over drinks. It was pleasant enough, and in some ways easier than being with relatives. She, however, grew increasingly aware of a difference. She was an odd person now, a detached wheel rolling about aimlessly.

Bobbie wanted her to buy a condo in the area, perhaps get her job back at the nursery school or take some courses at Western Connecticut State University in Danbury. Mrs. Slaton had suggested something like that in Tampa, Jack in Chicago. The options were always about the same, only the people and places varied. There was something wrong about it. Georgianne didn't know what, but she didn't like it. Freedom had a way of seeming to narrow down to practically nothing at all. It was true that she had more friends and acquaintances in the Danbury area than anywhere else, but after a few days at the Maddoxes, she'd begun to feel restless again. She didn't know if it was Foxrock, all the painful memories and the new feeling that she didn't, couldn't, belong there any more, or if it was some psychological compulsion to keep moving, but in either case she knew she had to leave.

"But why?" Bobbie asked, turning on the front burner to boil more water for the next round.

"I don't know," Georgianne said. "I've just seen my mother and my brothers, and their families, but I feel I have to go see them again. And there are other people and places I have to go. Friends I haven't seen in a while. I have to stay in touch, I have to see them."

"Whatever happened to that friend of yours?" Bobbie asked. "Oh . . . I can't remember his name now."

"Which one?"

"The one from California. Good-looking man. He came here with you one night last fall."

"Oh . . . Jeff Lisker."

"He's in computers or something like that."

"Yes, that's Jeff."

"Have you heard from him recently?"

"No, not in quite a while."

"He seemed nice."

"Yeah, Jeff's . . . nice."

"I thought he was showing signs of interest in you," Bobbie persisted. "I mean, as more than just a friend."

"Maybe he was."

"Didn't he call you every week for a while there?"

"Yes, for a while. Twice a week."

"Aha. But nothing came of it?"

"No," Georgianne said, managing a slight smile. "He wanted to come and see me again, but I . . . discouraged him, I guess. At the time, I just couldn't handle anything like that." The smile was gone. "Now, I don't think I'll ever be able to again."

"Now don't say that, Georgie."

"I mean it."

"Listen, that's what you think now," Bobbie said gently. "But sooner or later you're going to begin to feel you need someone. There's nothing wrong with that. It's perfectly natural. Your life is far from over, honey, but you just have to be careful. When the time comes, don't overreact. That's all. It's like after a divorce—so many people fall in love on the rebound, and it turns out to be a huge mistake. You know?"

"Yes, I know what you're saying." Georgianne didn't like comparing the violent and unnatural deaths of her husband and daughter with something as banal as divorce, but she knew Bobbie meant well. She gave a short pathetic laugh. "It's all so unreal, though. I'm not even ready to take on a one-room apartment, let alone another person."

Aunt Kitty and Uncle Roy gave Jeff the excuse he thought he needed to get in touch with Georgianne again. He could, of course, have picked up the telephone and called her anytime, just to say hello and chat, but he had always resisted the temptation to do that. He had to let enough time go by, he kept telling himself; he had to wait. And when he did eventually make contact with Georgianne again, he would have to have a reason, something specific to hang it on. He hadn't spoken to her in months, and somehow that meant it would be wrong to call offhandedly, out of the blue.

He had talked with his aunt and uncle twice since he'd been east for his father's funeral. Now, in October, they arrived in Los Angeles for a few days of whirl-wind sightseeing. They'd decided to spend some of the money from the sale of his father's house, and they'd joined the Ramblin' Rovers, a club that organized tours for groups of retired people. Aunt Kitty and Uncle Roy had already "done" Canada from Nova Scotia to Toronto, and had come to inspect fabled California.

Their days were well planned, with excursions to Hollywood, Disneyland, Knotts Berry Farm, the Cucamonga winery and the Getty Museum. That made it easy for Jeff, who had only to give them a tour of Lisker-Benedictus, show them his condo, and take them out to dinner a couple of evenings.

"Did you go to school with any of the Slaton kids?" Aunt Kitty asked at one point when they were filling Jeff in on odd bits of Brass Valley news.

"Sure. I knew the Slatons," Jeff replied. It would never have occurred to him to mention Georgianne to his aunt and uncle, and he was a bit surprised by the question. "Georgianne was in my class. We were good friends. Why?"

"Georgianne," Uncle Roy said, nodding. "That's the one."

They told him the whole story of Bonnie's death, which was still regarded as a suicide, and of Sean's murder the year before. The Corcoran double tragedy had been widely reported and gossiped about in Millville, since Georgianne had been a local girl. Jeff acted astonished and saddened, but he learned nothing new.

He could call Georgianne and honestly explain that he had just heard about Bonnie. It was an excuse, a reason, a hook.

They would have to get the subject of Bonnie's death out of the way sooner or later. Enough time had passed. He would have to find out where she was, and what she was doing now.

A call to the Corcoran home revealed that the phone number had been reassigned. So the house was sold. Directory assistance advised him that there was no new listing for Georgianne Corcoran (or Slaton) in either Foxrock or Danbury. Therefore, she was out of there. So far, so good.

Next he called Doris Slaton in Florida. She remembered him, of course, but wasn't very helpful. She hadn't heard from Georgianne in a week or more. At that time her daughter had been visiting friends in Connecticut, and might still be there. Or she could be somewhere else by now, with her brother in Chicago, perhaps. In any event, Mrs. Slaton did expect to hear from her soon and would tell her that Jeff had called. Did he want Georgianne to call him? Yes, please, Jeff told her. Neither of them referred to Sean or Bonnie.

It would have to do, he decided. He didn't want to

take it any further by calling the Maddoxes or Georgianne's brother in Chicago. And the more he thought about it, the more he liked the new situation. He had no doubt that Mrs. Slaton would keep her word and tell Georgianne about his call. It wasn't just an obligation, but something she would want to do. She knew Jeff from the old days and surely she'd want her daughter to talk with an old friend. Especially at a time like this. And Georgianne would have to return his call. That was it. Georgianne was incapable of being so rude as to ignore his call. All Jeff had to do was sit back and wait a little longer, a week, two at most. Georgianne would get in touch with him. And about time, too. Yes, he had done the right thing. It was turning out better than he had hoped.

A month later, he wasn't so sure. Thanksgiving was only a few days away. Georgianne had to be in Tampa again, to spend the holiday with her mother and brother. Where else could she be? Chicago, with the other brother? Possible, Jeff thought, but unlikely. The weather in Chicago would remind her too much of Connecticut, and Thanksgiving would be hard enough to take without that.

He hadn't heard a word from her. No call, no message, not even a click on the answering machine connected to his home phone. It didn't seem possible. Jeff didn't like it. It was worse than rude, it was a dismissal of their friendship, of . . . everything.

It didn't make Jeff bitter; it frightened him. What was he supposed to do? Hit the road and track her down? Then what? No, he didn't like it at all. The possibilities seemed to be narrowing to a single dark option. He would hold off as long as possible, because when you acted out of desperation you were no longer in control of things. For the last year and a half, he had followed an elaborate, evolving plan. He didn't always understand it, and at times he thought he was just drifting aimlessly, but at every crucial point the plan had worked, and his instincts had proved correct. It would be a disastrous mistake to rush things now. Patience and perseverance were still the order of the day, and faith. With the right moves at the right time, sooner or later she would fall into his waiting arms.

CHAPTER TWENTY-SIX

"It's been a great week," Georgianne said happily. "The best week I've had in quite a while. Thanks to you."

"So stay," Jan said with a bright smile. "Take my word for it, you won't find a better place to live."

"I'm not arguing. I like what I see."

And, Georgianne thought, You saved my life. Well, that might be an exaggeration, but there was no denying the fact that she had turned a corner since coming to visit Janice Tillotson. The two of them had been roommates at college in Boston, and had stayed in touch over the years with Christmas cards and the occasional letter or phone call, but they hadn't seen each other in a long time.

"You've been here—"

"Eleven years," Jan finished proudly. "And I'm never leaving. I've worked in Boston, Philadelphia, Houston, and . . . let's see . . . oh, Denver. Denver wasn't bad, but you can have 'em all. This is the place."

Jan was a nurse, had a broken marriage behind her and was "decidedly and permanently" single. She lived in her own cozy little ranch house and drove a perky old MG, lovingly cared for, that she was determined would last a million miles or the rest of her life, whichever came first.

When Georgianne stepped off the shuttle flight at the municipal airport, Jan had been there to hug her, hold her, and brush a few tears away. And from that moment everything started to get better. Jan was positive and full of life, and fifteen years of hospital work hadn't put a dent in her cheerful, optimistic nature. The darkness was squeezed out; it was as if she literally had pulled Georgianne around a corner and into the daylight.

Sean and Bonnie were mentioned hardly at all, to Georgianne's unexpected relief. It just wasn't necessary. Jan's sympathy and sorrow were communicated without words, and that was enough. For the first time, Georgianne didn't feel she was being treated like some special creature nobody knew what to do with—the bereaved. The years apart meant nothing. She and Jan were two friends together again, happy and comfortable in each other's presence.

Thanksgiving passed painlessly. Jan had taken the week off, and they'd been busy every waking hour. They even went to a couple of night clubs—something Georgianne wouldn't have dreamed of doing only a week before—not to pick up anyone, but for the simple pleasure of dancing until they were exhausted.

It was Sunday evening now, and Jan would be back

at the hospital in the morning, but she wanted Georgianne to stay on in Santa Barbara.

"I think I'll rent a car and go for a drive tomorrow," Georgianne said, unfolding a road map and spreading it out on the coffee table.

"Use mine," Jan said. "You can drop me off at work and then pick me up in the afternoon. Where are you thinking of going?"

"Let's see . . ."

"L.A. is about ninety miles from here."

"And here's Santa Susana." Georgianne put her finger on the spot and gauged the distance from Santa Barbara. "That's only about sixty miles."

"What's in Santa Susana?"

"Oh, just a guy I've known on and off since high school. Mostly off. But as long as I'm this close, I'd like to surprise him. He did it to me once. . . ."

Callie Shaw knocked once and entered Jeff's office, closing the door behind her. He glanced up from a desk covered with charts, print-outs, and other papers.

"Someone to see you."

"Who?"

"I don't know." Callie shrugged, but she had a sly smile on her face. "She just said, 'Mr. Lisker will see me,' and she wouldn't give her name. She's very attractive. You ought to take a look."

"Oh?"

"I don't think she's selling anything," Callie added. "I got the impression she does know you."

"Well . . . okay."

Jeff's mind raced as he got up from his chair and

crossed the room. He'd had a recurring paranoid fantasy that Diane and Knobs would track him down one day and present some outrageous blackmail demand, but he knew that really didn't make much sense. Who else could it be? A stray body from Triffids? But he hadn't been there in months.

Georgianne, a broad grin on her face, began to laugh merrily because Jeff looked so shocked. His cheeks turned pale, then red, and he stood frozen, as if he didn't know what to do.

Finally, he recovered his composure, and in the next few minutes he and Georgianne hugged each other, laughing and talking. Jeff introduced her to Callie, and then to Ted, whom he called in from the adjacent suite. He ordered some coffee and took Georgianne into his office.

He had been startled, he told himself, but not really surprised. *Hadn't he always believed that Georgianne would come to him sooner or later?* A year and a half of hard work and desperate risks had finally paid off. The only reason he'd been startled was that he hadn't expected it to happen this particular morning. But now that it had, he felt completely vindicated. It was as if twenty-one years had been erased, just like that, and he had achieved a new beginning in his life.

As soon as they were alone, Jeff put his arms around Georgianne and said, "I've been so worried about you. I called your house, your mother. You see, my aunt and uncle were here not too long ago, and they told me about Bonnie."

Georgianne's face tightened somewhat but she

maintained her smile. "I should have called you," she said. "That's twice, isn't it?"

"Georgianne, I'm so sorry. . . ."

"Thanks, Jeff. It was . . . terrible. But I'm better now, I really am." She spoke like someone who had taught herself how to acknowledge an unbearable fact without actually thinking about it. "Anyway, here I am, as you can see."

That's it? Bonnie disposed of in ten seconds? Jeff could hardly believe his luck.

"Yes, you are," he said happily. "And about time, too. I can't tell you how delighted I am. . . ."

And on, and on. Only one thing bothered him. Georgianne looked different. Still attractive, of course, as Callie had noticed. But her face did seem—older.

"It was very impressive," Georgianne said. "It's not really huge, not like a big factory, but it's very impressive. Everything about it is ultramodern and elegant. Jeff's office is beautiful. It's not flashy, but, like the rest of the place, it gives you a feeling of money and power. I've never actually been in that kind of environment before. He has a lovely walnut desk with brushed brass trim, and there's a sitting area with furniture you just sink into, and a great view of the mountains—the canyon, I guess. Anyhow, it was all like walking through the pages of a rich magazine."

"And this guy—Jeff—he owns the company?"

"Half of it. I met his partner."

"Sounds like your friend is a California millionaire," Jan said. "One of those high-tech success stories."

"Yeah, and it's kind of funny." Georgianne thought for a moment before continuing. "I saw him a couple of times last year, when he was back in Connecticut. But I guess I didn't really *see* him, or think much about him then. Now it's like seeing him in a whole new light."

"And you like what you see?"

"Well, it was different. That's all I meant. Maybe because I'm not so wrapped up in myself and my own . . . problems."

"So you had a good time."

"Oh, yes. Jeff wanted to take the rest of the week off so he could show me around Los Angeles. I said no, because I didn't want to take him away from his work. But then he more or less talked me into spending the weekend there. At his place."

"More or less?" Jan echoed wryly.

"Well, I said I would. He has a guest bedroom. I mean, I'd like to go, and I'd probably have fun if I did, and it's not that I don't trust Jeff, but . . . I feel kind of funny about it."

"You're not sure it's the right thing to do. Staying with him at his place."

"Yeah, I guess that's it."

"Go on, and have a good time," Jan said. She figured it might be very helpful for Georgianne to spend some time in the company of a single man, and an old friend had to be safer than a newly met stranger. "You're a big girl, you can take care of yourself."

"Oh, I'm not really worried about that."

"Well then, good," Jan said. "Go and have a good time. See L.A. while it's still there."

Georgianne smiled. Jan had a way of seeing and expressing things simply and clearly. You couldn't help feeling a little better for it. How different this same conversation would have been if Georgianne were talking with Bobbie Maddox instead. She felt healthier than she had at any time since Bonnie's death, and she attributed that to Jan. Until she had come to Santa Barbara, she had been drifting from one shuttered room to another. Her friends and relatives had always been on hand to comfort her. Jan was the first to show her the sunlight again.

Later, much later, Georgianne awoke in darkness. For a moment, she didn't know where she was, but she didn't move. She and Jan had been drinking that evening, and alcohol sometimes put you to sleep only to wake you up two or three hours later, well before dawn. It was a lonely, miserable state to be in, betrayed by drink that fails to get you through the night. The best thing to do was to lie still and wait for sleep to come around again. It would.

Something about Jeff stuck in the back of her mind. She still enjoyed the fact that she had been able to surprise him. He had looked more stunned than she had expected. And they'd had a pleasant time together, relaxed and free of tension. The tour of Lisker-Benedictus. The long lunch at the restaurant on the ocean, near Malibu.

So what was it? The way he looked at her? There had been moments when she thought there was something odd about it, almost as if he were studying her or thinking about something other than what they happened to be discussing. But thinking about it again, she felt it didn't seem that unusual. Jeff did give the impression at times that part of his mind was elsewhere; he'd been a bit like that the night they'd gone to the Maddoxes for drinks.

No—now she knew what it was. Bonnie. Aside from the first minute or two in his office, Jeff hadn't mentioned Bonnie at all. Perhaps he simply believed he was doing the right thing by not bringing up a very painful subject, but it was strange, all the same. You'd think there would have been *some* curiosity on his part, at least one delicately phrased question, regardless of how much his aunt and uncle had already told him.

Instead Jeff had talked about the glamour of his work, about the good living in Southern California, things to do, places to go—all the glittery, glossy surface of his life. In a way, that was the kind of mindless distraction Georgianne needed. But it was ephemeral. An hour later you couldn't remember half of it.

Oh, well, he probably just thought he was being considerate, she decided. That's all. It didn't matter anyway. No doubt they'd get around to more personal talk over the coming weekend.

"We get them every year at this time," Jan said, turning down the volume on the car radio. "They vary from bad to really terrible."

"Seems like the wrong time for it." Georgianne shook her head, smiling with disbelief. "This is autumn in New England. Almost winter. Remember?"

Friday. Wildfires had started at several scattered locations in Los Angeles and Ventura counties. Jan and Georgianne were driving south on the Pacific Coast Highway, which, according to the last report, was not in any immediate danger of being closed.

"Yeah, but not here," Jan said. "October and November, that's the fire season in this part of the world."

"Do you get them in Santa Barbara?"

"Santa Barbara zoning laws won't allow it," Jan cracked. But then she added, "Sometimes they come close, but generally the area around L.A. gets the worst of it. The Santa Ana winds come in off the desert that way, and if nature doesn't take its course, there's usually some nut standing by with a pack of matches to lend a hand."

"God."

Jan laughed. "Relax. You're on your way to be wined and dined by a millionaire. The only fire you're likely to see is the candle burning on your table in a romantic little restaurant in Beverly Hills."

"Oh dear." Then Georgianne laughed too.

Jeff was in the parking lot when the dusty old MG pulled in, circled around, and stopped nearby. Georgianne and her friend got out and walked toward him. He grinned proudly when he saw them blink. Their eyes widened.

"How do you like it?"

"Is that yours?" Georgianne asked.

"What is it?" Jan said.

"It's a Ferrari 328GTS," Jeff replied. "And, yes, it is mine. Picked it up a couple of hours ago."

"What happened to—"

"The Camaro? I just decided it was time for a change," he explained. "What do you think?"

"It's beautiful, of course," Georgianne exclaimed.

"Very," Jan said.

"Oh, Jeff, this is Janice Tillotson, the friend from college I told you about. Jan, this is Jeff Lisker."

"Hi, how are you?" Jeff said.

"Nice to meet you." Jan stepped forward and shook Jeff's hand. "I've heard a lot about you."

When they looked at each other, both Jan and Jeff experienced a sudden slight but distinct chill.

"Thanks for bringing Georgianne," he said politely. "I've been trying for a long time to get her to come out to California."

"Can I sit in your car?" Jan asked. "I've never seen a car this beautiful before. I've never even been close to anything like this."

"Be my guest."

"Nice shade of black," Jan said as she got into the driver's seat.

"Graphite," Jeff corrected.

"I'm glad you didn't get red," Georgianne said. "That would have been *too* much."

Jeff nodded, with a smile.

"It's . . . dazzling," Jan said. "Would you mind if I asked you what—"

"Sixty thousand." Jeff beamed. "The stereo system runs about three thousand by itself."

The numbers registered, but meant nothing. Jan was looking at the interior of the car, but her mind was elsewhere. She tried to make sense of the strange feeling of unease that had come over her. It stayed with her all the way back to Santa Barbara, where she still didn't know what to make of him.

He's a different person, Georgianne thought. But maybe he isn't—more likely it's just that I'm seeing him for the first time as he is on his home ground. She was interested, and curious.

At the moment, she was also scared. They were out for a drive, and Jeff was pushing the Ferrari too fast, she thought. It was like being strapped in the nose of a rocket. But he was obviously enjoying himself, so she said nothing. Oddly, it occurred to her that to feel even a tiny shiver of fear had to be a healthy sign. It was easy, in a way, to sit in Jan's kitchen and talk about how much of you had died, and it wasn't untrue, but it took only a little adrenaline in the bloodstream to remind you that you were still alive and wanted to stay that way.

Jeff sped down Topanga Canyon Boulevard. Just south of Woodland Hills, he turned onto a side road. The paving soon gave way to dirt and packed gravel. He was forced to drive a little slower, but the Ferrari spewed pebbles and a trail of dust in its wake.

"Did you ever hear of Mulholland Drive?"

"No," Georgianne replied.

"Well, this is it," Jeff said. "It's kind of famous in L.A."

"Why?" Georgianne looked around as they climbed up into the hills. There were few houses to be seen, and the landscape was unremarkable. "It just looks like a back road."

"Oh, movie stars have made love up here, or so they say. And a few murders have been committed. That kind of thing. It is just a back road, but it's also a bit of L.A. history."

When they reached high ground, Jeff pulled over and stopped the car. Georgianne was surprised to find that she was trembling. Her legs were shaky beneath her when they got out to look at the view, which was partially obscured by a thin haze. Jeff stretched his arm and pointed.

"Over there is Santa Susana, where we just came from," he said. "And then you have the San Fernando Valley, which is referred to simply as the Valley." His arm continued to swing. "That way is Beverly Hills, Hollywood, downtown L.A. And, behind us, Santa Monica, the Pacific, and on up to Malibu, although you can't see them from here."

There was, in fact, very little to be seen by way of distinguishing features. Georgianne spotted a bird on the road.

"Jeff, is that a roadrunner?"

"What? Oh, so it is. Now you know you're here."

The bird darted out of sight.

"Look," he said a moment later. He was pointing to the north and west again.

"What?"

"See those two grayish patches in the sky? They almost get lost in the haze, but you can just make them out."

"Oh. Yeah." Georgianne wasn't at all sure that the smudges she had picked out in the distance were the ones Jeff was talking about.

312

"That's smoke," he told her, "from the wildfires."

At once the gray-black blots seemed larger and more disturbing. But people out here accept the fires as a fact of life, Georgianne reminded herself. Like blizzards in New England.

"It's hard to believe that people go out and start some of those fires."

"They do, though," Jeff said.

Two things happened that weekend, so minor they could hardly be called incidents, that stayed with Georgianne and grew in her mind during the days and nights that followed.

The rough ride on Friday afternoon had covered a lot of ground. In addition to Mulholland Drive, Jeff pushed the Ferrari over Saddle Peak Road from Topanga Canyon to Malibu Canyon. Then he drove north on the coast road past Point Dume, really accelerating for a few miles, until he swung onto a secondary road that took them back to Santa Susana by way of Thousand Oaks and Simi Valley. Twice they spotted fires in the distance, and the spreading pall of smoke was always visible.

It was early evening when they arrived at Jeff's condo. Georgianne was still shaky, from bouncing over the back roads, and when she stepped out of the car, the heat seemed to settle on her like a lead cloak. It was dry heat, with virtually no humidity, but that was only a minor blessing.

Jeff had five rooms—a kitchen and dining area, a living room, two large bedrooms, and a room that he had turned into an office-study, with shelves of books neatly aligned, a personal computer, a sophisticated calculator, a three-drawer filing cabinet, a desk, a work table, and a leather sofa. It was so impeccably tidy and clean—every room was—that Georgianne found it hard to believe a single man lived there.

"I hope this is okay," he said as he showed her the guest room. He stood Georgianne's suitcase on the floor next to the bureau.

"It's lovely," she told him. "I mean, the whole place is. It's like something out of a magazine. And you've got more room than a lot of houses have."

"Yeah, it's very comfortable, and it's less than a mile from the office, so it's very handy too. Cost a small fortune, but I think it's worth it. Oh, I hope the bed's okay. It should be; it's brand new."

"What?"

"Yeah. I bought the furniture in this room only the other day," he explained, his smile a mix of sheepishness and pride. "You know, for the longest time I wanted to make this a proper guest room, but I never had any company—overnight, that is—and so, I never got around to it. But your visit took care of that. I went to a furniture store, picked this set out, and had it delivered the same day. What do you think? Okay?"

"Yes, it's fine. Very nice," Georgianne replied. Especially if you like black lacquer, she thought. She suppressed a smile. Anything would do; she wasn't that fussy. Then she deliberately added, "I'll tell you tomorrow how the bed is."

"Okay. Well. How about a drink?"

"In a few minutes? I hope you don't mind, but I'd

really like to take a quick shower. The heat really got to me."

"Oh, sure." He flicked a dial mounted on the bedroom wall, and a humming noise started somewhere. "Sorry. I forgot to put on the air conditioner. I usually keep the balcony door open when I'm home, so I don't think of it. . . . Let's see. The bathroom's through there," he said, pointing to a door next to the closet.

"Great. I'll be through in a few minutes."

"I put out some towels, and you'll find a small hair drier too, if you need one."

"I brought my own, thanks."

It would be a little weird if it weren't so amusing, Georgianne thought as she sat on the floor of the shower stall and let cold water pour down over her. Jeff was so considerate it was difficult not to laugh. There was something odd about coming into a person's home and finding that he had furnished a room for you with everything from a new bedroom set right down to a hair drier. He was trying hard, too hard really, not just to be the perfect host, but to impress her overwhelmingly. There was no other way to explain it all—the car, the deluxe treatment, and, most of all, the assertive new man-of-the-world style he was trying to project. She knew she would have to proceed cautiously, so that he wouldn't suffer a sharp letdown.

"Ah, you look much cooler now," Jeff said when Georgianne entered the living room. "Feel refreshed?"

"Yes, much better, thanks."

"Good. How about that drink now? We can sit out on the balcony. What would you like?"

"White wine?"

"Coming right up."

He reluctantly turned away from Georgianne, who looked stunning in shorts, bare feet, and a classy T-shirt printed with geometric patterns like an abstract painting. The shower had restored the healthy glow to her skin, and now he noticed that she had let her hair grow. It was much longer than a year ago, a dazzling, fluffy honey-gold mane. Just the sight of her made him feel weak—but very happy.

While he was busy in the kitchen, Georgianne wandered around the spacious, gray-carpeted living room. It was so sparsely furnished that it seemed Japanese in style. Maybe the black lacquer wasn't a mistake after all. A television set and a stereo rack in one corner, a sofa, easy chair, and coffee table opposite, and not much else. There were no lamps, only track lighting, and in another corner a huge salt-water aquarium housing a variety of anemones, shrimp, urchins, and other spiny creatures, along with some Fauvist fish. She noticed the pen-and-ink drawing she had given Jeff. It was hung by itself, all but lost in the middle of one long wall. It was the only thing on any of the walls, she realized.

The far end of the living room was all glass, with sliding doors to the balcony. She stepped out and looked around. Ravenswood Estate: the buildings set at angles to ensure maximum privacy, lawns well barbered, with no bare spots, white gravel paths, flowering shrubs, clusters of birch trees, wooded hills rising on all sides. Yes, it was very attractive.

Jeff's rooms were perhaps too austere and impersonal, but they were bachelor quarters and wouldn't necessarily acquire the cluttered, lived-in look of a family residence. Georgianne sat down on a deck chair. The heat seemed to have let up a bit, and there was even a hint of a breeze in the air.

Jeff appeared a minute or two later, carrying a large silver ice bucket. He set it down on a table, darted inside again, and was back almost immediately with a crystal goblet for Georgianne and his own drink. She didn't try to hide her smile now; she laughed aloud.

"You're trying to get me paralytic."

"Not really." He smiled. "You can add a little water if you want, and I've got a fat steak in the fridge whenever you feel you need some ballast."

Georgianne leaned forward to see exactly what was packed in the ice. There were two green Mosel bottles, a Wehlener Sonnenuhr 1976 and a Graach Himmelreich 1975. The third bottle was a liter of Contrexéville water. Jeff poured some of the Graach into her goblet.

"Cheers. It's great to see you again."

"And you."

They touched glasses, sat back, and sipped. The wine was too good to water down, Georgianne thought. She would enjoy it, but slowly. Had Jeff taught himself wines? No, more likely he'd gone into a good store and bought by the price tag. For her benefit, of course.

"What's that?"

"What?"

"Your drink."

"Laphroaig. It's a single malt Scotch."

"Oh." Then she seemed to be speaking mechanically, without thinking about it. "I was going to bring you a bottle, but I couldn't remember what you like. Is that your favorite?"

"I drink various things," Jeff told her. "But, yeah, I guess you could say I like this best. Ted introduced me to malt Scotches about a year ago."

Ted. Sure. Lots of people probably drink malt Scotch, Georgianne thought. It stood to reason. *Single* malt scotch, they call it. They'd even found some in Bonnie's stomach.

That was the first thing.

Jeff took her for a selective tour on Saturday. Wisely, he didn't try to cram too much into a single day. They cruised at a leisurely pace through Hollywood and Beverly Hills, taking in Laurel Canyon, Coldwater Canyon, the Strip, and Rodeo Drive. They ate a light lunch at the Polo Lounge, then drove on to Santa Monica and Venice, where they spent a while watching the crowd. The Ferrari never seemed out of place, and it drew many appreciative looks.

Georgianne felt out of place, though. L.A. was almost a foreign country. In a way that was healthy, she thought. Like fear, it was a form of negative definition. If she didn't belong here, she must belong somewhere else—but at least somewhere. She would just relax and enjoy the experience of being in a new and different environment.

Jeff's manner intrigued her. It was as though he was showing off his city, its exotic sights and people. There were moments when Georgianne was sure she saw pride in his expression. Steering his sixty-thousand-dollar car through the precincts of wealth and privilege, he looked proprietorial, and there was something amusing about that, because it seemed fairly obvious that he didn't really move in these circles on a regular basis. Georgianne would have bet that the glamorous side of L.A. life was as new to him as his Ferrari.

She didn't know what to make of the car. A ten-year-old Camaro was Jeff's style. The Ferrari was something else altogether. It seemed *too* extravagant, all the more so since Jeff made the point that he'd paid the entire bill in cash, on the spot. But then, Georgianne had to admit that after more than twenty years she probably didn't know what Jeff's style was, or even what kind of person he had grown into. Now she was seeing him on his home ground, and getting to know him all over again.

They returned to Jeff's condo, relaxed for a while, then showered and changed before driving back into the city for dinner at Spago's. Later, Georgianne couldn't remember the exact context, but at some point she mentioned Janice. And Jeff made a too-casual remark that upset her.

"Isn't she—oh, it's probably just my imagination."

"What?"

"Ah, nothing, really. Well, is she a little . . . uh . . . butch?"

"No," Georgianne replied after a momentary silence. "No, I don't think so at all."

Jeff shrugged in a way that suggested he wasn't willing to concede the point, but he sipped his wine and changed the subject. The rest of the evening seemed a bit cooler.

It was nothing more than a minor annoyance at the time. But when Georgianne thought about it later, again and again, it began to seem like a piece of calculated nastiness. Jeff had never been the kind of person to say something like that, either casually or inadvertently. Why would he even think it? Whether Jan was gay or not (and she emphatically wasn't), how could Jeff have formed an opinion and suggested it the way he had on the basis of one brief meeting.

That was the second thing.

The weekend went extremely well, Jeff thought, and he was quite pleased with himself when he looked back on it while driving home Sunday evening after returning Georgianne to her friend's house in Santa Barbara. Yes, yes, yes, he told himself. It's all here, it's all happening, it's all go now. He had been damn near perfect, he reckoned. Friendly, warm, attentive, lighthearted, generous, masterful, considerate—ah, let's see, did I say attentive? But never pushy, never too aggressive or forward or macho. Yes, it had all gone very well. So much so that Georgianne had agreed to come down again the next weekend. That said it all. Jeff had no doubt she'd be ready then for the one thing he'd been careful to avoid. Contact. Love.

"So, tell me, how was your weekend with Magnum, P.I.?" Jan asked sarcastically when she and Georgianne sat down with a nightcap. "Boozy? Automotive? Lavish? Sensual?"

"Yes, yes, yes, and no, respectively," Georgianne replied when she stopped laughing.

"Can you believe that car?"

"No, not yet."

"All he needs is a mustache. Not that it would turn him into another Tom Selleck, but . . ."

"I know what you mean," Georgianne said. "Jeff's not quite the same person here that I knew back in Connecticut."

"Well, I never saw him before the other day, but one thing was pretty damn obvious."

"What?"

"He wants you."

"Oh dear, that's what I was afraid of. Are you sure?"

"Are you blind? You really can't tell?"

"I guess I can," Georgianne said quietly. "I just haven't wanted to think about it."

"He didn't make a play for you? All that time the two of you were alone at his place?"

"No. No, he didn't."

"I don't care." Jan shook her head. "He will."

"I'm going to spend next weekend there too."

"Oh, you are, are you." Jan sat back, eyebrows raised. "So you're interested."

"No, I don't think so. Not really. Let's just say I want to get to know him better—better than I thought I did."

"Watch yourself."

"Why? What did you think of him?" Georgianne asked. If Jeff could make a snap judgment about Jan, then she was entitled to one in return.

"The truth?"

"Of course."

"Okay. I'm sorry if he is a good old friend of yours, but I didn't like him. I don't know exactly why, but I've been thinking about it all weekend, and it keeps coming back to the same thing. The minute I met him I felt a real chill—and he knew it. Something in his eyes maybe, or something *not* in his eyes; something missing. You know, we were standing just a couple of feet apart, but he gave me the feeling that he was far away, looking at me, watching from a distance. Do you know what I mean?"

"Well . . ."

"He gave me the creeps."

Why wouldn't it go away? It was the last thing, the very last thing Georgianne wanted to think.

She had found that she could live with almost anything. Her husband's senseless murder by strangers who mistook him for someone else? She had never been sure that's what had happened, but it was the best story, and she had come to accept it. Bonnie's suicide, arising from some terrible combination of loneliness, depression, and pain resulting from the loss of her father? Georgianne had never brought herself to believe that; it was impossible. But for six months, wherever she was, alone every night, she had cried for Bonnie, until she had reached the point where she had no strength left to rage against the possibility of her suicide, the fact of her death. And so, in a way, she had come to accept that too, or at least not to argue with herself about it. There were two gaping holes in her life, and all she had managed to do was surround them with scar tissue to contain them.

Then she had come to Santa Barbara, and Jan had been able to make her smile for the first time in ages. All Georgianne had wanted to do was to lose herself in the company of her friends, and she was beginning to succeed. Then everything was suddenly changed.

It was crazy even to think that Jeff—quiet, cautious, solid Jeff Lisker—could in any way be responsible for what had happened to Sean and Bonnie. But once the idea had entered Georgianne's mind, it wouldn't go away. Because the more she thought about it, the more she saw a certain perverse logic in it. The way Jeff had reappeared in her life after twenty years, shortly before Sean's murder. The way he had come back again after the funeral. The way he apparently—obviously, if Jan was right, and she probably was—felt about her. The fact that he drank malt Scotch, and his clumsy insinuation about Jan seemed more ominous when viewed in this light.

But there was nothing to it, she tried to reason. Nothing of any real substance. Suppose Jeff did have some kind of obsessive fixation about her. Wasn't it much more likely that he would have made some grand romantic play for her months before, even when Sean was alive? Married people fall in love, get divorced, and remarry all the time. He wouldn't have had to go to the deranged extreme of wiping out her whole family. And even if he had been happy to see Sean removed from the picture, there was no reason, no need whatsoever, for Bonnie to die too. It was crazy, that line of thought. Impossible.

The rest was the flimsiest of stuff. Coincidence and circumstance. During the week, Georgianne stopped at a pharmacy in Santa Barbara to buy something, and while browsing at the magazine rack she came across a full-page ad for a malt Scotch. She almost laughed and cried at the same time. You couldn't indict someone for drinking one thing or another, any more than you could for making an ill-considered remark.

The notion was so unspeakably awful that it had to be wrong. But it also had a horrible fascination, and it wouldn't go away. It was bad enough dealing with her thoughts; Georgianne couldn't bring herself to articulate them to Jan.

Jeff had a brilliant idea.

He decided to throw a party. It would be small but lavish. A caterer and a bartender. A stock of good wines, champagne, and the best liquors. He thought his condominium was just large enough for such an event.

He hadn't held a party since the minor fiasco he and Audrey had staged about ten years ago, when they were living in a boxy tract house in the Valley. All the top people at Lisker-Benedictus would come, of course. It would be a fine occasion for him to show off Georgianne. His woman.

What if?

That's what it came down to every time Georgianne thought about it. What if Jeff *was* the person responsible? It didn't matter if there was only one chance in two hundred million, she had to face the possibility.

And what if, somehow, she became convinced of it? She still wouldn't have any evidence to take to the police, and she knew she herself would be incapable of personally exacting revenge.

What if she might be at risk? If things somehow reached that appalling, impossible point, would she be able to defend herself or would she give in, perhaps even gratefully, and follow Sean and Bonnie?

I must be losing my mind, just to think like this, she decided. If I told anyone what's going on in my head, they'd recommend me for treatment.

But there she was, Friday morning, sitting at the foot of her bed in Jan's house, holding a gun in her hand. It was an ugly little weapon, so small and light it was hard to believe it could hurt anyone. The bullets were like tiny pieces from a child's board game.

The day she had arrived at Jan's, Georgianne was unpacking her suitcase and hanging up clothes in the spare bedroom when she found the gun and bullets in a shoe box on the closet shelf. Jan explained that she had bought it a few years ago, after there had been a number of attacks on nurses and women visitors in the area of the hospital. A suspect was caught, better lighting was installed, the attacks dropped off, and Jan eventually got tired of carrying the gun, so she put it away in the closet and forgot about it.

A cheap, trashy little pistol, so dusty it probably wouldn't even work. Idly, Georgianne began to clean it with a piece of tissue paper.

CHAPTER TWENTY-SEVEN

Friday evening they went out to dinner at Ma Maison and resumed a desultory conversation, begun the week before, about Georgianne's plans for the future. Jeff was cool. He didn't try hard to persuade her to stay on in Southern California, but he carefully reinforced the idea by the way he acknowledged its advantages and appeared to discount the alternatives. He assumed, correctly, that Jan also wanted Georgianne to stay and would be more direct and outspoken about it. So he took the softer approach.

Once again, it struck Georgianne as odd that Jeff had virtually nothing to say about Bonnie. No questions, no comments, no hint that he wanted to sympathize or share in her sorrow. It was as if Bonnie had been ruled ineligible as a topic for discussion. But because she wasn't really looking for sympathy and was herself reluctant to mention her daughter's death, she was still faced with the possibility that Jeff was simply being considerate.

After dinner, neither of them felt much like doing anything special, so they returned to Santa Susana and drank several nightcaps while watching *Hanover Street* and *Vertigo* on cable.

Georgianne made brunch late Saturday morning. When she turned on the radio, she heard the latest reports on the wildfires in Los Angeles and Ventura countries. Contained in some areas, the fires had nonetheless continued to burn and spread throughout the week. The desert winds, which had let up for a day or so, had regained force and were now said to be blowing at fifty miles per hour in some places. At Ravenswood Estate, it was another hot Saturday, with the temperature at about eighty degrees, twelve percent humidity, and a glorious sunny sky, clear but for a distant plume of gray.

Jeff had told her to bring her bikini, and she had bought one in Santa Barbara, but she wasn't in the mood to go anywhere. She didn't even want to take the short drive to the beach. Instead, they spent part of the afternoon at the Ravenswood pool, swimming and sunning, swimming and dozing. Aware of how pale she looked in the land of the permanent tan, Georgianne was glad to take on some color. She had the kind of skin that didn't burn easily, and she applied plenty of suntan lotion. The sun felt great on her body.

It was almost four in the afternoon when they picked up their towels and walked slowly back to the condo. Georgianne liked the feel of the chipped-stone path on her bare feet. But a strange, diffuse mood seemed to be gathering within her, trying to form itself into something more definite. She felt heavy and sluggish, not tired, but lazy.

Her room was cool and dark, with the drapes drawn, the lights off, and the air conditioner humming softly. A shower, followed by a tall cold drink? No, she didn't want either of those yet. She folded her towel and hung it on the bar in the bathroom. She tried to focus her thoughts, and wondered briefly if she hadn't wanted to go to the beach because she was afraid of seeing some girl there who would remind her of Bonnie, or because Bonnie had died at a beach. But her mind wouldn't settle. She stood indecisively in the middle of her bedroom until *the realization finally came that*—

The door to Jeff's room was ajar. He had taken off his swim trunks and put on his black robe. He was now laying out on the bed the clothes he intended to wear after he showered. They hadn't decided whether or not to go out for dinner. He didn't really care, though he would be a little happier to stay in. But broiling a steak was the limit of his ability in the kitchen. Was there a bag of French fries in the freezer, he wondered.

"Jeff."

Because he wasn't expecting it, he wasn't sure he'd actually heard it. He hesitated a couple of seconds, then tightened his robe modestly and went to Georgianne's door, which was slightly open too. He tapped on it once before entering. She was standing there, still in her bikini, with an uncertain look on her face.

"Did you call me?"

She gave a short, sharp nod, as if it required a special effort for her to move at all. She was waiting, helplessly it seemed, and she didn't speak.

"What are you doing?" Jeff asked delicately.

"Nothing." A hint of a shrug.

"Are you all right?"

"Yes." Then, "I don't know." Then, "No." Then, in a voice cracking with conflict, "Would you hold me?"

Jeff embraced her immediately. He couldn't think straight but that was good, because if he could think, he would say something and he knew this was not the moment for talking. She felt magnificent in his arms. He experienced a jumbled sensory rush. The texture of her skin. The trace of chlorine from the pool in her hair. The buttery smell of suntan lotion. The heat that radiated from her body.

"I need you"—she almost used the word "someone"—"to hold me."

Jeff squeezed her a little more tightly and lifted her chin so that she was looking up at his face. He smiled. In his mind, he could see the smile perfectly. It had warmth and tenderness. It was a smile that said, *It's all right*. It was a smile that communicated love. And when he felt the smile had achieved its purpose, he kissed her. He was a man in control. Sexual passion was building rapidly within him, and he let Georgianne know it with that kiss—but carefully, not too forcefully, not yet. He was rewarded. Her arms came up around his back as she responded to his embrace and kiss with her own enthusiasm.

The realization finally came that . . . she was going

to make love with Jeff. Part of her rebelled weakly at the idea, but she was surprised by the force of certainty she felt. How could she if she thought there was the slightest chance he had been involved in the deaths of Sean and Bonnie? But, paradoxically, that seemed to be part of the impulse, as if she knew instinctively that it would take more than dinners and drinks and scenic drives to get past his smooth, resilient façade. To learn what he really thought and felt. Maybe it was also the sun, the heat, the sight and proximity of his body, and the fact that Georgianne hadn't made love in more than a year. She seemed to have reached the point where intimacy could no longer remain implied, an abstraction, but had to be faced and tested. Now. Before they showered and dressed and sat down for another round of cocktails. Before the moment was lost.

Not that Jeff had any intention of letting it pass. He had waited more than half his life, and his time had finally come. The vague, inarticulate yearning, the doomed marriage, the years of total immersion in work, the substitute bodies, the intermittent but ever-recurring dreams and fantasies were all behind him, and he knew that he had succeeded in retrieving from the past the only thing, the only person he truly wanted.

Georgianne's desire was obvious as they moved to the bed, clenched in an embrace and kissing passionately, and it struck Jeff with all the power of a religious revelation: *She wants me.* The words repeated in his mind.

Her body was a delight. Not quite as firm and hard

as Diane's or Bonnie's; yet it was more beautiful than he had imagined, perhaps because he had it at last and could begin to savor its richness. This close, he could see the incipient lines around her eyes and feel the slight softening of her breasts—but those things didn't matter; nothing did. For once, the reality was greater than the dream.

Even as her body responded to his, Georgianne could sense the aching hunger in him, the enormous depth of his desire. It was like a force that had been held in check, perhaps too long, and was now breaking loose. It felt good to experience this, to be with a man again, but there was something awesome, almost frightening, about it too. She had nearly forgotten the kind of intensity that can be created between two people.

Everything changed in a few moments. As they rolled about on the bed, Jeff eased off her bikini bottom, unhooked the bra, and shrugged out of his robe. He moved on top of her, and as her legs opened to accept him, Jeff and Georgianne seemed to reach a clearing, a tender pause in their passion. She looked at him with half-open eyes, trying to hold back the tears that, for no reason she could think of, were trying to find release. He smiled lovingly at her and kissed the tears away. He had an idea how sensitive and emotional this moment must be for her. But it was his moment too, and he was so confident of his control that he thought he could hold himself there, rock-hard and ready, long into the night if need be.

"Jeff . . ."

So tiny and distant it might have been a dying echo,

so gentle and vulnerable it might have been the voice of a little girl.

"Mmm," he murmured, kissing her lightly about the face.

"Do you think . . ." She smiled as if she saw some minor silliness in her thoughts. "Can you . . . do I look like . . . Bonnie?"

The furious passion that had been about to sweep them up like a tornado skittered off in some other direction. Everything seemed to stop except his own blood, which he heard as a whirrushing whisper in his ears. Then, absurdly, he thought it had to be the air conditioner. It was the only thing his mind could fix on. He felt chilly and self-conscious, but unable to move or speak or think.

Georgianne could feel his erection dwindle away on her thigh until there was nothing left to it. She saw the vacuum in his eyes. He was still looking at her, but he had lost all focus. Finally, he seemed to relax, or sag from within, and he took his eyes from hers. They remained there, still and quiet in each other's arms, for a long time—until the room itself became a presence, cold, dark, and uncomfortable.

Tears. The damn tears came, and she didn't want them, but they came anyway, and all she could do was wipe them off her face and try to contain her jagged breathing. She thought she was doing a bad job—of everything. She couldn't even think clearly.

She had gotten out of bed, grabbed some clothes and her handbag, and shut herself in the bathroom. What, if anything, had that unfathomable moment actually meant? She was afraid, not just for herself but for Jeff. Had she seen something in his eyes and his expression in the sudden death of his desire? The most terrible possibility was that she had seen what she wanted to see, that her imagination alone was trying to render a verdict.

She sat on the toilet cover and awkwardly got the ridiculous bullets into the little gun, not at all sure she would need it or even be able to use it. Something to keep her busy while she tried to think. Maybe it was all her fault for saying the wrong thing at the wrong time, for thinking of her daughter when she should have been in tune with the man making love to her. Maybe. But then, maybe not . . .

She couldn't stay in the bathroom forever. If Jeff had moved, he hadn't made a sound. She put the gun in her handbag. She put on sneakers, jeans, and a light blouse. Her face in the mirror looked a wreck, but she couldn't do anything about it now. She just wanted to leave. What if he wouldn't let her?

When she opened the bathroom door, Jeff was in his robe, sitting on the bed. He gave her a pathetic smile, then sucked nervously on a cigarette. Twice he looked like he was going to say something, but he couldn't get it out.

"I'd like to go," Georgianne said quietly.

"You don't have to."

"I really think I should."

"Hey . . ."

"I'm sorry, Jeff. It's my fault. But I just don't think this is a good idea. Any of it."

"All right. Well . . . that doesn't mean—"

"I'll call Jan. She'll come and get me."

"No, don't bother." He got off the bed, as if to intercept her, but she hadn't moved from the bathroom doorway. "I'll run you up to Santa Barbara . . . if you really want to go."

"Thanks." She looked away from him. "I do."

"Okay. Well." He moved indecisively, toward his room, toward her, then stopped. "Georgianne."

There it was. She had to look at him.

"Yes?"

"You . . . don't . . . love . . . me?"

He sounded so weak and defeated that she despised herself for letting the situation get to this point. What had she been thinking? She felt nothing for Jeff, but that didn't alter the fact that she had behaved badly—or so she thought. When he was like this, it was impossible to imagine him hurting anyone, except possibly himself.

"I don't love anyone," she said. "Maybe I can't any more."

Jeff appeared to consider that for a couple of seconds, his face the picture of desolation. Then he nodded once and left the room.

Maybe that was worse than shooting him, Georgianne thought. Somehow the two of them had conspired to do nothing, and yet she felt dirty.

In his room, Jeff stood trembling so violently he wondered if his body was literally coming apart. His teeth bit together painfully, and he seemed to be sweating from his forehead to his crotch. He forced himself to sit down and swallow huge gulps of air. A few minutes later, he felt calm, maybe even serene.

There followed a ghastly interlude—leaving the condo, carrying her suitcase, getting in the car and starting out—that was like walking underwater, or trying to get out from under a dome of silence.

But when they reached the street, Jeff began to feel better. He could accommodate all the bitterness and frustration. He could bear the pain of final rejection. He could even fight off the nausea he felt when he thought of how she had cut him off, physically and psychically, just before the moment of penetration. A kind of castration—that was the only word for it. He could take it all, he could take anything. Shit on me, it doesn't matter. Because he knew what he was doing and where they were going.

He spun the wheel, and the car turned smoothly to the right. Then he slammed his foot down, and they accelerated sharply, streaking north into Topo Canyon on a road that went nowhere.

Georgianne knew immediately that something was wrong. The road looked wrong, the direction felt wrong, and the expression on Jeff's face frightened her.

"Where are we going?"

"A slight detour."

"Detour? Where?" No response. "Why? *Jeff.*"

"Relax," he said sarcastically. "I just want to get a look at the fire. That's all."

"I don't want to."

"There's a good vantage point I know."

"Jeff, I don't want to go anywhere near the fires. Please, let's turn around."

"It's not dangerous. Really."

Just then Georgianne spotted an unmanned barricade a couple of hundred yards in front of them. The road was closed. But before she had a chance to breathe easier, the Ferrari swerved off the asphalt into high grass and hardly lost any speed as it bounced along a rutted, partially overgrown trail. Branches whipped the windshield, scratched the roof, and raked the sides of the car.

"Jeff! What are you doing?"

He laughed, as if genuinely amused.

"They closed Topo Canyon Road, but there are a lot of these dirt tracks up into the hills," he said. "Bikers come here and roar around the countryside when they have nothing better to do."

"Jeff, please take me out of here."

"Yeah, yeah, in a minute."

"If the road is closed, it can't be safe. The fire must be close to this area."

"It is." Jeff laughed again. "The fire's *in* this area. I want to get a look at it."

There was no point trying to talk to him. Georgianne reached into the handbag on her lap and closed her fingers around the gun. She held it there, waiting.

Then she gasped as she noticed the sky. It was a black wall just ahead of them.

"You know," Jeff said, "I never thought of it before, but this area is a little like that place you have back in Foxrock. What is it—the Gorge?"

He said it without thinking—there was nothing to think about any more—and he was surprised at himself, but pleased as well. There was a certain mean

336

pleasure to be had in daring her, taunting her, and, most of all, scaring her. But he wouldn't hurt her. He could never hurt Georgianne—no more than he could let go of her.

But had he ever really loved her, or was he always in love with the idea of her and of having her? He couldn't tell now. It might be worth thinking about, as a matter of academic interest, but he was not inclined to do so. It would be too much like feeding on his own corpse.

They had driven two or three meandering miles away from the paved road. When they came up over the top of a rise and started downward, Jeff hit the brakes and Georgianne cried aloud. Below them, stretching from one end of a small depression to the other, was a shimmering curtain of fire. The air was suddenly harsh with smoke. A wave of heat hit both of them with physical force, like a blow to the forehead.

"Jeff, we have to get out of here!"

"In a minute. This isn't bad."

The fire was crawling steadily up the rise toward them. Jeff calmly put one hand on Georgianne's arm while he stared ahead. It felt good, his hand on her arm, and then he remembered. Of course. He'd made the same gesture with Bonnie at the beach. He had come through that scene all right, but he had to admit it was really a defeat to be where he was now with Georgianne. The situation had finally gotten away from him. The only good part about it was that he had learned the truth and he honestly didn't care any more. To hell with it.

"Isn't there something beautiful about it?" Jeff said.

"Fire on a scale like this? Raw, wild nature on the loose. It's spectacularly beautiful."

Georgianne flung his hand off and released her seat belt. She took the gun out and pointed it at him.

"It's getting hard to breathe," she said. "Please take us out of here. *Right now.*"

"Oh, this isn't bad. You should see what these fires can do. The wind isn't too strong here, but it can get up to a hundred miles an hour, and the temperatures can reach twenty-five hundred degrees Fahrenheit. Can you imagine what that's like? Houses implode; palm trees go off like giant firecrackers. The chaparral goes up like cellophane. They say if a bird gets caught in the middle of the worst zones, it blows up. Really. In midair, like a hand grenade."

"*Please.*" She felt sick.

Jeff sat back against the car door and smiled. He looked at the gun as if he were noticing it for the first time.

"I'm not moving yet," he said indifferently. "Did you ever play chicken? I bet I can stay here longer and let the fire get closer to me than you can."

Georgianne stared at him. It was very difficult for her to grasp that this was actually happening. She seemed to be trapped in a weird dream. They were like two complete strangers, but she couldn't afford to think about it. Her head was pounding, her eyes were running, and she didn't seem to get any air in her lungs when she breathed.

"Drive," she ordered hoarsely, waving the gun at him.

Jeff took the keys out of the ignition and studied them as if they were a fascinating relic from another age.

"I meant to tell you—"

"I'm going," Georgianne said curtly.

She started to open her door.

"Wait," Jeff cried, suddenly anxious and reaching for her.

"No!" She fired the gun, and kept firing as she screamed, "No, no, no . . ."

"Ah, Jesus." Jeff exhaled, slumping back against the door.

"God damn you, God damn you," Georgianne sobbed. "God damn you . . ."

"I wanted to tell you that I was thinking, and I really really, always always . . . loved you."

But she was gone, running back the way they had come. He glanced up at the rearview mirror. He couldn't see her any more.

Georgianne ran back the way they had come, and it was like fleeing down a tunnel or a corridor surrounded by orange flickering darkness. The black air scorched her throat and lungs. It swarmed with flying sparks that burned her arms and neck and singed her scalp.

She stopped for a second when she heard the loud, unmistakable sound of an explosion behind her. Then she drove herself on, stumbling, gagging on smoke, gasping for air. She was hardly aware of anything when she was finally grabbed by strong arms and taken out of that place.

You have to be philosophical, Jeff told himself. You have to look beyond all the pain and stupidity, the heartache, the waste . . . all the shit. Because that's what it is—just shit. All of it. Smile philosophically; nothing else is called for.

Oddly, his parents came to his mind. A plain, stolid couple with marginal expectations. Christ, why am I thinking about them now?

Georgianne was all wrong for him. He could see that finally. It must be the longest lesson in history, but he had more or less grasped the point. She had a limited imagination, a stunted intelligence, and an overriding self-interest that masqueraded as sweetness. She belonged in Foxrock, living her vacuous little suburban pseudo-life. He should have left her there and forgotten about her. What a mistake!

Still, he'd followed the damn trail all the way to the truth, nasty as it was, and that had to be better than perpetuating a fantasy. It was, in a way, a triumph for him.

The fire was much closer now, and the heat very nearly unbearable. Jeff examined himself. Five or six shots had been fired in his general direction, but Georgianne had shut her eyes and waved the gun wildly, like a little girl in a cornball horse opera. The only respectable wound was to his left knee, which looked quite bloody and generated a lot of pain. He tried to push that foot to the floor, but he winced and groaned, and his vision was blinded by a swarm of black spots. No, he wasn't going to walk anywhere on that leg.

He'd been grazed on the right shoulder too, but the damage there was trivial. It didn't even hurt. What else? He smiled. The Blaupunkt had taken a smashing hit, and another bullet appeared to be lodged in the door panel. That left one or two that had probably gone right by him and out the open window.

The gun was lying on the passenger seat. He picked it up, pointed it at his forehead, and pulled the trigger. Click. Nothing. Typical, he thought. She'd left him absolutely nothing.

It had been a brilliant try, a long effort full of dazzling moves and bold strokes. But Jeff could see now that he had missed an even greater brilliancy. He'd fooled himself with misguided nostalgia and childish sentiment. She was in every way unsuitable for him.

What he should have done was remove Sean and Georgianne from the scene. Then the way would have been clear for him with Bonnie. Dear, beautiful, bright, young Bonnie. She had liked him, she was in tune with him. He would have wooed her and won her, brought her to Southern California . . . oh, it all would have been so much better. How had he missed it? He could have done anything he wanted with Bonnie. She would have been Georgianne as she should have been. He could have taught her, molded her, composed her. It would have worked. He was sure of it.

The car was full of smoke. Jeff put the key in the ignition. He was dizzy and he could feel the air being sucked out of his lungs. The left front Michelin exploded while he was trying to recall the look on Georgianne's face in bed when she mentioned Bonnie. Did she know? She had to know. But then, why hadn't she tried seriously to kill him? There wasn't even enough substance to her to sustain a desire for revenge. He should have come right out and told her to her face, before she ran. Made her eat it—anything to raise a sign of life in her. But she was just another walking stiff. The right front tire detonated a few moments later. He didn't care. He wasn't going anywhere.

He'd gotten to the truth, and that was something. He tried to light a cigarette and eventually succeeded in spite of the fact that it was almost impossible to inhale now.

Ah, shit, shit, shit. But the truth. It abolished fear, and Jeff appreciated that.

FINISHING TOUCHES
THOMAS TESSIER

INCLUDES THE BONUS NOVELLA
FATHER PANIC'S OPERA MACABRE!

On an extended holiday in London, Dr. Tom Sutherland befriends a mysterious surgeon named Nordhagen and begins a wild affair with the doctor's exotic assistant, Lina. Seduced and completely enthralled by Lina, Tom can think only of being with her, following her deeper into forbidden fantasies and dark pleasures. But fantasy turns to nightmare when Tom discovers the basement laboratory of Dr. Nordhagen, a secret chamber where cruelty, desire and madness combine to form the ultimate evil.
